"Whatever happened to that good-looking army captain you were dating?"

"He escorted me to only two social functions, Gog. I would hardly call that dating. After the second time, every gossip column and tabloid in the country was spreading rumors about our pending engagement." The entire episode was one she still found irritating. "To be honest, Gog, I can't remember the last time I went on a date without a horde of photographers in tow, not to mention the Secret Service."

"My, I do believe I detect a trace of bitterness," Bliss murmured, a gleam of approval in her eyes.

Jocelyn missed it, her attention focused inward on all the resentment that churned inside, resentment that had been too-long repressed. "I'm afraid it's more than a trace. It's closer to a volcano, all hot and bubbling, about to explode."

"I'm relieved to see you are still human, after all." Bliss announced, practically beaming. "You have been such a paragon of charm and good manners these last three and a half years, that I was certain you were on the verge of sainthood. I was beginning to wonder if you were really my granddaughter."

In spite of herself, Jocelyn laughed, feeling some of her tension dissipate with it. "One day—that's all I want, Gog. One day to myself—without anyone watching me. One day to be Jane Doe, instead of Jocelyn Wakefield, the president's daughter."

Also Available by Janet Dailey

LET'S BE JOLLY
HAPPY HOLIDAYS
MAYBE THIS CHRISTMAS
SCROOGE WORE SPURS
EVE'S CHRISTMAS
SEARCHING FOR SANTA
MISTLETOE AND MOLLY
AMERICAN DREAMS
AMERICAN DESTINY
SANTA IN A STETSON

From the Calder Series

SOMETHING MORE
CALDER STROM
LONE CALDER STAR
CALDER PROMISE
SHIFTING CALDER WIND
GREEN CALDER GRASS

Published by Kensington Publishing Corporation

A
Capital
Holiday

JANET DAILEY

ZEBRA BOOKS
KENSINGTON PUBLISHING CORP.
http://www.kensingtonbooks.com

ZEBRA BOOKS are published by

Kensington Publishing Corp.
119 West 40th Street
New York, NY 10018

All Kensington titles, imprints, and distributed lines are available at special quantity discounts for bulk purchases for sales promotion, premiums,
fund-raising, educational, or institutional use.

Special book excerpts or customized printings can also be created to fit
specific needs. For details, write or phone the office of the Kensington
Special Sales Manager: Attn.: Special Sales Department. Kensington Publishing Corp., 119 West 40th Street, New York, NY 10018. Phone:
1-800-221-2647.

Zebra and the Z logo Reg. U.S. Pat. & TM Off.

ISBN-13: 978-1-4201-1222-1
ISBN-10: 1-4201-1222-8

First Printing: October 2001

10 9 8 7 6 5

Printed in the United States of America

PROLOGUE

WASHINGTON — U.S. SENATOR HENRY ANDREW WAKEFIELD THROWS HIS HAT IN PRESIDENTIAL RING Virginia Senator and Capitol Hill veteran "Hammerin' Hank" Wakefield announced today he will seek his party's nomination for president of the United States. On hand were his mother, Bliss Wakefield, and his daughter, twenty-three-year-old Jocelyn Wakefield. . . .

ATLANTA — WAKEFIELD WINS PARTY'S NOMINATION FOR PRESIDENT Wakefield is now his party's official candidate for president of the United States. In his acceptance speech, Wakefield declared. . . . A fresh roar erupted from the convention floor when Wakefield's daughter, Jocelyn, joined him on stage. . . .

MISSOURI — WAKEFIELD ON CAMPAIGN TRAIL Latest polls show Wakefield leads his opponent by hefty margin. Wakefield discounted the importance of the results at a campaign stop in St. Louis, quipping to reporters, "Everyone knows Jocelyn is more popular than I am." . . .

HOUSTON — JOCELYN CELEBRATES BIRTHDAY Presidential candidate Henry Wakefield made an unexpected appearance at a Houston fund-raising gala when he wheeled in a birthday cake, ablaze with twenty-four candles, surprising his daughter Jocelyn and delighting the two thousand guests on hand. . . .

RICHMOND — LANDSLIDE WIN FOR WAKEFIELD While daughter Jocelyn proudly looked on, President-elect Henry Wakefield made his victory speech . . .

WASHINGTON — JOCELYN WAKEFIELD, AMERICA'S "FIRST DAUGHTER" Jocelyn Wakefield confirmed today that she will assume many of the duties that usually fall to the first lady when her father takes office. Jocelyn is no stranger in Washington's political circle. She has frequently acted as her father's hostess, a role she assumed following her mother's tragic death in a car accident eight years ago. A University of Virginia graduate with a master's degree in education, Jocelyn has long been a staunch supporter of literacy programs. "We pare living in the Communication Age, where communication skills are the top job requirement," she explained. "Unfortunately, too many adults today have difficulty reading and writing. They are getting by when they should be getting ahead."

WASHINGTON — STUNNING JOCELYN STEALS INAUGURATION SPOTLIGHT Fashion critics applauded the simple but elegant Chanel suit Jocelyn Wakefield wore to her father's swearing-in ceremony on the Capitol steps. All were quick to cite that its rich hunter green color provided the perfect foil to her strawberry blond hair and creamy complexion. But it was her choice of Inaugural gowns that stole their breaths and drew spontaneous applause wherever she appeared. An original from the hands of a previously unknown American designer, Andrea Hart, the gown was a slender column of pink crepe de chine sprinkled with pearls. The soft color, described as "tea rose" by its designer, accented Jocelyn's model-slim figure and brought out the fiery lights in her hair, styled in a cascading mass of curls. Not since Jacqueline Kennedy has a woman in the White House so thoroughly captured the fashion eye and the hearts of the American public. This reporter predicts that soon the world will be watching her as well. . . .

WASHINGTON — JOCELYN CHARMS VISITING HEADS OF STATE The British prime minister joined the growing ranks of dignitaries singing the praises of America's "first daughter," stating that she is not only intelligent and witty, but a born diplomat as well—an essential trait for members of the first family.

WASHINGTON — JOCELYN DANCES WITH HOLLY-WOOD'S HOTTEST LEADING MAN AT TWENTY-FIFTH BIRTHDAY GALA Has America's princess found her Prince Charming?

WASHINGTON — JOCELYN ATTENDS "NUT-CRACKER" OPENING AT KENNEDY CENTER For the fifth time in as many weeks, Jocelyn Wakefield appeared in public with a different male escort, putting an end to further speculation about a budding romance in her life.

NEW YORK — AFTER TWO YEARS IN WHITE HOUSE, JOCELYN MORE POPULAR THAN EVER America's golden redhead Jocelyn Wakefield again heads the list of most admired women. Considered by many to possess the class of Grace Kelly, the mystique of Jackie O, and the savvy of Margaret Thatcher, Jocelyn has only to smile one of her sunny smiles and everyone within range of her warm brown eyes would agree that she is the ideal of American beauty.

CHAPTER 1

Marine One, the presidential helicopter, surrounded by its airborne military entourage, swept across the sky above the Potomac River. The loud drone of its engine made conversation difficult, a fact for which Jocelyn Wakefield was extremely grateful.

Eyes closed, she sat in her seat, too edgy with fatigue to relax. Her feet ached from the endless hours of standing and walking these last four days, and her hands throbbed from the endless times they'd been shaken. Even the muscles in her face quivered with fatigue from smiling so much.

It was one of the prices she paid for being the president's daughter, and an extremely popular one. A few pundits went so far as to suggest she was more popular than her father. More than one had dubbed her "America's Princess Di."

Popularity was not something Jocelyn had sought. But now that it had been thrust upon her, she tried to use it to benefit a host of worthy organizations, as well as her father's administration.

This past week it had put her back on the campaign trail, stumping for congressional candidates in her father's party. On Friday, Jocelyn had been joined by the president, and the schedule had become even more crowded and hectic.

The helicopter tilted and her stomach did a sickening little flip-flop as the craft veered to the right, bound for its landing site on the South Lawn of the White House. Flying had never been Jocelyn's favorite mode of transportation, and in a helicopter, she was an unabashed white-knuckler, despite the number of times she had flown in them.

Only a scant few of the staff were aware of her uneasiness at flying—Jocelyn refused to call it fear. It was something she had very early learned to conceal. Yet she couldn't stop her hand from double-checking to make sure her seat belt was tightly fastened.

As soon as the helicopter righted itself, she opened her eyes and forced herself to look out the window, trying to distract her mind from the sensations of the helicopter's descent.

The view of Washington, D.C. from the air was a sight guaranteed to do exactly that. Autumn's vibrant crimson and gold colors still clung to the trees along the National Mall, a perfect contrast to the green of its grass and the gleaming white of its monuments.

Her glance touched on the white marble obelisk that honored the nation's first president, George Washington. By law, it was the tallest structure in the city. The ring of American flags surrounding it waved idly in a late-afternoon breeze. Again Jocelyn made an oft-repeated vow to herself that one day she would ride the elevator all the way to the top—something she hadn't done since she was nine years old.

Just beyond the monument rose the familiar spires, towers, and turrets of the Smithsonian "Castle." Its museums were other sights on her private wish list of places to explore—alone, without a horde of reporters and officials surrounding her, or camera lenses trained on her. Unfortunately, there didn't seem to be much chance of that happening until she was around ninety.

Suppressing a sigh, Jocelyn looked beyond the row of museums that flanked the parklike Mall. At the far end stood the Capitol building, its familiar dome topped by a nineteen-foot-high statue of Freedom.

For a moment, she gazed down the length of Pennsylvania Avenue. A smile twitched the corners of her mouth as Jocelyn recalled a wry comment she had read a few weeks ago in the highly popular political column "Tucker's Take." In it, the columnist Grady Tucker had likened the famous street that stretched between the White House and Capitol Hill to a rope in a tug-of-war game. A singularly apt description, she thought, especially when she considered some of her father's recent battles with Congress over the budget.

Rising treetops blocked the Capitol building from her view as the helicopter descended below them. Involuntarily Jocelyn dug her carefully manicured nails into her palms and inwardly braced herself for that small jolt of touchdown. At the same instant, she jerked her gaze from the window, instinctively seeking her father's strong, square-jawed face and making contact with his warm blue eyes.

Henry Wakefield looked back at her, his gaze knowing in its softness. Instantly she drew strength from his rock-steady calm, a ridiculous admission for a twenty-six-year-old woman to make. But it was a true one, nonetheless.

As *Marine One* settled onto the South Lawn with only a gentle jar to its important passengers, her father quipped above the engine noise, "Home again, home again, jiggety-jog," drawing a faint smile from Jocelyn.

When she was small, the slightest amount of air turbulence had frightened her. Each time, her parents had recited that old childhood nursery rhyme; for some inexplicable reason, it had always calmed her fears. Now it had become a private joke between Jocelyn and her father.

Henry Wakefield, dubbed "Hammerin' Hank" by the reporters during his successful presidential campaign, glanced out the side window and sighed, "Just one more gauntlet to run."

Jocelyn knew without looking that he was referring to the White House press corps waiting on the South

Lawn, hoping for one final sound bite they could use on this nonpresidential election eve. The mere thought of more cameras, more shouted questions, was enough to set her teeth on edge.

Everything inside her screamed, "Stop! No more!" But that wasn't an option, and Jocelyn knew it.

The media pressure never seemed to faze her father, though. She supposed, when weighed against the demands of his office, the press was no more bothersome to him than a swarm of pesky mosquitoes.

Each time she considered the responsibility that sat on his shoulders, Jocelyn swallowed her own complaints. She had only to look at him to see the changes nearly two years in office had made in him.

The strands of gray in his hair had multiplied tenfold, silvering its brownness. A new soberness had ingrained itself in his features, firming the line of his mouth. And after the weekend's grueling schedule, there were new signs of weariness about him: a faint shadowing under the eyes, a deepening of the lines around his mouth, a slight sagging of his broad shoulders.

Yet, even as Jocelyn studied him, she watched him throw off the fatigue with a quick squaring of his shoulders and a determined lift of the chin. Before her eyes, Henry Wakefield recreated his public image of a vigorous, robust man.

Aware that she could do no less, Jocelyn slipped her toes back into her shoes and ignored the screech of protest from her aching feet.

*   *   *

The wash from the helicopter's rotating blades buffeted the throng of reporters stationed well beyond it. A shower of autumn leaves spun from the trees to whirl through the air. Grady Tucker stood slightly apart from his colleagues but still close enough to be counted as one of them.

At six feet four, he was a tall and lanky man with features that were strong and angular—handsome in a fresh, down-home sort of way. A lingering summer tan gave color to his skin, eliminating any suggestion of office pallor. His hair was a sun-bleached brown, on the shaggy side, and tousled by the helicopter-generated wind. The effect added to his slightly rumpled appearance.

He wore a tweed jacket with decorative leather patches at the elbows. Beneath it was a tan pullover sweater that gave some bulk to his otherwise lean frame. His jacket pockets bulged with a variety of items: the requisite notebook, pens, and pencils of his trade; a briar pipe and a pouch of tobacco; plus the odd slips of paper and occasional paper clips, two dog biscuits, an old tennis ball, and a roll of stamps; as well as last week's laundry receipt, matchbooks, and a dozen other things he thought he might need or forgot he had.

The overall impression was one of easy carelessness and fresh-faced innocence. All that was missing was a scattering of freckles to complete the look.

His appearance was part natural and part cultivated.

Only now and then did his hazel eyes reveal the keen intelligence behind the facade.

Tucker couldn't say what had brought him to the South Lawn that afternoon. The White House wasn't exactly his regular beat, although politics in general were. He certainly didn't need a quote for tomorrow's column; he had a week's worth already written.

He was there mostly because he didn't have anything better to do, and because he'd had an odd urge to come. And Tucker had always been one to follow the odd urges. They kept his life from getting into a rut. He abhorred ruts. Lately, he'd had the nagging feeling that he was slipping into one.

On the lawn, the helicopter pilot cut the engine, reducing it to an idle chug. As the blades slowed their rotation, a handful of Secret Service agents converged on the craft at a crouching jog.

An air of expectancy licked through the waiting press. Tucker felt the same quickening inside, even though his role was strictly one of a casual observer.

The instant the door to *Marine One* opened, the horde of reporters, photographers, and cameramen surged against the security barrier, jockeying for position. Tucker's mouth quirked in a wry smile at his colleagues' avidity.

With his hands stuffed in the pockets of his faded jeans, Grady sauntered a couple steps closer for a better view, then stood storklike with his weight on one foot, the other leg bent, and watched the unfolding circus.

As the president emerged from the belly of the

helicopter, there was an immediate click and hum of cameras. Tucker paid little attention, focusing instead on Hank Wakefield.

At first glance, the president looked like any other successful business executive, well dressed in a dark suit tailored to fit his athletic frame. The growing touches of gray in his hair gave him a distinguished air, and there were enough crags in his face to keep him from being too movie-star handsome.

Privately Tucker acknowledged that Henry Andrew Wakefield *looked* like a president. More than that, he possessed that indefinable something—something magnetic and forceful—that prompted people to automatically turn to him in time of trouble, confident he had the answer. Proof of that was in Wakefield's high confidence rating in the polls.

Wakefield glanced in the media's direction. Beside Tucker, the AP reporter Phil Aikens grumbled an irritated "What'd ya want'a bet he doesn't talk to us?"

"What makes you say that?" Tucker cocked his head at a curious angle.

"Because he looked at us," the man muttered, never taking his own eyes off the president. "When he does that, he almost never answers any questions, leaving us trying to read something into his body language. You know, one of those 'Today the president appeared confident—or concerned—or weary.' Take your pick."

Tucker smiled in commiseration. "You'd be better off with a 'no comment'."

"Tell me about it," the reporter grunted.

The president turned back to the helicopter's open door, a quick smile curving his mouth when his daughter stepped out. Phil Aikens saw her and flashed a grin at Tucker.

" 'Course, there's always Jocelyn," he said. "It's a whole lot easier making up a story about her. Any kind of exclusive item on the first daughter is worth its weight in gold."

Tucker shifted his gaze to the president's daughter. Like her father, Jocelyn Wakefield was tall, lacking only three inches of matching her father's six feet. She looked deceptively model-slender, but Tucker had seen enough pictures of her to know there were curves beneath that slimming business suit she wore. Its rich royal blue was a perfect complement to her fair skin and glorious red hair, a natural shade of strawberry-blond no hairdresser in the world could duplicate.

In the past three years, Tucker had seen Jocelyn Wakefield in person maybe a half-dozen times, always at a distance like this. Her clothes and hairstyles had varied with the occasion, but not the overall impression of elegance, poise, and an easy charm. There was no demure dipping of the head, no hint of shyness or reticence. Her head was always up, and her smile always appeared warm and friendly, making her seem approachable. There was nothing practiced or phony about her.

"Gorgeous, isn't she?" Phil observed the object of

Tucker's study. "The kind of woman you want to take home to meet your mom."

For a moment Tucker eyed Jocelyn with a purely male appreciation for her looks and figure, then dragged a hand out of his jeans pocket and scratched the back of his head. "I don't know. I can't quite see her fittin' into my mom's farm kitchen back in Kansas."

The president said something to his daughter that drew a wry smile and a nod from her. Together they moved out from the helicopter's shadow, with Jocelyn lagging a half step back from him, a position that gave the cameras a clear angle at the nation's chief executive. Her hair turned fiery in the afternoon sunlight, its sleekness gleaming with a more definite red.

The sight prompted Tucker to wonder aloud, "Has she got a temper to go with that hair?"

Phil shrugged. "If she does, I haven't heard a whisper of it."

Neither had Tucker, but he had never taken much interest in Jocelyn Wakefield, mostly because she hadn't provided him with much fodder for his column.

As the president moved within range, reporters shouted questions to him, microphones thrust out to catch his reply. But Wakefield shook his head and touched a hand to his ear, indicating that he couldn't hear them over the gathering roar of the helicopter now preparing to lift off. But it didn't halt the barrage.

"What about the Senate race in Ohio?"

"Does VanHorn have a chance of unseating Missouri's Scranton?"

"The polls show you might gain only two seats in the House. Do you think you waited too long to . . ."

"Mr. President, what chance does your budget package have of passing if you don't gain a majority in the House?"

"The *Atlanta Journal* claims your support for Dykes was too little too late. What's your comment on that?"

Smiling confidently, Wakefield waved at the cameras and kept walking toward the South Portico. Jocelyn mirrored his actions.

One of the network television correspondents yelled, "Why did you cancel your stop in Chicago, Mr. President? Do you consider that Senate race lost?"

Again, a wide-smiling Wakefield indicated he couldn't hear the question. Then his moving glance landed on Tucker and stopped in surprise. In a flash, he changed directions, his smile lengthening into a grin as he raised a hand in recognition.

"Tucker." His voice boomed the greeting.

Startled by her father's change of course, Jocelyn Wakefield stopped but didn't accompany her father when he walked straight toward the press corps. Her confused glance swept over the reporters' faces before colliding with Tucker's gaze.

For a split second, he felt the impact of her brown eyes. Then he switched his focus to the approaching president of the United States. All around him there was a mad scramble for position, reporters and cameramen jostling him from the side and behind, microphones bristling all around him while the Secret Service agents moved in to keep the press safely at bay.

"I never expected to see your face among this horde of reporters, Tucker," the president declared, coming to a stop before him and extending a hand.

Tucker shook it and ducked his head in his best aw-shucks fashion. "Everybody makes mistakes now and then, Mr. President. My granddaddy always said that's why we keep having elections."

Hank Wakefield threw back his head and laughed. Tucker had a brief glimpse of Jocelyn, enough to catch an echoing sparkle of laughter in her eyes. With both hands once again shoved in his pockets, he slouched a little more and shuffled his weight to the other foot.

"And I wouldn't be too hard on these guys here, Mr. President." He bobbed his head in the direction of the flanking reporters. "They're just trying to get an advance line on who's who and who's through."

"Wouldn't we all?" the president countered, his glance sliding over the group to Tucker's left. "But I'm afraid they'll have to wait like the rest of us, until all the votes are cast tomorrow."

Phil Aikens spoke up quickly. "Mr. President, what do you think Orrin Peters's chances are of winning Indiana's House seat from Clyde Renfrow?"

"It doesn't matter what I think," the president replied. "It's up to the voters to choose. But I do know the people of Indiana are as anxious as I am to get this budget issue settled, and Orrin Peters has voiced the same desire.''

A flurry of *Mr. President*s followed his answer, but Wakefield waved off any more questions. ''Sorry. That'll have to be it for now.'' He backed away, tapping his watch. ''I've got a meeting to attend.''

He walked off to rejoin his daughter, taking her by the arm and guiding her toward the White House entrance. The instant it was clear there would be no more remarks, the microphones and cameras were lowered, and the attention shifted to packing up and getting stories filed.

Pushed by no such deadline, Tucker went through the motions of patting his pockets, searching for the one with his pipe. Phil Aikens gave him a sideways glance, full of curiosity.

''I didn't know you were such good friends with Wakefield,'' he said, as if smelling something suspicious.

''It was news to me, too.'' After a show of searching his pockets, Tucker unerringly plunged his hand into the right one and pulled out his pipe, then the tobacco pouch out of another pocket, and dipped the pipe into the pouch to begin filling it. ''I guess it just goes to show you that you can always tell an election is near when a politician can recognize you at a distance.''

''Aren't you being a bit too modest, Tucker?'' cameraman Joe Grobowski scoffed from his listening post, where he crouched two feet away. He scribbled something on the tape in his hand and stuffed it into his bag.

"Modest? About what?" Frowning, Tucker tamped the last bit of tobacco into the pipe bowl and returned the pouch to his pocket with one hand while inserting the pipe stem between his teeth with the other.

The plea of ignorance drew a skeptical glance from Grobowski. "You mean you don't know that Wakefield regards you as his good-luck charm?"

Tucker blinked in unfeigned surprise and plucked the pipe from his mouth. "You're joshing me, Joe."

The roar of *Marine One* lifting off checked the cameraman's reply as the turbulent wind generated by its spinning blades lashed out, tugging at coattails and loose notebook pages before sending dry leaves whirling around them. The noise receded as the helicopter gained altitude and rejoined its hovering military escort. Like a flock of brown pelicans, they lumbered off toward Andrews Air Force Base.

When the noise abated, Tucker turned back to Grobowski. "Now explain yourself, Joe," he declared, wearing his most serious face. "What's all this about me being a good-luck charm? 'Cause I gotta tell you, Wakefield never struck me as the superstitious sort."

"It probably isn't him as much as it is his staff," the cameraman conceded. "But it all started when you attended the convention where he won the nomination to become his party's candidate. Everybody knows you don't usually go to such things."

"But I went to both conventions," Tucker recalled,

puzzled that any significance could be attached to his presence.

"And you also attended the first presidential debate, where Wakefield cremated Sy Cummings." Joe paused, his expression turning a little sly. "Do you remember the last time you went to a White House ceremony?"

Tucker chewed thoughtfully on the pipe stem while he searched through his mental files. Nodding, he recalled. "I came to see all the pomp and flourishes of Wakefield welcoming the new Israeli prime minister."

Afterward, he had taken more than a few jibes in his column at America's foreign policy. The most often-quoted item had been his claim that George Washington had set a poor precedent when he threw that dollar across the Potomac River, because ever since then, the government had tossed billions across the oceans.

"And do you also remember," Grobowski continued, "that not two days later came the big announcement of a new peace treaty between Israel and the PLO?"

Drawing his head back, Tucker cocked one eyebrow in a puzzled frown. "That's nothing but sheer coincidence. It had nothing to do with me being here."

With the videotape and camera stowed securely in their traveling case, Grobowski stood up. "Coincidence or not, there are some on Wakefield's staff who are convinced good things happen when you're around. I guess we'll see how true that is when the election results come in, won't we?'' Grinning, he sketched a salute to both Tucker and Phil Aikens and moved off. ''See you.''

Tucker absently lifted a hand in farewell, then dug a matchbook out of his pocket without the usual routine of a patting search. Still lost in thought, he tore off a cardboard match, scratched the head of it across the roughened strip, and held the flame close to his pipe bowl.

''Wouldn't that be an interesting headline,'' Phil murmured, eyeing him with amused thought. '' 'Grady Tucker, Wakefield's Lucky Rabbit's Foot.' ''

A puff of aromatic smoke came from Tucker's mouth. Wryness tugged at him as he lowered the pipe. ''You know, Phil, I never have figured out why people think a rabbit's foot is so lucky when you consider what happened to the rabbit.''

The AP reporter chuckled to himself and shook his head. ''On that note, I'm outa' here, Tucker. I've got a story to write. See ya' around.''

''You, too.''

Tucker stuck the pipe back in his mouth, clenching the stem between his teeth, and cast a last idle glance in the direction of the White House, catching a glimpse of the president and his daughter as they neared the steps to the South Portico. An instant later, the accompanying Secret Service agents and staff blocked his view of them.

Turning, Tucker stuffed a hand in his jacket pocket and fingered the dog biscuit inside it. ''Time for me to shove off, too,'' he muttered through the pipe stem to no one in particular. "Molly's gonna be wantin' her walk."

Unhurried, he strolled from the grounds. A dozen yards from the gates, an elderly and well-dressed gentleman approached him, the head of his cane raised in a silent request for his attention. Removing the pipe from his mouth, Tucker automatically cupped a hand around its bowl and slowed his steps, nodding in response to the man's grateful smile.

"I'm sorry to bother you, sir, but I was wondering if you could help me." He stopped before Tucker, planting the cane on the sidewalk directly in front of his feet and resting both hands atop it.

"I'll try," Tucker promised, his glance running curiously over this man whose skin was as dark as his beard was white. He was round and short, the crown of his black homburg coming no higher than the middle of Tucker's chest.

"I had understood it was possible to tour the White House, but the visitor center is closed."

"During the winter months, it is," Tucker admitted. "But the White House is still open for tours Tuesday through Saturday, but only in the mornings. Basically, you have two options now: you can either contact your local representative or senator to see if they can get you a pass; or you can go the Southeast Gate. But I think you have to be there before ten in the morning."

"The Southeast Gate before ten, Tuesday through Saturday," the man repeated, as if committing the information to memory, then tipped his hat. "Thank you very much, sir. You have been most helpful."

"No problem," Tucker replied and smiled to himself as the man set off with brisk, short-legged strides.

Jocelyn waited a beat after her father rejoined her before succumbing to her curiosity. "Who was that man you were just talking to?" she asked, resisting the urge to take another look in the man's direction.

"That was Grady Tucker." He gave her a look that suggested she should have recognized the man.

"Grady Tucker," she repeated with dawning cognizance. "You mean *the* Grady Tucker, the one who writes the 'Tucker's Take' column?"

"The very same." Her father nodded.

This time Jocelyn did crane her neck to take another look at the man. No photograph of its author accompanied the column—only a drawing of a hand holding a pipe with smoke curling from it.

"I thought Grady Tucker would be pudgy and bald, with wire-rim glasses." She stared at the tall, lanky man dressed in jeans, sneakers, and a tweed jacket, a pipe clutched in his mouth, then jerked her gaze to the front, trying to make the leap from imagination to reality. "He looks like some long-legged basketball player from Iowa."

Her father smiled drolly. "You're close. He's from Kansas."

"Kansas." Jocelyn wanted to laugh, but she suddenly couldn't summon the energy.

"Tired?" her father guessed, his astute glance traveling over her smooth face.

She refused to complain, or to lie. "It's been a hectic week."

He nodded wisely. "Your feet hurt, do they?"

Jocelyn all but groaned, "They're killing me." Each step she took brought a fresh stab of pain shooting from her feet. She measured the distance to the oval-shaped portico's ground-floor entrance and wondered if she could make it. "I can hardly wait to kick these shoes off," Jocelyn told him without moving her lips—an art she had learned early in her father's political career as a defense against all the networks that hired lip-readers.

In this town, image was everything and had to be protected. Hence, public complaints or criticisms were swallowed or muttered very softly under one's breath. To guard against embarrassing photographs of her skirt billowing up around her face in a strong wind, Jocelyn wore slim-fitting suits. To avoid mussed and untidy hair, she styled hers in a sleek French twist and plastered it with hairspray, not allowing a single strand to stray out of place. Rings were never worn on her right hand, to avoid the pain of one of those extra-firm finger-crushing handshakes. The list was endless and constantly being revised. At times, Jocelyn felt she was a prisoner, manacled and chained by a thousand dos and don'ts.

Waiting at the ground-floor entrance to welcome them back stood a tanned and athletically trim Alex Bakersmith, the White House chief usher. The bland-sounding title meant that he was in charge of practically everything at the White House: budget, staff, maintenance, entertainment, and more.

But it was the sight of Wally Hamilton, one of her father's advisors and his deputy chief of staff, who was also anxiously waiting for them, that gave Jocelyn pause. As usual, he was busy chewing his thumbnail to the quick.

"What does Wally want?" Jocelyn wondered aloud.

"He's probably waiting to walk me over to the Oval Office," her father replied.

"You have a meeting right away?" she said half in protest, aware that he had been on the go since four in the morning, just as she had.

"Dwight Hawkins is supposed to be there to brief me on the latest information about that terrorist bombing in Paris," he said, referring to his secretary of state.

"As worried as Wally looks, I hope the news isn't bad."

"Wally is always worried about something. I have never met a man so quick to see the bad in everything," her father stated without rancor. "That's why he is so valuable to me. With him, I know I'll hear all sides. But this time I don't think he's worried about the terrorist attack. He's probably received the latest election polls. Wait until he hears I talked to Tucker."

"What difference does Tucker make?" Jocelyn frowned.

"You aren't going to believe this," her father

warned, the beginnings of a smile dimpling his cheeks, "but Wally thinks Tucker is my good-luck piece."

His answer startled a laugh from her. "What? Why?"

"You'll have to ask Wally," he replied with an amused shake of his head. "He has a whole long list of reasons."

"You don't believe it, do you?"

"No, but ol' gloom-and-doom Wally does," he joked and started to split away from her to link up with his deputy. His glance traveled down to her feet. "You need to have Ernst come up and give you a massage," he said in parting. "Those aching muscles of yours will feel a lot better if you do."

At the moment, Jocelyn had no desire to see another living soul, even a masseur. She'd had her fill of people pushing and pulling and manipulating her.

But she didn't say that, replying instead, "Thanks, but I think I'll just settle for a long soak in the Jacuzzi."

Alex Bakersmith inclined his head in greeting. "Good afternoon, Mr. President, Miss Wakefield. Welcome back."

"Alex." Her father nodded an absent acknowledgment and clamped a hand on Wally's shoulder. Together the two of them set off for the colonnade that led to the Oval Office in the West Wing.

"Hello, Alex." Jocelyn managed a wan smile and walked through the door he held open for her, shadowed by her own personal Secret Service agent, Mike Bassett.

The minute she reached the ground-floor corridor, she stopped and slipped off her shoes and placed her hot and achy nylon-stockinged feet on the cool marble floor. There was relief—perhaps not total, but there was relief. She briefly paused to savor it, then forced herself to continue along the corridor.

At the moment, Jocelyn didn't particularly care how inelegant she might look walking through the White House in her designer suit and carrying her low-heeled pumps. Privately she thanked God that no photographers were around to snap this picture and plaster it all over tomorrow's papers.

Silently she made her way to their living quarters on the second floor of the presidential mansion. As always, Agent Mike Bassett left her at the elevator; the Secret Service didn't venture onto the second and third floors, giving the first family the illusion of privacy.

But Jocelyn knew it was only an illusion. The White House was served by a staff that numbered in the hundreds, ready to cater to her every need or whim—except the one Jocelyn wanted most: to be alone. Which was an impossibility. Even if she never actually saw the butler, the maid, or the valet going about their business, she knew they were somewhere about.

In her side vision, Jocelyn saw the evening newspaper lying on the table just inside the hall by the elevator. With it were messages that had been left for

Jocelyn and her father, the red-tagged ones indicating those that needed immediate attention.

Nerves frayed by the exhaustion and stress from the past week's activities, Jocelyn stopped to glare at the stack of red-tagged messages, hotly rebellious at the thought of even one more demand on her time. She took one furious step past the table, then swung back. Tucking her shoes in the crook of one arm, she snatched up the messages, angrily riffling through them to remove the ones addressed to her attention. There were seven in all, four with red flags. Her fingers curled around the slips of paper, crumpling them into the palm of her hand.

One day—that was all she wanted. Just one twenty-four-hour period all to herself, to do what she wanted, go where she wanted, wear what she wanted, say what she wanted.

One day of absolute and total freedom.

There had to be a way to arrange that. Jocelyn vowed to find it, convinced that if she didn't, she would go stark-raving mad.

A thought popped into her head, one that was so outrageous, so radical, that Jocelyn wondered if she hadn't already lost her mind.

But it could work.

It would just take some careful plotting and planning. But it could work.

CHAPTER 2

Energized by this new, wildly daring thought, Jocelyn practically flew down the hall, her fatigue and achiness temporarily forgotten. She stopped in her bedroom long enough to drop her shoes and call for her personal maid.

She met the short and stout gray-haired woman on her way out of the room. "Midge, draw me a bubble bath in the Jacuzzi, will you? And make sure the water is hot-hot," she instructed, calling the last over her shoulder as she swung into the room next door.

During past administrations, it had been used as a bedroom, but Jocelyn had converted it into a combination sitting room and home office. Without slowing a step, she went directly to her work corner, tossed

the messages on a desk once used by Eleanor Roosevelt, then switched on her personal computer.

She called up her calendar and waited impatiently
for it to come on-screen. After seconds that seemed
as long as minutes, it was there. Jocelyn scanned her
appointment schedule for the rest of November and
almost laughed aloud at what she saw.

There was the gap in her schedule. As big as life.
Next weekend she had only one commitment.

Could that possibly be right? She stared at the
screen, hardly able to believe her luck. There was
only one way to find out. Still she hesitated, adult
responsibility warring with rash impulse.

Rationalizing that a call to verify the accuracy of
her calendar didn't commit her to anything, Jocelyn
picked up the telephone.

"This is Jocelyn Wakefield. I need to speak with
Francine Rivers," she told the operator, confident
that no matter where her social secretary might be,
the operator would locate her. The White House
operators were famous for their ability to track people
down, at home or abroad, in the air or on the ground.

While she waited for Francine to come on the line,
Jocelyn began ferreting out the pins that secured her
long, spray-stiffened hair in its French twist. As she
tugged free the last one, a discreet knock came from
the doorway.

She half-turned in the cushioned office-style chair,
glancing back to see the maid, Midge Tidwell, standing in the opening. "Yes, Midge, what is it?"

"Your bath is ready," the maid replied, which

meant Jocelyn's robe and slippers would have been laid out for her as well. "Is there anything else you would like, Miss Jocelyn? Something to drink?"

"A tall glass of orange juice. With ice, please." As Francine Rivers's voice came over the line, Jocelyn cupped a quick hand over the telephone's mouthpiece. "Set the juice next to the tub, will you? Thanks, Midge." She removed her hand and spoke into the phone. "Hello, Francine. It's Jocelyn."

"Hi. Welcome back. Paula tells me it was a long, tough trip. Truthfully, I didn't expect to hear from you until late tomorrow morning at the earliest. What's up?"

Jocelyn tensed, almost guiltily, then mentally shook off the attack of nerves. "I was looking at my appointments for the coming week and noticed that I'm scheduled to attend the National Symphony's concert at the Kennedy Center Saturday evening. There are no special notations on my calendar about it, but I thought I'd better check with you and see if there would be any problem if I decided to cancel it."

"I don't think that's a problem, but let me look." There was a slight pause, filled by a series of faint clicks. "It's purely a social event, Jocelyn. Canceling might bend a few noses, but it shouldn't put them out of joint. So . . . is that what you want me to do? Cancel it?"

"Not yet. I'll let you know. Thanks, Francine." She hung up and clamped a hand over her mouth, trying to contain the exultant leap of excitement.

Did she really dare to do this? She felt positively

giddy at the prospect. It sounded so deliciously wonderful. One day of total freedom.

Her conscience reared up, scolding her to be sensible. She was the president's daughter. She had responsibilities, obligations. But that was the problem, Jocelyn thought as she pushed out of the chair. She was tired of being sensible. Tired of being the president's daughter. And tired of the responsibilities and obligations that came with it. She needed to escape from it, just for one day.

Impossible, her conscience scoffed.

"Probably," Jocelyn conceded out loud and sighed, then rallied her drooping spirits with the reminder that it wouldn't do any harm to fantasize about it. After all, there might be a way to do it without anyone getting hurt, including herself.

Back in the bedroom, she stripped off her clothes and tossed them one by one onto the bed, then padded into the steamy bathroom. The fragrance of lavender-scented bubbles wafted from the long tub. Jocelyn breathed in the relaxing aroma, then reached for the hairbrush lying on the sink's vanity top. Stroke after stroke, she dragged it through her hair until she had brushed out most of the crusting spray.

Straightening, she glanced into the mirror and came face to face with her own reflection. There was her biggest problem, Jocelyn realized: she had been photographed so much that she was instantly recognizable on any street.

She stared at the tumble of reddish hair about her face, the milky fairness of her skin, and the startling darkness of her brown eyes. Unlike the prince in the novel, she didn't know of a pauper with whom she could trade places—certainly no one with her particular shade of red hair.

A disguise was the obvious solution to that problem, of course.

Jocelyn wrapped a towel turban-style around her head, covering every strand of hair, then stepped into the tub and lowered herself gingerly into the hot, bubble-laden water. Leaning against the slanted backrest, she reached over and turned on the jets. Water churned in massaging currents over her sore muscles as a fresh froth mounded the blanket of bubbles higher.

Submerged up to her shoulders in pulsating water, Jocelyn let her mind wander back to her fantasy. A dark wig and different makeup and clothes would handle the recognition factor.

But how could she get away without her absence being discovered?

Slipping out of the White House unseen wouldn't be that easy, although it was far from impossible. Jocelyn glanced at the closed door between the bathroom and her bedroom. She couldn't hear any movement, but she knew the maid was currently in her bedroom, putting away the clothes she had just taken off.

As respectful as all the staff were of her privacy, sooner or later someone would call, someone would check, someone would question why she hadn't been seen. And they would check out of concern. When she wasn't found . . . Jocelyn shuddered to think of the ensuing hue and cry that would be raised.

If she was very lucky, she might be able to sneak out for a couple of hours without being discovered. But not for a whole day. Not from the White House.

Other children of past presidents had likened the mansion to a glass bowl. To Jocelyn, it was looking more and more like a glass prison.

She sighed and sank a little lower in the tub, accepting that she could never make a successful escape from it. Then a little voice inside her head whispered, *Then escape from somewhere else.*

Forget it, her conscience ordered.

Jocelyn argued that she was merely indulging in a mental exercise. She wasn't committing herself to doing it—merely exploring the possibility. On the basis of that reasoning, she gave her mind full rein.

Spur-of-the-moment trips did not sit well with the Secret Service. Which meant they would be three times as paranoid if she came up with one. Traveling any distance was clearly not an option because of the time factor.

Sighing again, she curled soapy fingers around the insulated tumbler of juice. Ice cubes clinked together when she tipped the glass to her mouth and took a drink of the chilled liquid.

The longer she thought about the problem, the more convinced Jocelyn became that her plan would never succeed unless she had an accomplice—someone who could cover for her.

But who?

Mentally she went through her list of friends. One by one she discarded them all. The reasons varied: some she knew wouldn't agree because they would regard it as too dangerous; others—well, she simply thought they would be poor liars; and sadly there were several she wasn't sure she could trust.

"Face it, Jocelyn." She stared glumly at the translucent cubes floating in her glass. "There isn't anyone. It was a crazy idea anyway."

She washed down her regrets with a swallow of orange juice, then set the tumbler back on the ledge and gave herself over to the pummeling jets. Surrounded by scented steam and moving water, Jocelyn closed her eyes and let her mind go blank. The hum of the water pump was soothing in its steadiness. For now, it was sufficient simply to lie there, limp and warm within the cocoon of bubbles and water, the fatigue and soreness draining from her.

A contented sound came from her throat. "Bliss," she murmured. "This is pure bliss."

Two seconds after she uttered the phrase, her eyes popped open, and Jocelyn sat bolt upright in the tub with a suddenness that sent a wave of water and bubbles sloshing over the edge.

"Bliss," Jocelyn repeated in discovery. "Why on earth didn't I think of Gog before?!"

If she scoured the globe, Jocelyn knew she could never find a more skilled accomplice than her very own grandmother, Bliss Wakefield. She might look like some dignified duchess, but behind that august face and sparkling brown eyes was a woman who was recklessly bold and adventurous—and easily the most convincing liar ever born.

In a flash, Jocelyn was out of the the tub, leaving the water to churn without her. Hurriedly she wrapped a towel around her wet body and charged into the adjoining bedroom, leaving a trail of frothy puddles in her wake. She snatched the phone off the cherry-wood nightstand and punched out her grandmother's number from memory.

The call was answered on the third ring by the gravelly English voice of her grandmother's longtime factotum, Dexter Cummings-Gould. "Redford Hall."

An edgy excitement had Jocelyn rushing her words. "Dexter. Hello, it's Jocelyn. Is my grandmother in?"

After a pregnant pause, he replied, "Are you quite certain you wish to speak to her, my dear? She is in a bit of a snit at the moment."

In the background Jocelyn heard the imperial sound of Bliss Wakefield's voice demanding, "Who are you talking to, Dexter? Bring me that phone at once."

"You mean to *whom*, Madam," he replied in a muffled aside.

"Give me that phone. And don't you dare correct my grammar."

Jocelyn laughed in spite of herself. "You two squabble worse than a pair of peahens."

"*She* is quite definitely in a 'fowl' mood," Dexter declared, placing heavy stress on the pronoun. "She and Colonel Harthcourt received a trouncing at bridge today. I—"

"Who is this?" her grandmother demanded, obviously having snatched the phone from her servant's hand.

"Hi, Gog," Jocelyn answered, using her pet name for the woman. It was a holdover from her days as a toddler, when everything was ma-ma, da-da and ga-ga. The latter eventually became shortened to Gog. "Trounced at bridge today, were you? I guess there's no need to ask how you are."

"Jocelyn." Her voice warmed instantly, then hardened again in irritation. "That impertinent British twerp has worked his last day for me."

"Gog, you are a marvelous liar." Jocelyn grinned at the woman's empty threat.

"This time I mean it," her grandmother stated. "I swear, that man may have a stiff upper lip, but his lower jaw is always flapping."

"Dexter is a positive sphinx with everyone outside the family, and you know it," Jocelyn chided in amusement.

There was an audible *harrumph* on the other end of the line. "If he's a sphinx, then it's high time he was mummified." His low, distinguished voice rumbled in the background, his words unintelligible. "I don't require prompting, Dexter. I am well aware she has been away. Honestly," she said into the phone again, "that man acts as if I were senile. So, tell me, Jocelyn, how was your trip?"

"Long, busy, and—thankfully—over."

"You certainly sound chipper. With the way you

were hopping all over the country, I expected you to return with your tail dragging.''

"A good, hot soak in the tub can be very reviving." She glanced at the wet footprints she'd left on the Turkish rug and got straight to the point. "I was calling to see if you were free for lunch tomorrow."

"Tomorrow? Dexter, fetch me my date calendar." There was a mumbled response. "It's a pity you aren't a dog, Dexter. My life would be much more peaceful if you were muzzled. I never said to *look* at my appointments for tomorrow. You know you can't see without your glasses. Just bring the book here. He delights in annoying me," she spoke the last to Jocelyn. "Ah, here we are. Tomorrow . . . You couldn't have picked a better day? I'm supposed to lunch with Maude Farnsworth at—"

"What about Wednesday?" Jocelyn interrupted.

"Nonsense. Tomorrow is fine. The woman is a first-class bore. What better reason could I have to cancel than a luncheon invitation to the White House?"

"If you're sure," she began.

"Very sure," her grandmother replied with a wealth of feeling. "I can't imagine why I ever agreed to meet her in the first place. I must have been desperate for entertainment. What time shall I be there?"

"I have a meeting at the State Department tomorrow morning at ten, which shouldn't last much more than an hour. But just in case it runs longer, let's say twelve-thirty."

"I'll be there with bells on." There was a slight pause. "Maybe I'll even wear Salome's veil and nothing else. Wouldn't that give the tabloids something to tattle about?''

She sounded so serious that, for a moment, Jocelyn was speechless.

Realizing it was another one of her grandmother's little jokes, she chuckled. ''Dad would have a fit, Gog.''

''I know. Poor Dexter is positively apoplectic at the thought. Which is just as well. He has been looking a trifle pale. I'll see you tomorrow, dear,'' she concluded cheerily and rang off.

With one hand still clutching the towel around her, Jocelyn returned the receiver to its cradle and walked back into the bathroom, deep in thought. So far, she had done nothing more than arrange to have lunch with her grandmother. If she started having second thoughts about the wisdom of this, there was still time to change her mind.

But the central issue hadn't changed. She was tired of being wise and cautious, guarding her every word and gesture, always concerned about doing the proper thing. It was time she did something unwise and improper.

Quite possibly, there was more of her grandmother in her than Jocelyn had realized.

Promptly at six-thirty the next morning, the telephone on her bedside table rang. Groaning, Jocelyn rolled over to acknowledge the wake-up call from the White House operator.

"I'm up," she mumbled sleepily.

"Would you like me to call you back in ten minutes?" the operator inquired.

She was briefly tempted by the thought, then flung back the covers. "That won't be necessary. Thanks." She hung up and pushed the button next to the bed, ringing a buzzer in the second-floor kitchen, signaling the steward on duty that she was ready for her morning juice and coffee.

Thirty minutes later, Jocelyn knocked at the door to her father's study, a second cup of coffee in her hand, her slippered feet and pajama-clad legs visible beneath the silk robe belted around her waist. Mornings were usually the only time during the day when she saw her father, unless there was a state visit from some visiting dignitary. This thirty-minute fragment of the day had become their family time together.

From inside the room came the mellifluous voice of James Earl Jones announcing, "This, is CNN."

On the heels of it came her father's muffled but equally familiar voice, calling, "Come in."

Jocelyn opened the door. Back during the days when it was customary for husbands and wives to sleep separately, the study had served as the president's bedroom. During previous administrations, it had been converted into a study. The carpets, drapes, and upholstery were all in a rich red, giving the room a definitely masculine and very presidential feel.

Cheery flames leaped and danced behind the fireplace's glass insert. Placed inconspicuously on the side of its marble mantelpiece was an inscription that read:

This room was occupied by John Fitzgerald Kennedy during the two years, ten months and two days he was President of the United States.
   January 20, 1961–November 22, 1963.

Elsewhere there was a second plaque:

In this room, Abraham Lincoln slept during his occupancy of the White House as President of the United States.

Every inch of the White House breathed history. There was no eluding it. Every time Jocelyn started to become comfortable living in it, she would turn her head and find herself staring at something of historic significance that reminded her of the temporary nature of her stay.

"Good morning." Her father sat in the overstuffed chair facing the television, his reading glasses perched on the end of his nose. The morning editions of the *Washington Post* and the *New York Times* lay on the floor next to his chair, indicating he had already read them. Three more newspapers were tucked next to him in the chair.

"Good morning, Dad." Jocelyn crossed to his chair and brushed a kiss across his freshly shaven cheek, something she had done every morning for as long as she could remember. "Mmm, you smell good this morning. Got a hot date?'' she teased and continued past him to curl into a second overstuffed chair, the twin to the one he occupied.

"Not unless you call a meeting with Cosgrove and his assistant from the Justice Department a hot date.'' He shook open another newspaper.

Jocelyn winced faintly in silent commiseration. "It sounds about as exciting as mine with State.'' She sipped her coffee, her glance straying to the television screen. "Is there anything new happening in the world this morning?''

"Not much. Rioting broke out when the first famine relief supplies reached the drought area in the Sudan. OPEC is talking about raising the price for crude—just in time for the winter fuel-oil season, naturally,'' he added with grim disapproval. "And the first winter storm is rolling into the plains states, which is bound to affect voter turnout.'' He gave her an inspecting sideways glance. "Did you sleep well?''

"After I finally got to sleep. Too tired, I guess,'' Jocelyn added by way of an explanation, when the truth was that she had trouble shutting her mind off from its plottings and schemings. "But I feel rested.''

Excited and energized was more like it, with a few nervous qualms to give it all some spice.

A knock at the door signaled the arrival of the butler with their breakfast. Her father had his usual order of one poached egg on toast, two slices of very crisp, dry bacon, and a bran muffin on the side. Jocelyn had never been able to eat a full meal so early in the morning, and settled for a side of whole wheat toast, spread lightly with honey-butter.

His breakfast was served on a tray drawn up to his chair. Between bites, he read from the folded newspaper held in one hand and propped next to his plate. Jocelyn nibbled at a corner of her toast and pretended to watch the news, but her mind was busy compiling a list of things she wanted to do on her "free day."

Her fanciful flight was interrupted by a low chuckle. Jocelyn turned with an almost guilty start and saw the amused curve to her father's mouth.

"Tucker's in fine form today," he remarked.

Tucker. For a moment, the name didn't register. Then Jocelyn remembered that tall, gangly columnist her father had spoken to yesterday afternoon.

"What's he say?" she asked, feigning interest.

"He starts talking about all the fuss that was raised when it came out that Paul Cunningham's—the candidate going up against Rockwell from Alabama— that his grandfather was a wizard in the Ku Klux Klan. Then Tucker goes on to say, and I quote, 'Now I don't know what difference it makes that his granddaddy was a big chief in the Klan. But the whole affair sure does prove that the cheapest way to get your family tree traced is to run for public office.'"

"That's definitely a fact," Jocelyn agreed wryly.

Nodding, her father inched the paper up to focus on another section of the column. "Farther down, he writes, 'You all got to understand now that the whole purpose of a political campaign is to stay cool, calm, and elected—which is probably why so many candidates develop *straddle* sores.' "

"Ouch." She winced at the humorous barb.

"Listen to his closing comment." His grin briefly widened. " 'People have been complaining about all the political jokes going around lately. They claim they're bad for our country's morale. I gotta admit they're probably right. So, when you cast your vote today, make sure you don't elect any of them.' "

"Unfortunately, I think I met a couple of them while I was out on that campaign blitz," Jocelyn recalled cynically.

"Haven't we all?" Her father unfolded and folded the newspaper to another section.

She thought back over the quotes he had just read to her. "The wit of most political humorists tends to be acerbic. But this Tucker guy just pokes fun. He hits the target without being vicious about it. That's very rare these days."

"Isn't it, though." He cut off a bite of egg and toast, then speared it with his fork.

"What's his background?" she wondered, suddenly curious about Grady Tucker. "I know you said he's from Kansas. But what did he do before he started writing this column?"

"I've heard he went to work straight out of college as a speechwriter. Better at the jokes than he was at explaining political positions, from what I understand," he recalled with a smile. "Supposedly he did some freelance work, writing copy for various lobby groups when he first came to the Capitol." Pausing, he peered at Jocelyn over the top of his reading glasses, his eyes twinkling. "There's a story that he twice offered his column to the *Washington Post,* but they turned it down. As popular as his column is getting, don't you know they're gnashing their teeth over that one?"

"Undoubtedly," Jocelyn agreed and took another bite of her toast.

"Why do you ask? About Tucker, I mean."

"No particular reason. Curious, I guess," she replied with an idle shrug. "It occurred to me that I know practically every other reporter in Washington on sight, and I just realized I've never run into Grady Tucker before."

"That's not surprising. On the rare occasions when Tucker does go to some political function, he tends to stand back and observe. He isn't one to mix and mingle."

"He didn't look like the type who would be big on socializing," Jocelyn commented, recalling that shy ducking of his head. "He reminded me of a bashful schoolboy."

"Maybe." The paper rustled and crackled as her father turned to another page. "But I wouldn't underestimate him. He has a sharp eye and a keen mind."

"Obviously, but I don't think it's likely that I'll ever run into him." Stretching, Jocelyn reached over and helped herself to more coffee from the insulated pot on his tray. "What's the weather supposed to be like today?"

"Sunny and warm, the high in the seventies. An Indian summer kind of day. Why?"

"I invited Gog to have lunch with me today." She lifted her cup and blew lightly on its steaming surface. "It sounds like it could be warm enough to eat outside on the Truman Balcony. It might be the last chance this year."

"Mother's coming here?" He frowned in surprise, then lapsed into concentrated thought. "If I can't slip over to say hello, tell her to drop by my office before she leaves. But ask her not to answer the phones when they ring; I don't care how busy someone is."

Jocelyn laughed. "The staff is still talking about that last time she took the call from the Russian ambassador."

On that occasion, Bliss Wakefield had informed the ambassador that he would have to wait to speak to the president until after she had seen him.

"Rimsky hasn't forgotten it either. And the press had an absolute field day with it," her father recalled dryly. "Sometimes it amazes me, the things my mother can get away with. Yet everybody loves her."

"Mostly because they know she doesn't care what they think. They envy that about her." Jocelyn certainly did.

"You're probably right. Age does have its advantages. And my mother uses them all," he added.

CHAPTER 3

The state visit by Britain's newly elected prime minister and his wife was only two and a half weeks away, leaving a myriad of last-minute details to finalize. Nothing was too small to be considered, even their preference in toothpaste brands. As a consequence, Jocelyn's meeting with officials from the State Department and protocol office, a meeting that shouldn't have taken more than an hour, stretched into two.

It was half past eleven when Jocelyn arrived at the White House. A line of tourists trailed from the East Gate, waiting to tour the mansion's public rooms.

Noticing them, Jocelyn remarked to her personal Secret Service agent, Mike Bassett, "Everybody seems to be taking advantage of today's warm weather."

"You can't blame them," he replied. "It's a beautiful day outside."

"Yes." Perfect for lunching on the Truman Balcony, Jocelyn thought. As she approached the private elevator, she spied the security guard on duty. "Has Mrs. Wakefield arrived yet, Tom?"

He hesitated, stretching his neck a little as if his collar had suddenly become too tight. "In a way."

Jocelyn stopped, little alarm bells going off in her head. "What do you mean? Is she here or not?"

"She's here," he admitted, his glance skittering off her face. "But instead of going up, she ... uh ... joined a group of fourth-graders touring the rooms."

"Why am I not surprised?" Jocelyn sighed and fought back a smile. "I'd better go find her."

Even as she spoke she was conscious of Agent Bassett's low voice speaking into his microphone. When she took a step toward the public rooms, he laid a light hand on her arm.

"Wait until Mavis and Frank get here."

It was on the tip of her tongue to remind him that it was a group of schoolchildren; they could hardly constitute a threat to her. But this was not a time to make waves and go charging off, not if she ever hoped to slip away from them in the future. Stifling her impatience, she waited for the rest of the security detail to arrive.

The sound of giggling children and her grandmother's regal voice led Jocelyn directly to the East Room on the mansion's first floor. Security guards, stationed to keep the stream of visitors moving along, stood helpless while Bliss Wakefield held court, regaling her audience of schoolchildren, their accompanying teachers, and a handful of other adults with the exploits of Theodore Roosevelt's children.

"I can't imagine a room better designed for roller-skating, can you?" A chorus of noes greeted her grandmother's question. "Too bad none of you brought your Rollerblades. Then we could try it out. I'm quite good at Rollerblading; did I tell you that?"

A more incongruous picture couldn't have been painted than that of this tall, elegant woman wearing a pair of Rollerblades. Unless, of course, they had been dyed a sapphire blue to match her cashmere suit, Jocelyn decided.

"After the White House was first built," Bliss continued with her lecture, "this room remained unfurnished for a good number of years. In fact, Abigail Adams instructed her servants to hang the laundry in here. That was back when people didn't have clothes dryers—or electricity, for that matter." She spied Jocelyn watching from the rear of the group, flanked on three sides by her Secret Service escorts. "There you are, Jocelyn," she declared, an outrageous twinkle in her eyes. "I'm so glad you could join us. I was about to tell these children about the time those rascally Roosevelt boys snuck a pony into the White House and tried to take it up the elevator. You all know my granddaughter, Jocelyn, don't you?"

For the Secret Service agents, the ensuing scene was like a nightmare with the children mobbing around her, bombarding her with questions. With their usual tact, they managed to deter the more aggressive and restore some semblance of order.

After Jocelyn had fielded several of the youngsters' queries, a short, elderly man of African descent raised the head of his cane, seeking her attention. "Excuse me, Miss Wakefield." His voice was in that low bass register, rich and beautifully modulated. "If you would be so kind as to answer one more question?"

"Of course." Smiling politely, Jocelyn reached deep into her reserve to summon up another handful of patience.

"With the holidays coming up, I was wondering in which room does the official White House Christmas tree stand?" He stood at the rear of the group, his topcoat unbuttoned, a cane in one hand and a hat in the other. But it was the shining brightness of his dark eyes and the contrast of gleaming brown skin and a neatly trimmed snow-white beard that drew Jocelyn's eye.

"It's always in the Blue Room," she replied, "although we have trees in other rooms as well. Those trees decorated with ornaments of past Christmas themes are usually displayed in the East Colonnade."

"Have you chosen this year's theme yet?" he inquired.

"That was done some months ago." *After much discussion and planning,* she could have added.

"May I ask what it is?" There was something eager and childlike about the smile on his face. Then concern flickered across his expression. "Or is that something you don't wish to announce yet?"

"I don't think this year's Christmas theme falls under the category of a state secret." She smiled back at him, this time with a natural warmth. "We have chosen 'A Child Is Born' for this year."

An even bigger smile lit his face. "An interesting and highly appropriate choice."

His obvious pleasure in the theme prompted Jocelyn to explain, "The inspiration for it came from the exquisite eighteenth-century crèche that has been displayed here as part of the holiday celebration ever since it was given to the White House in nineteen sixty-seven. In all, there are forty-seven wood-carved and terra-cotta figures that make up the crèche. It will be the focal point of our decorations here in the East Room."

"And the ornaments for the official Christmas tree?" The rising inflection of his voice turned the phrase into a question.

"We have invited three separate organizations to create ornaments in various ethnic styles that depict the birth of Christ," Jocelyn told him. "America is, after all, a melting pot, peopled by immigrants from every country in the world. It's that diversity that has made us strong. We wanted to celebrate that, as well."

"A most laudable decision." His warm smile held both wisdom and approval.

A curly-haired girl waved frantically from the middle of the group, anxious to ask her question. Jocelyn pointed to her and nodded. "I was just wondering . . ." the girl began, then hesitated, suffering a momentary attack of shyness, "with all the fireplaces you got, which one does Santa come down?"

The boy directly behind her hooted at the question and punched her in the back. "You don't still believe in Santa Claus, do you?" he scoffed.

Red-faced, the girl turned on him hotly. " 'Course I don't, but my little sister does, so Santa still comes to our house at Christmas."

"I'm glad he still visits you," Jocelyn inserted, drawing the group's attention back to her. "Don't we all love it when Santa comes?" There was an instant chorus of agreement. "And here at the White House," Jocelyn added, "Santa can come down whatever chimney he wants to."

On that note, she managed to extricate herself from the tour group. The Secret Service agents instantly whisked both Jocelyn and her grandmother to the elevator.

"Can you believe all those questions about Christmas?" Jocelyn murmured in exasperation when the doors slid shut. "It isn't even Thanksgiving yet."

"Still, it isn't too early to be thinking about it," Bliss replied over the low hum of the elevator engaging.

"Unfortunately I've been talking about Christmas for months." She caught her grandmother's skeptical glance. "It's true. Last year's decorations were barely down before the planning sessions started for this year. First the theme had to be chosen, then a decision on how it was to be carried out. After that, it's all the fine details. And when I wasn't meeting about that, then it was about the design for this year's White

House Christmas card, or choosing the inside verse or updating the mailing list. By the time Christmas finally gets here, I'll be so tired of it, I won't care."

"I think the schoolchildren were interested in how you decorate the White House for Christmas, though," Bliss mused. "They were a fun group, weren't they?"

"I think I will strangle you for that, Gog," Jocelyn declared as she stepped off the elevator onto the family quarters' second floor.

"I probably deserve it," Bliss agreed, unconcerned. "But we both know you made those children's day. They'll be talking about it for the rest of their lives."

"You seemed to be doing a fine job of making their day before I ever arrived."

"I couldn't help it. Those poor children looked so horribly bored wandering from room to room. You really need to do something about livening up those dreadful guide books. They spend far too much time identifying the furnishings in a room and giving their provenance. Only someone interested in antiques—a dealer or collector—could possibly care that the Steinway grand piano in the East Room was designed by Gugler, that it has gilt American-eagle supports, or that it was decorated with gilt stenciling by Beck. The guidebooks make the White House sound like some dry, dull museum instead of a place where people laughed and loved and lived—and where some of the most important moments in our nation's history were played out."

"So you took it upon yourself to correct the situation by recounting the exploits of Teddy Roosevelt's children and the East Room's former use as a kind of laundry room." Smiling at her grandmother's irrepressible logic, Jocelyn glanced through the handful of messages on the hall table.

"You can't deny the White House has had its moments of frivolity, Jocelyn. Wonderfully undignified ones, I might add. But I would have also told them of the room's more somber use as the place where Lincoln's body lay in state on a black-draped catafalque following his assassination." Finger by finger, Bliss Wakefield pulled off her black gloves. "And I would have told them about Dolley Madison and the way she refused to flee the White House, despite the advancing British Army, until the portrait of George Washington had been removed from its frame and included with her things. Imagine that moment, Jocelyn!" She paused, one hand dramatically lifted as she peered off into the past. "British soldiers on the outskirts of the city, friends deserting her right and left, officials urging her to flee, the Capitol and the White House about to fall in enemy hands. Think of the panic that must have been in the air. But Dolley stood fast, refusing to leave without Washington's portrait. Of course"—she lowered her hand and turned to Jocelyn with a decided twinkle in her eyes—"the wise woman also took her own portrait. Which tells me the painting of Washington wasn't the only item rescued from the White House before the British burned it."

"But Washington's portrait is the only item to survive the fire that has been in the White House ever since eighteen hundred.''

Prior to moving into the presidential mansion, Jocelyn had made an extensive study of its history. In college, she had carried a dual major, earning a degree in both education and American history. As a result, there were few facts about her temporary home and its past residents that she didn't know.

"Except, of course, for those times when the White House was being reconstructed or renovated,'' her grandmother inserted, as always, determined to have the last word, and in the process dismissing Jocelyn's point with a wave of her gloves. "As dramatic and stirring as that episode must have been, it's much more fun to imagine John Adams's drawers and Abigail's pantaloons hanging on drying racks in the East Room—or the Roosevelt children racing around it on their roller skates.'' She slipped her folded glove inside her small clutch purse and mused idly, "I wonder what Dexter did with that old pair of skates I had. I used to be quite good on them.''

Jocelyn raised one eyebrow, then lowered it, smiling. Forewarned, she could be forearmed. "The next time you spend the night in the White House, I'll make sure someone goes through your luggage. Any roller skates—or Rollerblades—will be confiscated. But don't worry.'' She flashed her grandmother a quick smile. "I'll see that they're returned to you when you leave.''

Bliss Wakefield gave her a long, assessing look, then released an exaggerated sigh of despair. "I worry about you, Jocelyn. You are fast becoming too proper and correct," she declared with a sad shake of her head. "You need to do something outrageous before you become a deadly bore."

"Don't think I'm not tempted. But I also dread the thought of becoming the media's lead story. As things stand now, I can't even cough without someone reporting it." Finding no messages marked to her attention, she placed the stack back on the table and turned from it, avoiding direct contact with her grandmother's suddenly intent gaze. "It's such a beautiful day, I thought we'd lunch on the Truman Balcony."

"An interesting choice," Bliss murmured on a thought-filled note.

The luncheon setting was magnificent with its sweeping view that drew the eye across the immaculate green of the South Lawn and the Ellipse all the way to the Mall and the soaring marble obelisk of the Washington Monument. Beyond the gleaming white tower, the smooth waters of the Tidal Basin reflected the cloudless blue of the sky. At the end of the grand vista sat the Jefferson Memorial, in perfect alignment with the White House.

The axial view was one of two designed by Pierre L'Enfant, the young French engineer and Revolutionary War veteran who laid out the plan for the new capital city, destined to be built on the banks of the Potomac River, back in 1791. A second eye-stretching view used the Mall and the Reflecting Pool to join the Lincoln Memorial with the Washington Monument and the Capitol building.

Seen from the mansion's second-floor balcony, the scale and graceful symmetry of the scene had never failed to stir Jocelyn—until today, when she gave it little more than a cursory glance before sitting down to the lunch the staff had prepared.

Uneasy and edgy, Jocelyn struggled to conceal the tension that had her stomach in knots. She disinterestedly poked her fork first at the mixed green salad topped with mandarin oranges and sugared almonds, then at the delicate omelet. As usual, her grandmother dominated the conversation, allowing Jocelyn the freedom to entertain all the last-minute doubts about her venture, requiring of her only a nod or an occasional word now and then to hold up her end of the exchange.

After the coffee was poured, the steward paused by the table. "Is there anything else I might bring you?"

Before Jocelyn could reply, her grandmother spoke up. "Nothing, thank you. Just leave the coffee pot on the table. We'll manage from here."

The subtle request for privacy was not lost on the steward. He withdrew from the balcony, discreetly closing the doors behind him. Jocelyn went through the motions of sipping her coffee, conscious of her grandmother's bright eyes studying her over the rim of her own china cup.

"Have you decided yet?"

"Decided what?" Jocelyn lowered her cup in surprise, a guilty heat creeping into her neck at the accidental accuracy of the question.

It had to be coincidental. Her grandmother was many things, but a mind reader wasn't one of them.

"I don't know. You haven't told me," Bliss countered smoothly. "But I can see the wheels turning in your head. You have something on your mind, and it clearly isn't the pleasure of my company. So out with it."

This was it—the turning point. Jocelyn could choose either to abandon her foolish fantasy or to plunge ahead with it. It was time to decide.

"Actually, I—I was wondering whether you had any plans for this weekend?" Jocelyn asked, stalling for more time to make up her mind.

"This weekend?" Her grandmother blinked, thrown off balance by the unexpected question. Recovering with aplomb, she replied, "I have nothing earthshaking planned, certainly nothing that can't be canceled if I choose. Why do you ask?"

"I thought I might visit you." Jocelyn tried to sound very offhand about it.

"You know very well that you are always welcome at Redford Hall," Bliss chided.

"But you could have been busy this weekend—"

"I am never so busy that I can't make time to be with my favorite granddaughter," Bliss declared, a genuine affection softening her otherwise regal features.

"I am your *only* granddaughter," Jocelyn reminded her dryly.

"So you are," she agreed, an impish curve to her lips. Pausing, she tipped her silver-white head to one side, studying Jocelyn with bright and curious eyes. "There's more to this than just coming to visit me, isn't there?" she challenged with a knowing look.

Jocelyn hesitated, then made up her mind. "Yes, there is." A new calmness settled over her.

Bliss leaned forward with avid interest, resting both elbows on the damask-covered table. "What's his name? Do I know him?"

"Whose name?" Jocelyn frowned in bewilderment.

Bliss sighed in disappointment and sat back in her chair. "If you have to ask, you obviously don't have a new man in your life. I had hoped you were planning an assignation at Redford Hall, out of sight of the prying press. Dexter would have loved that."

"A new man." Jocelyn scoffed at the idea. "I don't even have an old one."

"More's the pity, if you ask me," her grandmother declared with true regret. "Whatever happened to that good-looking Army captain you were dating?"

"He escorted me to only two social functions, Gog. I would hardly call that dating. After the second time, every gossip column and tabloid in the country was spreading rumors about our pending engagement." The entire episode was one she still found irritating. "To be honest, Gog, I can't remember the last time I went on a date without a horde of photographers in tow, not to mention the Secret Service."

"My, I do believe I detect a trace of bitterness," Bliss murmured, a gleam of approval in her eyes.

Jocelyn missed it, her attention focused inward on all the resentment that churned inside, resentment that had been too long repressed. "I'm afraid it's more than a trace. It's closer to a volcano, all hot and bubbling, about to explode."

"I'm relieved to see you are still human, after all," Bliss announced, practically beaming. "You have been such a paragon of charm and good manners these last three and a half years, that I was certain you were on the verge of sainthood. I was beginning to wonder if you were really my granddaughter."

In spite of herself, Jocelyn laughed, feeling some of her tension dissipate with it. "One day—that's all I want, Gog. One day to myself, without anyone watching me. One day to be Jane Doe instead of Jocelyn Wakefield, the president's daughter."

"That's a tall order." Her grandmother's dark eyes widened expressively. "Unfortunately, grandmothers aren't given magic wands, you know. Only fairy godmothers have those. I wish I could help, but—"

"You can," Jocelyn broke in as excitement began to take hold inside.

Bliss drew her head back in a mixture of doubt and interest. "How?"

It was Jocelyn's turn to lean forward. "Remember that hidden staircase in Granddad's old room. And that old tunnel between the house and the carriage house?"

"Of course I remember them. I happen to be the one who showed them to you when you were just a scruffy little tomboy in braids." An ambulance plowed its way through the traffic on Constitution Avenue, lights flashing and siren wailing. "You were fascinated with that tunnel. Every time you came, you insisted on going through it. Dexter was convinced you were going to grow up to be a spelunker.'' Bliss laughed suddenly, a rich, hearty sound, rife with amusement. ''How he hated going in that tunnel and wiping down all those webs before you would arrive! The man has a positive aversion to spiders; did you know that?''

It had never been the tunnel itself that fascinated Jocelyn. It had been its use by runaway slaves back during the days when Redford Hall had been a station on the Underground Railroad. Little did she know then that her fascination with it would eventually lead to her interest in American history.

''What condition is it in now?'' Jocelyn asked and held her breath, conscious of how much depended on her grandmother's answer.

''I really don't know.'' Bliss thoughtfully considered the question. ''I don't think anyone has been in it since the Secret Service people checked it out. Such a fuss they raised about it then,'' she recalled in amusement. ''If it had been up to them, they would have filled in the passage. But the historical significance of it made that impossible, so they settled for padlocking the doors at both ends.'' She chuckled at another thought. ''I think it was that very same day when they told me their great revelation about Dexter. How grave their faces were, Jocelyn, when they informed me that he wasn't from England at all, but the Lower East Side of Chicago, and that his name wasn't Cummings-Gould but some Polish thing that I can't begin to pronounce. They were quite put out when I told them your grandfather had uncovered the same information nearly forty years ago when Dexter first came to work for us. That was back in the days when having a houseman with a British accent had a certain cachet. Now, Dexter has become more British than the Brits, but a false name hardly makes him a security risk. Not that the Secret Service ever really suggested he was, but—''

''The padlocks, Gog,'' Jocelyn interrupted, anxious to get back to the matter at hand. ''Who has the keys to them?''

''The keys? I don't remember,'' she murmured and stopped to think. ''I can't imagine that they didn't leave us a set at Redford Hall. Dexter will know. Why?'' she asked curiously, then gasped as understanding flashed in her expression. A split second later, a smile of utter delight broke across her face. ''You plan on slipping away from the Secret Service through that old underground passage, don't you?'' When Jocelyn nodded, her grandmother's expression turned a little wicked. ''They aren't going to like it one bit when they discover you're missing.''

''That's where you come in, Gog,'' Jocelyn explained, unconsciously lowering her voice to a conspiratorial level. ''You need to cover for me, convince them that I'm still there. You'll have to tell them I'm sick or something—anything so they won't become suspicious when they don't see me around. But you only have to keep them fooled for twenty-four hours.''

"You certainly can't be very sick, or they'll insist on bringing a doctor in," her grandmother commented, already mulling over the possible excuses. She paused, her gaze traveling to Jocelyn's distinctive red hair. "You do realize that you'll need some type of disguise, dear. You wouldn't get ten feet without someone recognizing you."

"I know. You'll have to help me with that, too, Gog. I'll need a wig, preferably a dark-brown one, and some different clothes, nothing like the styles or colors I usually wear. We both know I can't go shopping without the whole world knowing what I've purchased. And I can't send any of the staff to buy clothes like that without raising all sorts of questions in their minds. As closemouthed as all of them are, they still talk among themselves."

"You're absolutely right," Bliss agreed, her quick mind turning its thoughts to this new request. "Actually, shopping for a disguise will be quite fun. A real adventure." Her glance, sharp and probing, flashed back to Jocelyn's face. "You do realize that Dexter will have to be told about this." Her lips thinned with a mixture of disgust and irritation. "If I know him, the pompous old bat isn't going to approve of it either. I can just hear him now, raving on about how selfish and irresponsible it would be for a woman in your position to do such a thing. Why, before he's through, he'll have you kidnapped and held for ransom by some radical terrorist group."

"That's ridiculous," Jocelyn protested, not entirely sure how to get around this obstacle.

"Of course it is, but Dexter watches way too many Bruce Willis movies." She sipped at her coffee and pondered this new problem.

"Somehow you have to convince him, Gog, that with the right disguise, I won't look any different than the average tourist," Jocelyn reasoned.

"True," her grandmother murmured thoughtfully. "But even if I convince him of that, he will want to know everything: what you plan to do; where you will go."

"In only a twenty-four-hour period, I won't have time to go anywhere. About all I can do is wander around Washington and see the sights; visit some of the places I haven't been to since Mom took me when I was—what?—nine or ten."

The thought brought back a flood of warm memories of the many and varied picture-taking excursions around the capital Jocelyn had gone on with her mother. Photography had been her mother's favorite hobby, and Audra Wakefield had been good at it. Better than good, Jocelyn corrected herself, recalling some of the more memorable portraits her mother had taken.

"You keep saying 'twenty-four hours.' Does that mean you plan on being gone all night?" Bliss asked. "Where will you sleep?"

"In a hotel, like any other tourist." Jocelyn considered the answer to be obvious.

"But what will you do for identification? How will you pay for the room? That's something else you need to decide," Bliss stated, returning her cup to its saucer.

"With cash, of course," Jocelyn said with a shrug. "I can't very well use a credit card, can I? Not when I'll have to register under a fictitious name."

"But if you pay for the room with cash, the clerk will probably think you're a hooker."

"Not if I'm dressed like some dowdy plain Jane," Jocelyn reasoned.

"True. It's a pity, though," her grandmother replied, a naughty twinkle in her eyes. "It would be much more fun dressing you up like a hooker. Think of the clothes I could buy."

"And if some cop arrested me, what would I do for identification?" Jocelyn chided. "No one else is likely to ask for any."

"Unless you're in an accident," Bliss added, then sighed in concern. "Dexter will worry about that, you know."

"You'll simply have to assure him that I will be extremely careful not to have one." Jocelyn lifted the silver coffeepot and refilled her cup. "Heaven knows, if anything like that happens, the game is up anyway. There'll be news bulletins all over the place, not to mention a lot of red faces and painful explanations."

"But it will be a marvelous adventure for you, dear." Her grandmother practically beamed with excitement. "The risk of discovery merely adds that delicious element of spice to it."

"That reminds me, I need to write you a check before you leave. Don't let me forget, will you?" Jocelyn raised the china cup to her lips.

"A check? For what?" Bliss gave her a blank look.

"For the clothes, the wig, and the cash I'll need to pay for my room and meals, plus whatever else I might want."

"You can forget that." With a downward flip of her hand, Bliss dismissed the idea. "This entire little adventure is on me. You can consider it an early Christmas gift." When Jocelyn opened her mouth to argue, Bliss gave her a quelling look down her aristocratic nose. "I insist, Jocelyn."

"All right, but—" Catching the warning rattle of the balcony door latch, Jocelyn quickly changed what she was about to say. "This Indian summer weather makes it difficult to remember that winter is just around the corner, doesn't it?"

"It certain does. I—" With the skill of an actress, her grandmother cast a seemingly idle glance toward the opening door. A smile of genuine warmth and affection instantly transformed her expression. "Henry! What a delightful surprise."

Crossing to the table, the president dropped a kiss on his mother's offered cheek. "Hello, Mother. I heard you were here."

"Oh, dear." Glancing at Jocelyn, Bliss made a poor attempt at feigning concern. "That means he's heard about me talking to that group of schoolchildren, I'm afraid."

"Talking?" Henry Wakefield questioned her choice of words. "Wasn't it more like taking them on a personally guided tour of the public rooms?"

"They were bored—and singularly unimpressed by room after room of stuffy old furniture," she offered in defense.

"I should have known it would be something like that." He grinned with a kind of approval.

"Sit down. I'm getting a crick in my neck looking up at you." Bliss motioned him into one of the vacant chairs at the table.

As if on cue, a steward stepped onto the balcony, carrying a tray with a fresh pot of coffee and a clean china cup and saucer. He placed the latter in front of the president, filled it with steaming coffee, then topped off both Jocelyn's and her grandmother's cups before withdrawing back inside the house.

"Have there been any early reports on voter turnout?" Jocelyn asked automatically. Politics had always been a part of any table conversation as long as she could remember. Talking about various issues and stands came as naturally to her as discussing the weather did to others.

"It looks like the turnout will be right around average. Down in some states and up in others, depending on the local issues on the ballot." Henry Wakefield reached for his cup, taking an appreciative sip from it.

"There's both good and bad in that," Bliss remarked and ran an inspecting glance over her son.

"You are looking fit and rested. Obviously you have recovered from the campaign whirl."

"Sometimes I think he feeds on the frenzy of it all," Jocelyn teased.

"The mark of a true politician." Bliss lifted her coffee cup in a mock toast to her son.

"Thank you, I think." He inclined his head, his eyes sparkling as bright as his mother's were. "Actually, I do feel quite rested, but I'm still looking forward to a quiet weekend at Camp David. Why don't you join us, Mother?"

Jocelyn stared at her grandmother, seeing all their schemes dissipating like smoke in the air. But Bliss Wakefield didn't turn a hair.

"Your invitation comes a bit late, Henry. Jocelyn and I have already made plans for the weekend," she announced. "She's spending it with me at Redford Hall. We haven't had a good old-fashioned gab session in months. You are welcome to join us, of course—"

The President held up a hand, good-naturedly staving off the invitation. "Thanks, but no thanks. I'll pass."

In that instant, Jocelyn knew it was handled. "Dad," she began hopefully, another thought occurring to her, "instead of using *Marine One*, could you arrange to go by car to Camp David? That way, with any luck, the press will think I'm there with you, and won't notice that I've slipped over to Redford Hall. It would be wonderful not to have photographers camped outside the whole weekend."

"I don't see why not," he agreed readily. "With all the fall foliage, it should be a beautiful drive."

Jocelyn almost laughed in triumph. The last major hazard had just been removed. Short of an act of God, nothing could possibly go wrong now.

CHAPTER 4

At half past four on Friday afternoon, minutes after the presidential motorcade left for Camp David, Jocelyn walked out of the White House and climbed into the rear of a dark, nondescript sedan. With her lone suitcase stowed in the trunk, the vehicle pulled away from the mansion and onto the city streets, followed by a second unmarked car carrying two more members of the security detail assigned to her.

Jocelyn made a show of settling back in her seat and gazing idly out the tinted-glass window, a pose that didn't invite conversation. But it was an idleness she didn't feel. Inside she was a jumble of nerves and excitement, skittering pulse, and tense muscles. Fortunately, none of it showed. That mask she had learned to wear in public was firmly in place. In the back of her mind, she knew that if she seemed unusually quiet and distracted, it would ultimately make the excuse that she wasn't feeling well seem all the more genuine.

"Tired?" Mike Bassett's gentle question pulled Jocelyn's gaze from its sightless stare out the window.

"Very," she said and sighed on the heels of it, a sigh that was heavier with tension than fatigue.

"I take it that means you'll be staying in tonight," he guessed.

"Tonight and tomorrow," Jocelyn told him. "In fact, I don't plan to do anything more strenuous than read or play Scrabble the whole weekend."

"But what plans has your grandmother made? That's the real question," he said, as much to himself as to Jocelyn.

"Whatever they are, she can count me out of them," she replied. "I've already warned her that if she invites anybody over this weekend, she'll have to entertain them. All I want is some peace and quiet." Leaning her head back, Jocelyn closed her eyes.

"I'm surprised you didn't go to Camp David with your father," he remarked.

She could feel the curious inspection of the agent's glance. Without opening her eyes, Jocelyn replied, "I thought it was time he had a weekend with just the guys. That way he and Doctor Jim can sit around the table puffing on their cigars, trading fish stories, and playing poker to their hearts' content—without giving me a second thought."

Obviously satisfied with her explanation, the agent fell silent.

Using side streets and avoiding the more heavily traveled thoroughfares and the congestion of DuPont Circle, they crossed the bridge over Rock Creek and entered the Georgetown district. Redford Hall stood in a forgotten corner of one of the area's more fashionable residential neighborhoods, remote yet easily accessible, the type of location favored by the ever-cautious Secret Service.

Ivy twined around the tall gateposts at the entrance to Redford Hall. Its wine red autumn leaves blended with the red brick of the posts. The elaborately scrolled black iron gates stood open, awaiting their arrival.

At the foot of the curved driveway stood the two-and-a-half-story manor house, Georgian in style. Two more agents, Donna Travers and Don Hubbard, waited outside the imposing front entrance, having arrived two hours earlier to make a final check of the premises.

But it was the sight of the tall, stoop-shouldered Dexter Cummings-Gould holding open the driver's-side door of a navy blue Mercedes parked in the driveway that drew Jocelyn's attention. Standing before the open car door was an older, slightly heavyset woman, dressed in an uninspired aubergine suit, her gray locks dyed an obvious champagne blond.

Jocelyn almost groaned out loud when she recognized Maude Farnsworth, pawing through her purse, making a great show of looking for her car keys. Fairly or not, Jocelyn was convinced it was a stall tactic on Maude's part. The woman obviously knew Jocelyn was expected—if not from Bliss herself, then the presence of the Secret Service agents would have indicated it. The instant she saw the car pulling into the driveway, Maude miraculously located her keys.

When the sedan came to a stop in front of Redford Hall, Jocelyn remained in the back seat until Agent Hubbard opened the door for her. Resigned to the idea that she couldn't avoid exchanging a few words with her grandmother's friend—although Jocelyn wasn't sure that *friend* was the right word to describe their relationship—she stepped out of the car, accepting the hand the stocky agent offered in assistance.

While Maude didn't stoop to something as undignified as a waving "yoohoo," she did call out, "Jocelyn, it's been ages since I've seen you. How are you?"

"Fine, thanks. Give my regards to the judge, will you?" Jocelyn said, referring to Maude's husband, and continued toward the front entrance, determined to keep this exchange as brief as possible.

But Maude wasn't about to let it end this quickly. "I mentioned to your grandmother that the judge and I would love to have you over for lunch tomorrow," she said, forcing Jocelyn to pause at the base of the steps, both agents at her side. "But Bliss tells me you already have other plans."

"Yes. Perhaps another time," Jocelyn suggested without enthusiasm.

"Wonderful," Maude declared, choosing to read

more into the statement than Jocelyn intended. With a farewell wave to her, the woman slid behind the wheel of the Mercedes.

Dexter was quick to close the car door and stride stiffly from it. Automatically Jocelyn waited for him to join her. He had on his bulldog face, the corners of his mouth severely down and his chin tucked against his neck to give the appearance of jowls. She smiled when she saw the sternly disapproving look he directed at her, a clear indication he did not like her plans for the weekend.

To upset him more, Jocelyn planted a kiss on his cheek, which was not at all the proper gesture of affection to show a servant in public according to the rigid code Dexter had adopted years ago.

"It's good to see you," she said when he reached ahead of her to open the door. "It's been a long time since I've been able to spend a weekend at Redford Hall."

"Yes." He dragged the word out in his best British fashion, loading it with a wealth of other meanings. "It's such a pity that your stay can't be a longer one."

His pointed look was cool with censure, which only made Jocelyn want to smile all the more. "I'll have to make sure to enjoy the time I have, won't I?"

"Indeed. Who knows when—or if—you'll ever return again." He deliberately injected an ominous ring to his voice.

"You're such an alarmist, Dexter," she chided and walked past him into the manor's grand hall that showcased its dramatic imperial staircase of polished oak. It rose in a single cantilevered flight to a half landing, then divided into a double sweep of stairs. "Where's Gog?"

"Madam awaits you in the sun parlor," he said, using the grand name he had given to one of the smaller rooms facing the rear gardens.

Leaving Dexter to deal with her luggage and her security detail, Jocelyn crossed the inlaid marble floor and turned down a side corridor. When she reached the sun parlor, she saw her grandmother fussing over a drooping Boston fern and muttering to herself.

"Talking to your plants, Gog?" she said, unable to hold back her good humor a moment longer. She was too filled with a nervous, charged energy to make any further attempt to conceal it.

Straightening into perfect posture, Bliss Wakefield turned from the plant. Even in slacks and a long, flowing tunic vest over a simple turtleneck, she managed to appear queenly.

"As a matter of fact, I was. I told that sickly fern if it didn't get better soon, I was going to throw it out." She glanced past Jocelyn. "What did you do with your shadows?"

"I left them with Dexter." She entered the room made cheery by the soft yellow color of its walls and the pastel floral patterns of the furnishings' upholstery.

"Yes, they've set up shop in the kitchen, as usual. With any luck, we won't see them again until it's time for you to return to the White House." Her grandmother held up a pair of crossed fingers.

"Let's hope," Jocelyn agreed. "Guess who was on hand to welcome me when I arrived?"

"Maude managed to dally long enough outside, did she?" Bliss surmised, making a small grimace of distaste.

"She did," she confirmed.

"It took me a full twenty minutes just to shoo her outdoors. Sometimes that woman simply refuses to take a hint," her grandmother declared irritably. "I don't know why I put up with her nosiness."

"Face it, Gog. You have a soft heart." An inner restlessness carried Jocelyn to the French doors with their view of the garden beyond them.

"Nervous?" her grandmother guessed, astute eyes studying her closely.

"That's one way to put it." She sighed, but it didn't release any inner tension.

"You aren't getting cold feet, are you?" Bliss accused.

"No. No, I'm not." Jocelyn turned from the garden view and smiled crookedly. "Although I think Dexter hopes I will get a bad case of them."

Her grandmother pshawed that idea. "Don't pay any attention to that old fuddy-duddy," she insisted. "He's just going through the motions of objecting for the sake of appearance. Trust me, he's totally in favor of this."

"Dexter?" Jocelyn wanted to make sure they were talking about the same person.

"Yes." The woman's beaming smile was naughtily triumphant.

"How did you manage to convince him?" she wondered. Once Dexter made up his mind about something, he wasn't a man easily persuaded to change it.

Bliss sat down in one of the high-backed cushioned chairs. "I didn't convince him of anything. I left it to Audrey Hepburn and Gregory Peck to do that."

"Wait a minute. Come again?" Jocelyn shook her head, unable to make sense of that answer.

"Audrey Hepburn and Gregory Peck, they were in that movie *Roman Holiday*. After Dexter put his foot down and absolutely refused to participate in your little adventure, I had him take me to the video store so I could rent the movie. We watched it Wednesday night." Tilting her head to one side, she studied the blankness in Jocelyn's expression. "You've seen it, haven't you?"

"Actually, I've never even heard of it." Jocelyn sank onto the sofa's plump cushion, angling toward her grandmother.

"How perfectly dreadful! The movie is a classic, Jocelyn. Audrey Hepburn's debut film," she added for good measure. "She plays a princess from some obscure little country who comes to Rome on an official visit. But she is weary of the endless ceremonies and protocol and trotted-out speeches. Like you, she wants a day to be an ordinary person, to laugh and sing and see the sights. So she escapes from the palace—or maybe it was a villa; I'm not sure. And one of the first people she meets is Gregory Peck. He plays a cynical reporter," Bliss explained, then paused, a smile dimpling the corners of her mouth and bringing a wickedly amused gleam to her eyes. "That was a bit redundant, wasn't it? How many reporters do you know who aren't suffering from an overdose of cynicism?"

"Not many." Truthfully, Jocelyn couldn't think of a single one whose view of the world hadn't been colored by it.

"Anyway, Gregory Peck ultimately recognizes the princess, Audrey Hepburn, and realizes he's onto a hot story. So he gets this photographer friend to follow them around Rome and take pictures. Of course, before the day is over, he falls in love with her, and she with him. But she is a princess with duties and responsibilities. So she returns to the palace and Gregory Peck tears up his story," Bliss concluded on a sighing note. "It's an absolutely marvelous story, light and humorous, yet wonderfully warm and poignant."

"It must be, if it succeeded in changing Dexter's mind," Jocelyn agreed.

"Dexter only pretends to be a curmudgeon, dear. At heart, he's an unadulterated romantic." She darted a glance at the doorway to the hall, causing Jocelyn to do the same, then leaned forward, confiding in a whisper even though there was no one within hearing, "You see, Dexter is nourishing the fantasy that you'll meet Gregory Peck while you're on your little holiday."

Jocelyn didn't blink an eye. "I think he'd be a bit old for me, don't you?"

Bliss Wakefield threw back her head and laughed

uproariously. "You're absolutely right," she declared, struggling to control her mirth while she delicately dabbed at her watery eyes with a fingertip. "He would be much more suitable for me, wouldn't he? Gregory Peck—the mere thought of dating him is enough to make my heart race."

"Gog!" Jocelyn feigned shock to cover her amusement.

"You find that funny, do you?" Bliss chided, looking wise rather than offended. "Darling, no one is ever too old for love. Even at eighty-three, you can still have those silly flutterings over a man. Probably at ninety-three as well. I'll let you know when I get there."

Looking at this remarkable woman, Jocelyn couldn't help but believe every word she said. Affection welled, strong and deep.

"You are a treasure, Gog," she said in absolute sincerity.

"Old people invariably are," she declared with a blithe certainty. "Unfortunately, most people take one look at the white hair and wrinkles and never realize that the gold is still there. It's just covered by the crusty accumulation of years. But speaking of treasure"—Bliss rose from her chair—"come see what I dug up on my shopping spree for you. At the moment, I have it all tucked away in my bedroom. After all, the Secret Service are never surprised by anything they find in my closets. That's one of the advantages of being old and more than a little eccentric."

For a wistful moment, Jocelyn envied her grandmother, thinking it would be wonderful not to have to explain or justify her actions. But her grandmother was already exiting the room, allowing Jocelyn no time for idle reverie. Walking swiftly, she caught up with her at the stairs.

When they reached the second-floor corridor, Dexter emerged from the onetime master bedroom now relegated to the use of overnight guests—the same room that contained the hidden staircase.

"Your luggage is in your room, Miss Jocelyn," he intoned with great formality. "Would you like me to unpack your things for you?"

"No, I'll do—" Before Jocelyn could complete her refusal, her grandmother broke in.

"The unpacking can wait till later, Dexter. I was about to show Jocelyn some of our special purchases," she declared with an almost smug glee.

He winced as if the news pained him. "Regrettable choices that they are, Madam."

Cupping a hand to the side of her mouth to conceal the formation of her words from Dexter, Bliss said to Jocelyn, "He doesn't approve of them, dear."

"I gathered that." But the news suddenly made her uneasy.

For the most part, her grandmother had impeccable taste. But there was that bronze statue of the Venus de Milo in her grandmother's bedroom—the one with a clock face where her navel should be.

"Wait until you see them," Dexter stated, his eyebrows arching high in dour criticism. "They are highly inappropriate."

"Nonsense. They are perfect." With an indignant toss of her head, Bliss Wakefield preceded them into her bedroom suite.

"Remember," Dexter murmured near Jocelyn's ear, trailing behind her when she followed her grandmother, "I warned you about them."

With visions of a red leather miniskirt, high-heeled patent-leather boots and a white, frowsy fake-fur coat dancing in her head, Jocelyn entered the bedroom. No matter how much she tried to assure herself that her grandmother would never have gotten her clothes suitable for a prostitute, there was just enough doubt to make her worry a little.

The room's decor offered little comfort. Done in dramatic blues and golds, there were just enough touches of whimsy evident—such as Venus and her belly clock—to reveal the unpredictability of its occupant.

"What exactly did you buy me, Gog?" Jocelyn stared at the blue lava lamp on the ormolu side table. Behind her, Dexter discreetly closed the door to the hall, insuring their privacy.

"You mustn't allow yourself to be influenced by Dexter's opinion, Jocelyn." Bliss threw open the doors to her large walk-in closet and disappeared inside it, her voice taking on a hollow sound. "If I had allowed him to choose, your wardrobe would have been straight out of *Roman Holiday*, complete with a full-skirted dress and acres of starched petticoats."

Dexter had the grace to redden a little. "Please, Madam. I am well aware that starched petticoats are passé."

"Unless you are going to a fifties sock hop, of course." She poked her white head out of the closet, her eyes rounded by the thought. "Maybe we should throw a costume party. That would be fun."

"The clothes, Gog?" Jocelyn prompted, her curiosity now reaching the anxiety level.

"Coming." Bliss ducked back in the closet and a rustling of paper sacks followed.

Hearing the sound, Dexter sniffed his distaste. "I feel you should know, Miss Jocelyn, Madam purchased these items at a thrift shop."

"Not the wigs." Bliss swept out of the closet, carrying two hat boxes and a brown grocery sack. "They are brand-new, and the very best quality."

"*Wigs.*" Jocelyn stressed the plural as her grandmother dumped all of it atop her bed. "You bought more than one?"

"Of course." She lifted the top off one of the tall hatboxes and removed a long red wig, almost the exact strawberry blond shade as Jocelyn's hair. "This goes on the head of the mannequin that's still in the closet. I didn't see any point in dragging it out."

Jocelyn stared at her, a confused frown puckering her forehead. "Excuse me, but I think I'm missing something here. What are you planning to do with a mannequin and that wig?"

"Dress it in your pajamas and put in your bed—purely as a safety precaution, of course. In the event that one of your guard dogs insists on peeking into your room to make sure you really are there, they'll see your hair and maybe an arm outside the covers."

"Very good." Jocelyn applauded the clever and inspired deception.

"And this"—after returning the red wig to its box, Bliss lifted out a second one—"is for you to wear."

The wig was a deep, dark brown, styled in a shoulder-brushing bob cut with full bangs—almost exactly what Jocelyn had envisioned for herself. She carried it to the dresser mirror and slipped it on.

The change in her reflected image was instant and dramatic. The dark frame around her face made her brown eyes appear nearly black, while the bangs and the boxy cut deceptively altered the shape of her face.

"That doesn't even look like me." Jocelyn stared at her reflection in amazement. For now she ignored the red wisps of her own hair that peeked out in places from beneath the wig, and concentrated on the overall effect.

"It definitely won't when we are all done with you," her grandmother agreed.

Jocelyn turned from the mirror, the last of her doubts flying out the window. "This is really going to work, Gog. No one is going to recognize me. Absolutely no one." Excitement bubbled for a minute before her grandmother's last remark finally registered. "What do you mean, done with me?"

"With that hair, you'll need to wear a darker shade

of makeup. One look at the fairness of your skin and it just screams, 'Wig!' " Bliss pulled a smaller sack out of the brown grocery bag. "I bought some for you. Actually, it's more like body paint."

"Body paint. Isn't that going a bit too far?" Jocelyn stared uncertainly at the sack.

"My dear, we can't do your face without doing your hands—or any other part of you that might show," her grandmother pointed out. "But don't worry. It will wash right off with soap and water, I'm told."

"She purchased it at a theatrical store," Dexter inserted and flashed a look of rebuke at his employer. "She told them she had been invited to a costumed Thanksgiving dinner, and that she planned to go as Pocahontas."

Bliss shrugged off the remark. "He's upset because I said he was going as Chief Stick-in-the-Mud."

Smiling at their oh-so-typical exchange, Jocelyn slipped off the brunette wig and ran a smoothing hand over her own hair. "I'm almost afraid to ask what I'm wearing with this. Just tell me it isn't beaded buckskin," she joked.

"You would be much too noticeable in buckskin, Jocelyn," her grandmother chided.

"That's a relief," she murmured under her breath as Bliss reached into the brown sack.

"I got you this at the thrift store to wear when you make your escape." She held up a navy blue sweatsuit with a narrow white stripe running vertically down the pant leg and a second one running horizontally around the chest of its matching sweatshirt. Both looked a little faded and worn.

"They are clean, Miss Jocelyn," Dexter hastened to inform her. "I washed them the instant we returned to Redford Hall."

"Thank you, Dexter." She was both amused and touched by his gesture. "That was very thoughtful of you."

"One can never be too careful," he said, nostrils flaring when he glanced at the garments. "Who knows what sort of person wore that last? Personally I still think you should have purchased a new jogging costume."

Bliss strongly disagreed. "New clothes are almost as conspicuous as buckskin."

Moving closer, Jocelyn examined the sweatsuit with a critical eye. "It looks too big for me, Gog."

"It won't when you get the padding on," she announced airily.

"Padding. What do I need padding for?" Jocelyn frowned at the idea.

"To fill you out, give you some heft and bulk, of course." Bliss dived back in the sack and came out with a pair of knee-length drawers, padded at the thighs, seat, and hips, and a thick, eight-inch-wide band that went around the waist.

Shaking her head in refusal, Jocelyn backed away from them. "I don't need that, Gog."

"Of course you do, dear. Men don't look twice at a chunky girl out jogging, but they would if she were tall and slim like you are. And we don't want anyone taking a second look at you when you leave here. This"—she held out the padded articles for Jocelyn's inspection—"will do the job nicely, completing the disguise. Originally it was designed to be used by some skinny Santa impersonator, but I removed some of the stuffing to thin it down."

"Thank you—I think." Jocelyn took the drawers and held them against her. "Let me guess, you bought these at that theatrical store, too."

Her grandmother made an agreeing sound while studying the new fullness the drawers gave to Jocelyn's figure. "No one—not even your father—will be able to recognize you by the time we're done with you. But this will clearly require some acting on your part, Jocelyn. It isn't enough to *look* out of shape; you must act it as well. Round your back; pretend you're winded; puff a little," she instructed. "And whatever you do, don't lapse into that high-headed walk of yours. It's almost as distinctive as your hair."

"How do you know all this, Gog?" Jocelyn stared at her in amazement, glimpsing a side of the woman she hadn't known existed.

"When I was much younger, I seriously toyed with the idea of pursuing a career in the theater," her grandmother confessed, her eyes bright with amusement at Jocelyn's surprised expression. "I fancied myself as the next Tallulah Bankhead—that is, when I wasn't seeing myself as the new Mae West." Bliss struck the latter's famous pose, a hip thrust to the side, one hand lifted, holding a long imaginary cigarette holder, her lips pouting in a sexy smirk while she uttered the notorious line, " 'Why don't you come up and *see* me some time?' "

The impersonation was flawless—and absolutely ludicrous coming from this dignified woman. Jocelyn clamped a hand over her mouth, smothering the laugh that gurgled in her throat.

Stiff-necked Dexter was neither amused nor entertained. "You couldn't possibly look more absurd, Madam, if you portrayed Betty Boop."

"You didn't know me when I was young, Dexter," she informed him haughtily. "For your information, I was the flappiest of the flappers. At the black bottom and the Charleston, I was superb. I can still dance you under the rug any day of the week, 'boop-boop-e-doop' and all."

As her grandmother launched into the Charleston, dah-dahing the melody, Jocelyn's mind flashed back to an earlier comment. "Wait a minute, Gog. What did you mean, when you're done with me? What else did you buy at that theatrical store?" Jocelyn tossed the padded items on the bed and reached for the sack. "Not a molded nose like Barbra Streisand?"

"Of course I didn't get you a fake nose." Bliss regarded the very suggestion as ludicrous. "Only a skilled makeup artist could make one look real enough to fool anyone."

"How refreshing that Madam admits to having no skill in that area," Dexter murmured cuttingly.

"Where's the rest?" Beyond a pair of running shoes and a pair of athletic socks, Jocelyn found no other clothes in the sack. She turned to her grandmother.

"You surely don't expect me to wear this jogging suit the whole time I'm gone."

"Of course not. The sweatsuit is merely to get you clear of Redford Hall without any suspicions aroused," she explained. "The rest of your clothes, along with some toiletries, are in an old Samsonite weekend bag, safely stowed in a locker at the main bus terminal."

"The bus terminal." Jocelyn struggled to make sense of this while a part of her wondered whether she had made a mistake giving her grandmother a free hand.

"It seemed the best choice," Bliss declared in unconcern. "After all, people don't tote a bag along with them while they're jogging—certainly not in this neighborhood. And you won't exactly be dressed appropriately for the airport. But one sees all types at the Greyhound bus terminal. Believe me, I know. I had Dexter take me there just to be certain."

Unable to argue with that logic, Jocelyn asked instead, "Where is the bus terminal?"

"On First Street Northeast, at the corner of L, I believe," she replied absently.

"A dubious area, to be sure," Dexter inserted with censure.

"I prefer to regard it as interesting and colorful," Bliss countered, directing him a saccharine smile of reproof.

He sniffed in disagreement. "I regret that I took you there in the morning rather than the evening.

Seeing it in the darkness of night, you may have revised your opinion."

Her confidence faltered a little. Recovering it, Bliss dismissed his concern with a faint lift of her chin. "Be that as it may, the bag is in one of the terminal lockers. It's much too late now to move it somewhere else."

"How do you propose I get to the terminal?" Jocelyn asked with a wary frown. "You don't really expect me to jog all the way there, do you?"

"I imagine you could if you chose," Bliss said with a careless little shrug. "But it's little more than a fifteen minute walk from Redford Hall to the subway station at DuPont Circle. I assumed you could ride the Metro, at least as far as Union Station."

"Ride the Metro," Jocelyn murmured, intrigued by the thought. "I've never done that before."

"Oh, you'll quite enjoy it," her grandmother stated with certainty.

Jocelyn looked at her in surprise. "Don't tell me you've ridden the Metro?"

"Yes, just this past Wednesday. After I hatched the idea of you taking it, Dexter insisted that we check it out first." Leaning forward, Bliss laid a confiding hand on her arm and whispered behind her hand, "You see, he was worried you might be mugged, dear."

"One hears dire stories about subways, Madam," Dexter spoke up in his own defense.

"Well, they aren't true of the Metro," she retorted, then assured Jocelyn, "You'll find it is remarkably clean and safe; not a single soul accosted us asking for handouts. I spoke to some subway riders from other cities who said the Metro was like dying and going underground to heaven." She laid a hand on Jocelyn's arm, an afterthought occurring to her. "By the way, I had Dexter buy you a one-day pass. It's good for an unlimited number of rides."

"That's nice, but . . . the other clothes you bought for me, the ones in the suitcase at the bus terminal," Jocelyn began, suddenly leery as her glance strayed back to the padded getup on the bed.

"Yes, what about them, dear?" Bliss prompted.

"Exactly what did you buy for me to wear? It's not anything like this, is it?" With her thumb, she indicated the sweatsuit and padded drawers on the bed.

"Unfortunately, your other clothes are quite ordinary," her grandmother replied with real regret. "A pair of brown corduroy jeans, a nondescript tan pullover, a beige turtleneck in the event you need to layer, and a rather tacky plaid anorak. And, of course, pajamas, some clean underwear, and good pair of walking shoes."

"None of the clothes need padding, do they?" she asked, none too sure what the answer would be.

"Good heavens, no." Bliss laughed at the idea. "If the weekend is as warm as it's predicted, you would roast."

"Thank goodness," Jocelyn breathed in relief.

"Now . . ." Bliss dug back into the sack. "In addition to these sneakers and socks, I also bought you one of those pouch purses that fasten around the waist. It's adjustable so you can wear it even with the padded sweatsuit. After you get your bag from the locker at the bus terminal, I thought you could slip into the ladies' room and change clothes." She handed the leather waist purse to Jocelyn. "The cash you'll need is in that middle zippered compartment along with your Metro pass. There's a hidden pocket in that last area. That's where you'll find the extra set of keys to the stair door and the tunnel."

Locating the keys first, Jocelyn felt excitement bubbling all over again when she touched their cool metal. "Then you've already checked them both out?"

"Oh, yes. I had Dexter do that yesterday morning before Harriet arrived," she said, referring to the woman who served as both housekeeper and cook. "You should have seen him before he ventured into the tunnel to sweep down the cobwebs. He was garbed like a beekeeper about to check his hives."

Jocelyn bit back a smile at the image. "Thank you for doing that, Dexter."

"You are most welcome." He inclined his head in acknowledgment, then sent a cutting glance at his employer and sniffed, "It's reassuring to know that *someone* appreciates my efforts."

"Your efforts are always appreciated by me, Dexter," her grandmother stated loftily, then allowed a faint smile to show. "It's the way you go about them sometimes that I find so amusing."

"Amusing," he repeated, his nostrils flaring indignantly.

"Don't get your feathers ruffled," Jocelyn chided. "She's only saying that to irritate you." When she started to put the purse back in the sack, her fingers closed around something boxy and oblong tucked in the front compartment. "What's this?" She fingered the shape of it through the leather, then reached to unzip the compartment.

"A beeper," her grandmother replied.

Lifting it out of the purse, Jocelyn demanded half angrily, "Why do I need this?" It felt as if she had just been put on a leash again, the very thing she was trying to escape.

"It was Dexter's idea." Bliss left the explanation to him.

"In the event of a crisis that might necessitate your immediate return, we must have a means to contact you, Miss Jocelyn," Dexter stated somberly. "The beeper accomplishes that."

"So much for being free for one day," Jocelyn murmured, tasting bitterness.

"I promise we will only contact you if something truly horrible has happened, Jocelyn." Bliss took both the beeper and the purse from her and returned the former to its appointed pouch in the purse. "In the meantime, simply forget it's there. The odds are in your favor it will never be used, right?"

"Right." Jocelyn smiled, a little ashamed of herself for making such an issue of it, if only in her mind.

"When do you plan to do this deed?" Dexter inquired. "Have you decided?"

"Yes." Jocelyn nodded. "First thing tomorrow morning."

Something told her she would be lucky to sleep a wink tonight.

CHAPTER 5

The blinds in the onetime master bedroom were drawn, blocking out the blush of dawn that tinted the eastern sky. With her grandmother's help, Jocelyn lengthened the purse's waist strap and fastened it around her padded middle, then pulled the heavy sweatshirt over it.

Bliss Wakefield stepped back to view the finished product. The scarlet silk of her kimono-style robe shimmered in the lamplight with the movement.

"There you are. All set to go." She clasped her hands together in satisfaction.

"Yes." A last minute attack of nerves gave Jocelyn's voice an edgy and breathless quality.

Out of the corner of her eye, she caught a glimpse

of her reflection in the dresser mirror, and turned with a start to gaze at the tall and slightly stout woman in the mirror. She felt a sense of shock at the sight of this stranger looking back at her. A stranger with dark hair and eyes and an olive complexion.

"Even I can't recognize myself," she murmured.

"Who could? As disguises go, this one is perfection," her grandmother declared proudly.

There was a soft rap at the door. Jocelyn swung around to face it, her glance flying to her grandmother, her mouth opening in wordless alarm. Bliss held up a silencing hand.

"Who is it?"

"May I enter, Madam?" The heavy door partially muffled the low request, but it couldn't mask that very upper-crust British accent Dexter had long ago adopted as his own.

"Yes, and don't dawdle about it," Bliss responded in a clipped undertone.

Soundlessly the door swung open. Dexter stepped into the room and silently closed the door behind him. There was the smallest flicker of surprise in his eyes when his glance traveled over the transformed Jocelyn; otherwise there was no change in his customarily sober expression.

"It is a bit brisk out this morning," he stated solemnly. "No one would think it untoward if you have your head covered with that hood, Miss Jocelyn."

"Good idea." Reaching back, Jocelyn caught hold of the sweatshirt's hood and flipped it over her wig.

But when she tried to tie the strings to secure it in place, she was suddenly all thumbs.

Bliss came to her rescue. "Nervous?"

"That's an understatement," Jocelyn admitted. "It feels like there's a fleet of butterflies in my stomach."

"That's as it should be. It keeps the adrenaline up." With the strings fastened, Bliss turned to Dexter. "Did you bring the flashlight?"

"Naturally." He handed it to Jocelyn, then checked the watch on his wrist. "It shouldn't take you more than five minutes to make your way down the stairwell and through the tunnel. At exactly twenty minutes before eight o'clock I will take fresh coffee to the agents watching the street. I'll leave the side gate unlocked when I go out. I will converse with them for precisely five minutes. That should provide you with sufficient time to make your way from the carriage house to the side gate and onto the street."

"Right." Jocelyn nodded in quick acknowledgment, then waited, half-expecting Dexter to suggest that they needed to synchronize their watches.

He gave her a stern look. "Be certain to leave the flashlight hidden in the carriage house. You will need it on your return tomorrow morning."

"And don't forget to call first so we'll know you are on your way," her grandmother added. Jocelyn nodded again, her glance sliding from the stranger's image in the mirror to the mannequin dressed in her pajamas lying in the bed. "All this subterfuge seems so ridiculous," she murmured.

"It isn't too late to change your mind, Jocelyn," her grandmother reminded her.

Jocelyn thought about it for all of two seconds, then dragged in a deep, marshaling breath and shook her head. "No, I'm not going to change it, not after putting on this getup."

Tightening her grip on the flashlight, she crossed to the far end of the room's ornately paneled fireplace. The hidden stairwell was contained in the space next to the chimney flue, a common practice in colonial architecture. Its door was flush with the wall, the fireplace's decorative pilasters and cross moldings serving as its frame.

Jocelyn hesitated a split second longer, her thoughts suddenly flashing to the secret staircase in the White House that led from the second floor to the third. Merely recalling her life at the White House was enough to stiffen her resolve to steal this one day of anonymity.

Under the firm push of her hand, the door opened and the steep stairway corkscrewed down before her. She snapped on the flashlight, its bright beam piercing the interior shadows.

Releasing the breath she had unconsciously been holding, Jocelyn directed a tense smile toward her grandmother and Dexter. They stood side by side watching her.

"Here I go," she murmured. "Wish me luck."

"I am reminded of the epigram: 'God looks after fools, drunkards and the United States,'" Dexter stated.

Bliss gave him a disgusted look. "There is absolutely

nothing foolish about Jocelyn," she declared, then smiled at her granddaughter. "If you run into Gregory Peck, give him a kiss for us."

Jocelyn laughed, as she was meant to do, then ducked through the opening, aiming the flashlight at the steps before her. Descending, she hugged the stairwell's outer wall, where the treads were at their widest. The thick soles of her sneakers made almost no sound. Her heart was making more than enough racket, though.

Down and down, and even farther down, Jocelyn went until she was swallowed by the musty darkness of the enclosed and seldom-used stairwell. At last the flashlight's beam picked out the padlocked door at the bottom. Dust motes danced in its light, adding to the air's stuffiness.

It seemed to take an eternity to dig the key out of the hidden compartment in her purse, unlock the door, and return the key to its proper place. Jocelyn winced when the hinges creaked, sounding loud in the absolute silence of the stairwell. She took comfort from the knowledge that she was deep in the bowels of the house; the chance of anyone hearing the creaky hinges was so remote as to be nonexistent.

Still, she waited a full beat without moving.

When Redford Hall was first built, the stairwell opened into the basement larder. Later, to conceal the underground passage, a false wall was erected, hiding the entrance to the tunnel. Now the stairwell opened to the small anteroom created by the false wall.

Jocelyn moved into the anteroom, closing the stair door behind her. Fumbling a little, she extracted the second key from her waist purse and unlocked the passage door, tucked the key back in its hiding place, and ducked through the opening.

The tunnel's low ceiling forced her to walk crouched over, which prevented her from traveling with any haste. Busy spiders had spun new webs along the way. Thanks to the flashlight's broad beam, Jocelyn managed to dodge the worst of them.

The air in the tunnel was warm and heavy, redolent of damp earth. By the time she reached the tunnel's end, she was perspiring from the combination of its stuffy warmth, nerves, and the extra padding she wore.

She paused long enough to run the flashlight beam over the ladder, checking for any areas of rot to avoid, then put a hand on a rung, switched off the flashlight with the other and tucked it in a side pocket of her sweatpants, and started up. Reaching the top, she eased open the trapdoor in the carriage house floor and peered out. A stack of boxes blocked her view.

Birds twittered somewhere outside, a cheerful and reassuring sound. With as much stealth as she could manage, Jocelyn clambered through the opening and carefully lowered the trapdoor. She stowed the flashlight in a corner behind some boxes, then tiptoed to the side door and peeked out its dusty pane.

There went Dexter, carrying a thermos of coffee and two plastic cups. Jocelyn watched as he unlocked the side gate and ventured onto the sidewalk, quickly disappearing from her view. She took a deep breath and started to blot the perspiration from her face with a sweatshirt sleeve, then realized it would succeed in making her all the more convincing as a jogger. She settled for brushing off the wisps of cobwebs and dust from her clothes, then slipped outside.

The cool freshness of the air was like a deep gulp of water to the thirsty. She threw an anxious look around her, then dashed to the gate. Reaching it, she flattened herself against a post, then peeked around it to verify that Dexter was occupying the agents' attention.

A chattering squirrel scolded her from the limb of a nearby tree. She glanced up, murmuring under her breath, "I feel so silly, kind of like I'm some kind of fugitive from the law."

But she had already come too far, gone through too much to call it quits now. Jocelyn pushed the newly oiled gate open a crack, then darted through the narrow opening, nearly catching the sleeve of her sweatshirt on its protruding latch. Immediately she broke into the slow jog of runner, arms pumping.

As she approached the agents' car, she was careful not to glance at either it or Dexter. Her heart pounded in her throat, and her mouth was desert dry when she trotted past it. Any second she expected to hear her name called.

Two blocks from Redford Hall, Jocelyn knew she had made it. She was free, completely and totally free. There was no one discreetly following her, no one watching her, no one checking out the path ahead of her.

A laugh started low in her throat, emerging first as a chuckle, then escalating into full-blown laughter. Funnier yet, no one paid any attention to her.

The day was hers and Jocelyn intended to savor every minute of it.

The year-old black Labrador gamboled around Tucker's long legs like the overgrown puppy she was. Stopping, he bent to unwrap the leash the dog had wound around him. The black Lab instantly took full advantage of the opportunity to wash his face with kisses.

"Would you just settle down for two seconds, Molly?" Tucker pushed her away with a grin. "We're gonna play some ball, but not yet."

Out of all his words, there was one the dog understood. It was "ball." She crouched low on her front feet, her rear end high in the air, a posture that invited play. She barked once, the full-throated and deep sound of an adult dog, then ruined the illusion by breaking into a puppy's excited yelping.

"You have to wait." With the leash untangled, Tucker straightened and looked around the Mall.

Usually he waited to turn Molly loose so she could run off some of her energy until they were on the other side of the Reflecting Pool. But few tourists visited the nation's capital in November, and fewer still ventured out at eight-thirty on a Saturday morning. In fact, Tucker saw no one in the immediate vicinity.

He turned back to the young Lab, still poised in her play stance and panting with eagerness, her moist breath turning into puffs of steam in the crisp morning air. Her bright eyes were trained on him, alert to the smallest shift in his body language.

Looking at her, Tucker sighed and shook his head in amused surrender. The dog instantly went wild, leaping in the air and bouncing back and forth in front of him.

"You have to sit now, Molly," he told her, and the dog promptly plunked her rear on the grass, vibrating with eagerness. Tucker crouched beside her and reached to unsnap the leather strap. "You know this is illegal, don't you? Dogs are supposed to be kept on a leash."

She took a swipe at his cheek with her tongue. Tucker managed to dodge it and pushed himself upright, coiling the strap in his hand. He stuffed it in one of the many pockets in his lined jacket, then patted the rest of them.

"Now, where did I put that ball?" he murmured, keeping one knowing eye on the black Lab.

Instantly Molly flung herself at him, banging her nose against the round bulge in his right side pocket. Acting surprised, Tucker pulled out the old tennis ball along with an article torn from yesterday's newspaper. Molly jumped up and down, barking for him to throw it.

Obliging her, Tucker cranked back his arm and

lobbed the ball farther down the grassy strip that ran along the concrete bank of the Reflecting Pool. With an excited yelp, Molly charged after it, nearly tumbling to the ground in her haste to get her ungainly legs and big paws all headed in the same direction. Watching her chase after the ball, Tucker decided Molly didn't exactly race after it; it was more like she galumphed after it.

The faded yellow ball hit the ground about twelve feet ahead of Molly and took a wild bounce. Tucker winced, anticipating that it would careen into the glass-smooth waters of the Reflecting Pool. He knew Molly would dive in after it.

Instead, the ball sailed toward the row of trees that lined the area, and straight toward a tall brunette in olive-plaid anorak, just strolling out of the trees into view.

Her head was turned toward the Lincoln Memorial just beyond the foot of the long pool. She didn't see the ball—or the clumsy dog careering after it.

"Look out!" Tucker shouted the warning, but it came too late.

Molly had already sideswiped the brunette, knocking her to the ground. With a mixed groan of dismay and concern, Tucker broke into a run, offering up a silent prayer that the woman hadn't suffered anything more serious than a bruise or two.

For a full second, Jocelyn was too stunned by the sudden fall to move. While her mind worked frantically to figure out how she had ended up on the ground, she felt one of the bobby pins that held her

wig in place dig into her scalp. She instantly realized
that her wig had somehow gotten pushed forward.
Hurriedly she righted it, glancing furtively to see if
anyone had noticed.

That was when she saw the black Labrador, proudly
holding a tennis ball in its mouth as it trotted toward
her. "You're the culprit, aren't you?" Jocelyn guessed
and gingerly pushed herself up into a sitting position,
automatically cupping a hand to the sore spot on her
hip.

Wagging its tail, the dog whined what could have
passed for an apology, then swung its head toward
the man loping toward both of them, his jacket tails
flapping about him.

One look at his country-boy face, and recognition
sent a shaft of fear slicing through Jocelyn. Of all
people, why did it have to be him?

Ducking her head to hide her face, she tried to
scramble to her feet, convinced this whole thing was
her grandmother's fault for wishing Gregory Peck on
her.

And by no stretch of the imagination was Grady
Tucker a Gregory Peck. Tom Sawyer or Huck Finn,
maybe, but not Gregory Peck.

Before Jocelyn could get one leg under her, a tall
and gangly Grady Tucker was hunkering over her,
his big hands earnestly reaching to help.

"Careful. Are you all right?" Unlike the rest of him,
his voice had a solid, male ring to it, rich and warm
with just a trace of Kansas in it. It was the disarming

kind of voice that made a person want to respond. "You didn't hurt yourself, did you?"

"I'm fine." Jocelyn kept her face turned from him, letting the shoulder-length wig partially curtain it.

"Are you sure?" His hands started moving over her as if checking to see whether anything was broken.

"Positive," she insisted as the black Lab came bouncing up to them.

The dog immediately stuck its nose between them to affectionately nuzzle at Jocelyn's face. In near panic, she pushed the dog away before it accidentally licked off her makeup.

"Cut it out, Molly." Tucker grabbed the dog by the collar, dragging it away from Jocelyn. "Just sit down and behave. You've done enough damage for one morning."

"Hear, hear," Jocelyn muttered the agreement under her breath, then quickly extended an arm when Tucker turned back to her. "Help me up."

There was a lot more strength in his grip than she had expected. One minute she was on the ground, and in the next, she was shooting to her feet with a quickness that took her breath. Grady Tucker might look tall and scrawny, but that leanness was all hard muscle and bone, she realized.

Fighting to ignore the hammering of her pulse, Jocelyn drank in a deep, steadying breath and glanced at the dog sitting near her feet, somehow managing to wiggle in place while grinning happily.

"I take it that giant bowling ball belongs to you." Jocelyn indicated the dog with a flick of her fingers.

Then she made the mistake of looking at Tucker and seeing the adorably sheepish grin that crooked his mouth, and the sudden glint of humor in his eyes.

"I guess Molly must have seemed like an overgrown bowling ball when she slammed into you, huh?" he said, absently rubbing the back of his neck, looking shy and embarrassed. Something inside Jocelyn melted a little.

She almost smiled back, then noticed the curious probe of his gaze and quickly shifted her attention to the dog.

"Your dog's name is Molly, is it?" The dog immediately thumped her tail on the ground.

"Yup, Molly." Tucker nodded in confirmation. "I named her after the song."

"The song?"

"Yeah, you know, 'Good Golly, Miss Molly,' " he explained and watched the dawning smile of comprehension. "She's caused me to say that a lot since I brought her home from the pound. She's kind of an overgrown pup yet, barely a year old and still awkward and gangly, always running into things and knocking them over."

"Don't I know it," Jocelyn murmured dryly and brushed at the odd bits of dried grass and leaves that clung to her coat and slacks.

A soft chuckle came from him. "I guess you have experienced that firsthand, haven't you?" He paused a beat, then bent low to get a look at her face again. "Are you sure you're okay? You look a little shaky."

If she was, Jocelyn chalked it up to nerves and the

fear of being recognized. "Other than a couple sore spots, I'm fine. Honestly," she insisted.

"I guess I'll have to take your word for that." There came that lopsided smile again. "My name's Grady Tucker, by the way. You've already met Molly."

"Yes." Jocelyn glanced at the dog before taking Tucker's outstretched hand, conscious of the close study of his eyes. She had the uncomfortable feeling her wig was slightly askew, but there was nothing she could do about correcting it without drawing attention to it at the same time. "How do you do, Mr. Tucker?"

"My friends call me Tucker." He was slow to release her hand, causing the sensation of his warm grip to linger when he finally did. "I don't think I caught your name."

Trapped, Jocelyn scrambled to remember the name she had used not thirty minutes ago when she had signed the hotel's registration card. "Believe it or not, it's Jones," she lied boldly. "Lynne Jones."

"I guess you're from that family everybody is always trying to keep up with," he said with an answering grin. "I always did want to meet one of you."

She couldn't think of a suitable rejoinder to that, so she simply smiled and nodded. The dog, thankfully, provided a distraction by snatching up the faded tennis ball and prancing over to drop it at Tucker's feet.

"I think Molly is trying to tell you she's tired of standing around," Jocelyn observed and used it as an excuse to end this little encounter. "It was nice to meet you, Mr. Tucker," she said, backing away.

"Wait a minute," he said before she completed her turn, his long legs carrying him to her side in a single stride. "Can I buy you a cup of coffee or something?"

"It isn't necessary, really." She started walking toward the memorial to Lincoln.

"Maybe it isn't," he said, falling in step with her, his body angled sideways toward her while he shoved his hands in first one pocket, then another before finally pulling out the dog's leash. "But it doesn't feel right to just let you walk off without apologizing somehow for the way Molly bowled you down."

Jocelyn shook her head in refusal. "That's very kind of you, but I would just as soon forget it. After all, there was no harm done."

"That right there alone is cause to celebrate. Whatd'ya say?" he coaxed. "There's a street vendor up there by the memorial's steps. His coffee is always steaming hot and fresh."

She halted, exasperation and resignation mingling in the look she gave him. "Is this how you pick up girls, Mr. Tucker?" she chided. "Did you train your dog to knock them down to give you an excuse to meet them?"

"To tell you the truth," he rubbed the back of his neck again in that self-conscious gesture and studied her with a head-down, sideways glance, "this is the first time Molly has ever crashed into a beautiful woman like you." He held up a hand to stave off any response. "Now, I know that sounds like an old line. But it's the truth, I swear," he declared, crossing his heart.

"Right," Jocelyn countered in dry disbelief and tried not to be moved by his earnest, little-boy expression.

"Will you have that cup of coffee with me?" Bending down, he snapped the leash to the dog's collar. "I'll feel better about this if you would."

After another moment's hesitation, she relented. "One cup, then we're quits."

"Deal," he agreed.

As they set off together, the dog bounded ahead of them, straining at the leash one minute, then pausing to investigate a new scent or watch a bird flying by.

Jocelyn was painfully conscious of the long and lanky man ranging alongside her. She was playing with fire and she knew it. Every additional moment in Tucker's presence increased the risk he might recognize her, regardless of the elaborate disguise she wore. It heightened her awareness of him. She could actually feel his gaze on her, making a curious study of her profile.

Remembering some of the tidbits of advice her grandmother had given her, Jocelyn tried to alter her walk, making sure to keep her chin angled down, forcing a curve to her shoulders and a slight slouch to her spine.

"Are you from around here?" Tucker asked after they had traveled a dozen feet.

"No." That was a half-truth. The White House was strictly a temporary residence. Jocelyn considered Virginia her home.

He nodded, as if her answer confirmed his own thoughts. "I was positive Molly and I would have remembered seeing you if you had taken morning walks along the Mall before. We're here bright and early every day, rain or shine, sleet or snow. Kinda' like the postman," Tucker added with a small smile. " 'Course, we're not here to deliver any mail. We just come and wander around until Molly loses some of her zip."

"Clever." Jocelyn smiled at his analogy.

"So, is this your first trip to the capital?" He cocked his head toward her, his attitude one of avid interest— the straightforward, boyish kind that was impossible to ignore.

"No, it isn't my first time." She lifted her gaze to the columned temple of the Lincoln Memorial directly ahead of them. "But it's been years since my mother brought me here."

"It can't be that many years." From most men the remark would have been all smooth flattery. But from Tucker it had a ring of simple observation.

"Enough. I was only ten at the time." She kept her eyes on the famous landmark, pretending to give it the whole of her attention.

"Magnificent, isn't it?"

The morning sun bathed the marbled front of the Lincoln Memorial. Its reaching rays penetrated into the monument's open chamber and touched Daniel French's statue of the seated president. Tucker turned his gaze to the monument as well.

"It's a sight that never fails to move you," he mused,

his steps automatically slowing. "It doesn't seem to matter how many times you see it; there's still an impact. Something inside you kinda' lifts up. Even the most jaded and cynical politician will tell you that," he added with a dry and knowing gleam.

Impishly Jocelyn couldn't resist asking, "Do you know many?" then wondered at her own daring. The disguise was giving her a false sense of security, she decided.

"Jaded and cynical politicians, you mean?" A raised eyebrow sought confirmation. At her nod, Tucker sent his glance traveling toward the city's northern skyline. "Living here, a fella can't help but meet some."

"I suppose not." The concrete steps rose before them, leading from the banks of the Reflecting Pool to street level.

"Where do you live?" Tucker asked as they started up the steps in perfect unison. The dog, on the other hand, chose an investigating, zigzag route up the steps, following its nose.

"Iowa."

"Whereabouts in Iowa?" he persisted.

"Waterloo." Jocelyn had no idea why she had listed that as her home when she filled out the hotel registry, unless she had acted on the subconscious belief that she was going to meet hers.

"That makes us distant neighbors in a way." He flashed her a quick, engaging grin. "I'm originally from Kansas myself—the Wichita area."

"I'm surprised you didn't name your dog Toto," she joked.

"Yeah, it's for sure we're not in Kansas anymore," Tucker replied, borrowing that famous line from *The Wizard of Oz*, the gleam of shared humor in his eyes.

"You've got that right," Jocelyn agreed, a smile widening her lips.

At the top of the steps, Tucker altered his course and headed toward the vendor cart parked near the street curb. Jocelyn trailed along with him, drawn by the tantalizing aroma of coffee that drifted from it. Halfway there, Tucker came to an abrupt stop, looked from the dog to the leash in his hand, then at the cart before turning to Jocelyn, all gauche and uncertain, endearingly so.

"Uh . . . maybe you'd better hang on to Molly while I get the coffee." He thrust the leash toward Jocelyn. "This way—hopefully—I won't spill any. You don't mind, do you?"

"I—" Before she could get an answer out, the leash was in her hand and Tucker was striding toward the cart with a kind of long, loping gait.

Snapping his fingers high in the air, he stopped again and swung back to her. "I forgot to ask, how do you like your coffee? Cream? Sugar?"

"Black, no sugar." Jocelyn took a tighter hold on the leash when Molly perked her ears at a strutting pigeon searching for morning crumbs on the sidewalk.

Tucker gave her a thumbs-up sign, then called, "Why don't you and Molly head on over to the memorial? I'll bring the coffee and we can drink it on the steps.''

Nodding, Jocelyn tugged on the leash and called the dog to her. The young black Lab threw a glance at her master, then padded over to Jocelyn with the fickleness of a pup, eager for attention from anyone. Amused, Jocelyn rubbed the shiny black head that the dog shoved under her hand.

"You are anybody's friend, aren't you, Molly?" Jocelyn murmured, glancing Tucker's way as she spoke.

There he stood at the vendor's cart, his elbows jutting every which way as he dipped his fingers into pocket after pocket, obviously pulling out everything but money.

For an instant, there was something Lincolnesque about him, something that was more than just his height and leanness of frame. It was that air of awkwardness, she decided, coupled with an unassuming country-boy way he had about him, plus that touch of wit. But the resemblance stopped at the face. There Tucker didn't have Lincoln's gauntness and bony angles. His features were smoother, cleaner—good-looking in a plain, Jimmy Stewart kind of way.

Jimmy Stewart. There she was, thinking about old movie stars again, Jocelyn thought with disgust. All because of her grandmother and that nonsense about Gregory Peck.

"Come on, Molly." Shortening the leash, Jocelyn made a quick check for traffic, then headed across the street, the dog trotting happily by her side.

CHAPTER 6

When they reached the opposite curb, Molly lunged at a strutting pigeon, then pounced on a stray feather that fluttered to the ground when the bird took flight. Picking it up, the dog pranced after Jocelyn with all the delight of a child with a new toy.

Jocelyn paused at the base of the memorial and looked up the long flight of steps that led to the massive statue of a somber Lincoln. Doric columns surrounded the white marble structure. Thirty-six in all, Jocelyn remembered—one for each of the states that were in the union at the time of Lincoln's presidency.

Molly's excited *whoof* dissolved into a happy whine of greeting as she bounded away from Jocelyn's side.

When she hit the end of its slack, she yanked on the leash, straining forward. Jocelyn turned, thinking it was Tucker with their coffee.

Instead the young dog was writhing ecstatically before a short, rather stout gentleman, dressed in a dark topcoat and a black homburg covering crisp, white hair. In any other city but Washington, his style of dress might have seemed unusual, even out of date. But here, where foreign embassies were almost as numerous as federal buildings, clothes styles were as wide-ranging as the cultures. Jocelyn was too accustomed to such variety to give his choice of attire any thought.

"Aren't you the friendly girl." Bending, the man fondled the dog's ears, a ripple of laughter in his voice, a voice full of the rich, deep tones of a bass viol. He straightened and looked directly at Jocelyn, while reaching up to tip his hat to her. "Good morning. Fine day, isn't it?"

For a second, she could only stare at his face, certain she had seen it before. The white of his neatly trimmed beard contrasted sharply with the milk chocolate color of his skin, and his eyes were as black and shiny as polished coal.

"A fine day," Jocelyn echoed vaguely, still trying to remember when and where she had met this elderly black gentleman.

His brow knitted slightly as he peered at her a little closer. Then a smile of recognition wreathed his face, rounding his cheeks into brown apples. He placed the tip of his cane directly in front of his feet and rested both gloved hands on its curved head.

"The transformation is remarkable." He nodded, an approving twinkle in his eyes. "Truly remarkable. Slipped out to take in a few of the sights, did you?"

"I—" The denial lodged in her throat as the memory suddenly clicked into place.

This man . . . he had been one of the adults with that group of children touring the White House—the man who had asked all the questions about the White House Christmas tree and this year's theme.

A touch of chagrin edged his smile. "You are incognito, of course. I should have guessed," he declared softly, his voice low and musical. He leaned a fraction of an inch closer, a mischievous gleam in his eyes. "Not to worry, I won't tell a soul."

"I . . . I don't know what you're talking about." A heat scorched her cheeks. Jocelyn was certain it showed despite the concealing makeup.

"Of course, of course, I understand perfectly," he said and gave her a knowing wink before switching his attention to the monument before them. "It's a rather grand tribute to a man of such humble beginnings, isn't it?"

"Yes." Her mouth was as dry as dust, and her heart was pounding like a frightened rabbit's.

She wanted to run, but how could she when she had Tucker's dog? Jocelyn thought seriously about shoving the leash in the old gentleman's hand and taking off. Common sense told her such an act would only arouse unnecessary suspicion.

"Such a profoundly pensive pose the artist chose." The white-bearded man thoughtfully studied the seated marble figure, then cast a faint smile at Jocelyn. "But don't you know how his face would light up if one of his children ran up and crawled onto his lap right now?"

"I always wanted to do that when I was a girl," Jocelyn remembered, surprised by how fresh and sharp that long-ago wish suddenly seemed—so sharp and fresh, she forgot to be cautious. "Just sit up there and talk to him."

A low, rumbling chuckle came from the man's throat. "Wouldn't we all? Rather like sitting on Santa's lap, confiding all our secret hopes and dreams to him."

"Please," Jocelyn sighed in barely concealed annoyance, "let's not talk about Santa Claus or Christmas now."

"You don't like Christmas?" He looked hurt and surprised.

"I like Christmas well enough—at its proper time. But it isn't even Thanksgiving yet and the stores are already putting up decorations and setting out shopping reminders." Jocelyn knew she was climbing onto her own personal soapbox, but she couldn't seem to stop herself. "Christmas is a celebration of Christ's birth. I don't think God intended for it to be *the* big buying event of the year."

He listened patiently, then smiled in gentle reproof. "Isn't it a bit presumptuous to think God didn't know exactly how Christmas would turn out?"

The question had never occurred to her before. Jocelyn had absolutely no answer for it. In her heart she had always believed God to be all-seeing, all-knowing and all-powerful. She was dumbfounded by the elderly gentleman's suggestion that God had foreseen the commercialization of Christmas. That He had not only foreseen it, but allowed it to happen.

"You hadn't considered that possibility, had you?" The man grinned, his eyes bright with a merry wisdom.

"No, I—" Her arm was jerked by the dog's sudden tug on the leash. When Molly came to the end of it, she rose up on her hind legs and started barking with joy.

Here came Grady Tucker loping across the street, a tall, plastic-lidded cup of coffee in each hand, the front of his coat flapping open, revealing its plaid lining. Molly jumped at him in greeting, and Tucker stopped at the edge of her reach, holding both cups aloft.

"Get down, now, Molly. Don't be jumping on me. Good golly, girl, you're gonna' be having me spilling this coffee," he warned good-naturedly.

Obediently, the dog sank onto all fours, winding herself around his legs and banging him with her rapidly wagging tail. Still holding the coffee high, Tucker worked his way to Jocelyn, miraculously without getting tripped by the dog or tangled in the leash.

"Sorry it took so long." He checked the lids on both cups, then offered her the one in his right hand. "This one's yours, I believe. Black, no sugar."

"Thanks." Taking it, she passed the leash to Tucker, conscious all the while of the white-bearded gentleman watching them both with undisguised interest.

It was impossible for Tucker not to notice him.

"Morning." Tucker acknowledged the man's presence with a somewhat absent nod. Then his glance caught on the man's face and stayed there to probe curiously.

"Good morning," the gentleman responded, continuing to stand there, showing no inclination whatsoever to leave.

"I've met you somewhere before, haven't I?" Tucker asked, his brow furrowing in a perplexed frown. Then he held up a hand, shaking a finger at the man in a waiting gesture while he searched his memory. "I know." He pointed to him. "We bumped into each other outside the White House fence. You asked me about the tours through it. Did you ever get to take one?"

"Indeed, I did," the gentleman replied, inclining his head in visual confirmation of it.

Jocelyn held her breath, fearing he would glance her way and somehow reveal her identity. But his twinkling gaze remained on Tucker.

"A most entertaining time I had, too." Lifting a hand from his cane, he extended it to Tucker. "The name's Obediah Nicklaus Melchior."

Tucker juggled a minute with the leash and his coffee cup before finally freeing himself to shake hands with the man. "Mine's Tucker. Grady Tucker.

This here is Miss Jones," he said, pointing to Jocelyn. "Miss Lynne Jones from Iowa," he added, then paused, glancing from one to the other. "Sorry, I guess you two have already met."

"Not formally," Jocelyn murmured, growing more uncomfortable by the minute, yet unsure how to extricate herself from the situation.

"Yes, Miss Jones and I hadn't progressed that far in our conversation about Christmas to actually introduce ourselves," Obediah Melchior admitted.

"Christmas?" Tucker drew his head back in surprise. "Why would you be talking about Christmas? It's only November, for heaven's sake."

Obediah Melchior chuckled. "Your sentiments are shared equally by Miss Jones."

"And you don't agree, I take it." Tucker pried off the cup's plastic lid and took a blowing sip of coffee, eyeing the elderly man over the styrofoam rim of it.

The man didn't deny it. "It has occurred to me that the life of Christ is something to be celebrated all year long."

"It would be if that's what people did. Instead they spend all their time figuring out what to buy this person and shopping for that one," Tucker declared, gesturing broadly. "Gifts, that's all they think about."

The old man thoughtfully stroked his white beard. "Yes, giving presents is a bad thing, to be sure."

Jocelyn almost choked on her coffee as a laugh bubbled in her throat at the subtle gibe.

"It isn't a bad thing," Tucker protested, getting a little flustered.

"Hardly," she inserted. "Christmas is about the greatest gift of all."

"True," Tucker conceded. "But that isn't the gift people are thinking about."

"Yet it's the one you are thinking about right now," Obediah pointed out in a perfectly reasonable tone, then paused a beat in thoughtful reflection. "Interesting, isn't it? The earlier the Christmas season comes, the quicker people are to remember that it is supposed to be a holiday to celebrate the birth of the Christ Child." He directed a bright and twinkling glance at Jocelyn. "Do you suppose it could have crossed God's mind that such a thing might happen?"

It was a direct reference to his earlier suggestion to Jocelyn that perhaps God had known all along how the holiday of His Son's birth would evolve—known and planned for it. It gave Jocelyn something else to think about.

"Maybe it crossed His mind," Tucker conceded. "But people still don't like the idea of thinking about Christmas before December gets here."

"But that's understandable, isn't it?" Obediah countered smoothly. "We humans tend to be very self-centered. Christmas, with all its commercialism, forces people to think about the wants and wishes of someone other than themselves. Not just friends and family, but the poor and the hungry and the homeless in our midst. Perhaps that's why people would secretly like Christmas to come and go fast, so they can return to their favorite pastime: dwelling on themselves."

"Now, that's a depressing thought," Tucker observed with a troubled frown.

"Isn't it?" Obediah replied dryly, then stirred himself. "I have bent your ear with my opinions long enough. You two young people have better things to do with your time on such a beautiful morning than chat with an old man." Tipping his hat, he bowed briefly to Jocelyn. "It was a pleasure meeting you, Miss . . . Jones."

He hesitated just enough over her alias to scramble her pulse. "And you, Mr. Melchior," Jocelyn murmured, fighting breathlessness.

"Among friends, I am simply Obediah," he told her, then nodded to Tucker. "I have enjoyed our little talk, Mr. Tucker."

"Just plain Tucker is fine, Obediah," he replied, once again juggling cup and leash to shake hands with the man. "Have yourself a good day, sir."

"I will. I definitely will." With a swing of his cane, Obediah set off up the steps, chuckling softly to himself.

Tucker watched him a moment, then turned, his glance flicking over Jocelyn, first measuring in its study, then warm. More than warm, actually, but Jocelyn wasn't ready to deal with that thought.

"Whatd'ya' say we find ourselves a comfortable step and sit down and enjoy this coffee?" He gestured to the concrete stairs behind them.

"Sounds good."

They climbed up three steps and lowered themselves onto the fourth one, joined by a reluctant

Molly, who longingly cast her gaze toward the top. Tucker stretched his long legs in front of him, angling them down the steps, then took another sip of steaming hot coffee. His glance once again sought out the retreating figure of Obediah Melchior.

"Interesting old codger, wasn't he?" he commented idly.

"I'm not sure I would call him a codger." Jocelyn lifted her cup to her mouth and blew on the coffee's steamy black surface. The heat from it touched the coolness of her skin.

"Maybe not," Tucker agreed. "That beard, though, is straight out of Uncle Remus."

"But not his voice," Jocelyn remembered. "It's deep and rich, with beautiful modulation. It has, almost, a cultured ring to it—like a Shakespearean actor."

Tucker lowered his cup, slanting her an amused glance: "King Lear he's not, though. And I can't see him spouting that line from Othello either: 'O thou weed, who art so lovely fair and smell'st so sweet.' "

Jocelyn laughed faintly. "No, it isn't a role that would fit him either. He's probably a minister."

"My granddaddy is a preacher." He noted Jocelyn's slightly skeptical look. "It's true. Reverend Matthew Grady Tucker is a born-again, baptized-in-the-Holy-Ghost, God-loving and God-fearing preacher of the Good Book." He dragged his legs up and rested his forearms on his bent knees. "He's never been much impressed when he sees people wearing crosses around their necks. I remember one time he stood at the pulpit and admonished the congregation, saying,

'What God needs is fruit-bearing Christians, not religious nuts.' ''

She laughed, convinced she knew where Tucker had inherited his warm but pointed humor. "I think I would like your grandfather."

"He is one of those rare truly good men." His mouth crooked at some distant memory. "I'll tell you, though, if you aren't in church Sunday morning, you need to have a really good reason."

"Like death's door," she suggested lightly.

Tucker nodded emphatically. "It has to be just about that good. Funny," he mused. "I can't remember the last time I went to church. Not since I left home, I guess." He turned his interested gaze on her. This time it stayed to study and watch. "How about you?"

She avoided his eyes, finding them a bit too disconcerting. "I still go nearly every Sunday."

"Back in Waterloo?"

For a split second, Jocelyn couldn't think what he was talking about, then remembered her fictitious hometown. "Yes, in Waterloo."

She took another tentative sip of the hot coffee, wishing it would cool down so she could drink it and be on her way.

"You like it there in Iowa, do you?"

"It's a good place to live." She pretended to admire the view from the memorial's steps.

The Reflecting Pool was as still as a silver mirror, flanked by its groves of elms wearing the last of their autumn leaves. The Washington Monument rose high and white beyond it, drawing a line that pointed to the crowning dome of the Capitol building at the far opposite end of the Mall.

"It's postcard perfect, isn't it?" she said, trying to direct Tucker's attention away from her.

But he wasn't so easily distracted. "How long will you be staying in Washington?"

"Not long." Unnerved by his continued study of her, she finally said, "I wish you wouldn't stare at me like that."

"Sorry." A smile of apology twitched over his mouth. "I thought you'd be used to people staring at you by now."

Alarm sizzled through her nerve ends. "What's that supposed to mean?" Jocelyn tried to laugh, but it came out thin and weak.

"Back in Kansas, guys always stared at beautiful girls, and beautiful girls always knew it. In fact, most of them got to where they expected it," Tucker explained.

"I'm flattered, but—"

"You're right. These days, it's smart to be cautious of strangers in a big city." Molly butted her head against Tucker's arm, looking for an ear-scratching. Smiling, he obliged her. "Especially ones with clumsy dogs like this one."

Jocelyn laughed when the big dog tried to climb into his lap. "You two definitely look dangerous."

"Only accidentally," Tucker promised and managed to push the dog away before any coffee spilled from his cup. "What all are you planning to see while you're here?"

"As much as I can," she said, being deliberately vague.

"That narrows things down considerably," he said dryly.

"I know, but it's true just the same. And I don't have a lot of time." She looked pointedly at her watch, then stood up, her cup still nearly full. "Thanks for the coffee—and the company."

"You aren't going already, are you?" Tucker shot to his feet, with none of the ungainly awkwardness that usually marked his movements. "You haven't even drunk your coffee yet."

"I know, but . . ." Shrugging, Jocelyn descended a step. "I've got places to go, things to do, and I'm running out of time to do them." When Molly bounded to her side, Jocelyn gave the dog a farewell pat. "Don't get into any more trouble, okay?"

With a wave to Tucker, Jocelyn skipped down the last two steps to the sidewalk and headed swiftly for the street. She knew without looking that Tucker still stood there, stunned and surprised by the suddenness of her departure.

"Hey, Jonesy, wait!" he called and leaped to the sidewalk in one long, striding jump.

Short of breaking into a run, Jocelyn knew she had no choice but to stop. Nervous and annoyed, she swung back just as Tucker took a second long and bounding stride. At that same instant, the dog decided to switch sides and race ahead of him to

Jocelyn. The shortest route to accomplish that goal was between Tucker's legs.

Jocelyn gasped in alarm, but it was already too late to shout a warning. For Tucker, it was like running into a trip wire that cut him off at the knees without checking his forward momentum.

He seemed to hang in the air for an instant, completely overbalanced, one foot on the sidewalk and the other high in the air, pointing at the sky, coffee flying from the cup in a brown arc. An arm reached as if to ward off the onrushing concrete; the other held on to the dog's leash while Molly tried to scurry out of his way.

In that last second before Tucker made actual contact, Jocelyn squeezed her eyes shut, inwardly bracing herself for the sound of it. He landed with a thud, a scrape, and an *"oomph!"*

She peeked through her lashes and saw him lying there, his face contorted with pain as he tried slowly and carefully to untangle arms and legs.

The sight instantly dissolved that momentary paralysis. Dropping her own cup, Jocelyn rushed to his side, but Molly beat her there, nosing around his face, her black body a wriggling mass of contrition and happiness.

"Ow! Ooh. Molly?!" Mixed with the exasperation in Tucker's voice, there was pain as he tried to fend off the dog over the protest of hurting muscles and limbs.

Reaching them, Jocelyn grabbed a section of leash and dragged the dog off him. But the end of the strap was still wrapped around Tucker's wrist. In pulling the dog off him, Jocelyn yanked his arm halfway across his body, drawing another sharp grunt of pain from him.

Instantly she let go of the leash. "Oh, my gosh. I'm sorry. I—" She dropped to her knees beside him, helplessly reaching, wanting to do something. But there was Molly again, trying to push her way back to Tucker's face. Jocelyn shoved her away, ordering sternly, "Molly, sit!"

Looking shamefaced, the dog sat. Satisfied for the moment that the dog would remain there, Jocelyn turned back to Tucker. He was lying more or less on his back, moving this arm and that hand in a testing fashion.

"Where are you hurt?" She immediately set to removing the leash from around his wrist, using extreme care in moving his arm just in case something was broken.

"All over," Tucker answered, and winced when he tried to lever himself up onto his elbows. A fresh stab of pain quickly prompted him to give up that effort. "Give me a hand, will you? If I could just sit up . . ."

Jocelyn hesitated. "Are you sure you should move? If something's broken—"

"Naw, I didn't break anything." Tucker finally looked at her, a rueful smile edging the corners of his mouth. "Except my pride, maybe. The rest of me's intact, just a little twisted and battered. Scraped, too," he added, examining the raw and bloodied area on the heel of his hand. I didn't know concrete could be so rough and hard. I'll tell ya' one thing, it's a lot harder than that grass you landed on.''

It was all the talking, more than the actual words he said, that convinced Jocelyn his injuries were minor but painful. Relieved and showing it, she bent to help him into a sitting position.

"Put your arm around me," she instructed, lifting it and ducking her head under it to let it settle around her shoulders while she slid a bracing hand underneath him.

Their faces were close—close enough that Jocelyn could see the minute gold flecks in his hazel eyes. Her heart did an unexpected flip-flop at the heat that suddenly glittered in them, little sexual sparks flying. The fresh scent of soap and some woodsy aftershave lotion drifted around her, tinged with a hint of tobacco.

At almost the same moment, Jocelyn discovered there was a lot more hard flesh and muscle covering his bones than the leanness of his frame had led her to expect.

"I've heard of falling hard for a girl before," Tucker murmured, a dazzling light in his eyes as he lazily studied her. "But I always thought it was a figure of speech."

Her mind seemed to be absolutely blank. Jocelyn couldn't think of a single response. Certainly nothing that would defuse this intense awareness that seemed to grip both of them.

The spell—or whatever it was—was broken by the scuffle of hurrying feet descending the memorial steps, a sound accompanied by the tap-tap of a cane striking one step then another.

"Mr. Tucker." The familiar bass voice of Obediah Melchior reached both of them at the same moment, its tone riddled with concern. "Is he badly hurt? Will we need an ambulance?"

"No, I don't need an ambulance." Tucker was definite about that. "Just a little help to sit up, that's all."

His arm tightened on Jocelyn's shoulders, gripping it for support. Bracing herself to take more of his weight, she clamped an arm behind his back. With Jocelyn pushing and Tucker pulling, they had him sitting up by the time the elderly gentleman's short legs succeeded in propelling him to the scene.

"Are you certain you are all right, Mr. Tucker? You look a bit shaken." Bending, Obediah hovered over him, huffing a little from his haste in reaching him. "That was a very nasty fall you took."

"In more ways than one." There was something bright and tender and a little bemused in the smiling glance Tucker slanted at Jocelyn.

Then he was looking away, leaving her to wonder if she had imagined it—and why she felt these stirrings of disappointment if she had. As Tucker withdrew his arm from her shoulders, Jocelyn removed her supporting hand from his back. Immediately she missed the contact, the warmth and strength she had felt.

Tucker started to gather himself for the push to

his feet, then stopped, hissing in a breath. "My knee, I must have twisted it."

Leaning forward, he took a look at it, then flung an irritated glance at the dog. "Would you look at what you did to my pants, Molly? A perfectly good pair of pants, and now they've got a hole in the knee." The dog whoofed in answer and flopped onto her stomach, her wagging tail sweeping the sidewalk. "Well, you're wrong, Molly," Tucker informed her. "It's not the fashion anymore to go around with holes in your pant knees."

He examined the rip in the fabric and the shredded patch of scraped flesh oozing blood near the base of his kneecap. Wincing, Tucker picked out a bit of embedded cement and tossed it aside.

"You definitely need a doctor to look at that knee," Obediah announced.

"No, all I need is some soap and water and a little iodine to take care of this." Tucker tried bending the knee and paled. "Maybe a couple of good wraps with an Ace bandage for support, too."

"You didn't tear something in your knee, did you?" Jocelyn asked, suddenly worried.

"No, I've done that before. I know how that feels," Tucker assured her. "I just twisted it good and probably strained something." He started to shift his weight and get the other leg under him. "Ouch!" He rolled back.

"What's wrong?" Her glance flew to his opposite hip in alarm.

"Something poked me." Tucker pulled the tail of his jacket out from under him, then dug a hand into the pocket, searching for the offending item. "My pipe." He held it up in two pieces, the stem snapped off an inch from the bowl. "Molly, you broke my pipe."

Guiltily the dog lowered her head to the sidewalk and whined. Jocelyn didn't mean to laugh, but the entire exchange struck her as comical.

"I'm glad somebody thinks this is funny," Tucker grumbled. "This happens to be my favorite pipe, and Molly knows it." He shoved the pieces into a different pocket.

"I believe she does," Obediah agreed with a smile. "She looks so sorrowful, you would think she was human."

"Why is it when people say that, they think they're paying the dog a compliment?" Without the broken pipe in the pocket to jab him, Tucker rolled onto his right side, bending his knee under him while trying to keep the injured one straight.

"A profound observation, Mr. Tucker. Now, let us help you up." Reaching down, Obediah hooked a hand under Tucker's arm and instructed, "Miss Jones, you take his other arm. We'll see if he can stand as well as he thinks he can."

With all three of them working more or less together, Tucker made it to his feet—an effort that produced more than one grimace. He stood for a minute, his weight centered mainly on his right leg, then cautiously swung his left foot forward, testing to see if the knee would hold him.

"It's going to work fine," Tucker insisted, more to himself than to Jocelyn and Obediah, then hobbled forward a couple more steps, noticeably favoring his left leg.

"I think you should see a doctor," Jocelyn said after watching him, "and have that knee X-rayed."

"No point," Tucker rejected the idea. "He'll just send me home, tell me to wrap it in ice and keep it supported, write me a prescription for some pain pills, and charge me for the office call, the X ray, and who knows what else."

But—" she began.

"You're from Iowa, Jonesy," he reminded her. "You know, when you live on a farm, you do most of your own doctoring. If the animal doesn't get well in a reasonable period of time, or gets worse, that's when you call the vet. You sure don't pay him to come out for every sniffle and limp."

"You are not a cow," Jocelyn declared in irritation.

Tucker shot her an indignant look. "I should hope not. A young range bull, maybe, but—"

"That's not what I meant and you know it," she flashed in exasperation.

"I know, I know." He waved off her protest. "But the principle is still the same, animal or human."

Jocelyn folded her arms tightly in front of her. "That is a ridiculous attitude, Tucker—" She started to inform him that if he was too cheap to go to a doctor, she would pay for it. Then it hit her: what if she didn't have enough extra cash with her to pay it?

Fortunately, Obediah intervened, gently reminding her, "But it is Mr. Tucker's prerogative whether he wants to be examined by a physician or not. What we should concern ourselves with now is, how is he to get home so he can do his own doctoring?" He turned to Tucker. "Is your car parked nearby?"

"No, Molly and I walked here." The two words *Molly* and *walk* brought the dog bounding to Tucker's side, barking with excitement. Tucker tried to shush her. "No, Molly, you've got it wrong. We're gonna have to cut our walk short this morning and head back home."

That last word silenced her. She stared at him as if unable to believe it could be true.

"Don't give me that look," Tucker told her irritably. "It's your fault for tripping me."

"Your master is quite right, Molly." Obediah gathered up the loose lead. "Now, back to the matter at hand. Do you live far from here, Mr. Tucker?"

"A few blocks. And call me Tucker," he stated somewhat sharply. "I'm not comfortable with that 'mister' business. My dad is the *mister* in the Tucker family. I keep wanting to look over my shoulder and see if you aren't talking to him."

"Don't you go getting grouchy with Mr. Melchior," Jocelyn scolded. "He's trying to help. You could be a little more grateful."

"I am grateful," Tucker retorted, getting his back up a little. "Forgive me if I don't get down on one knee and kiss his hand in thanks, but mine happens to be hurting a little."

"And whose fault is that?" Jocelyn wanted to know. "And don't go blaming Molly. You're the one who came leaping off those steps after me."

"What was I supposed to do? I couldn't just let you walk off like that!".

"Now, now, children." Obediah stepped between them, holding up a placating hand. "How the accident happened, whose fault it was or wasn't, is immaterial now. Tucker has injured his knee. We need to get him off it as quickly as possible."

"Thank you." Tucker made a mock bow of gratitude.

"You're welcome." Obediah nodded, a small smile showing within the white of his beard. "In the meantime, let's get you situated over here on the steps. Then I'll see about whistling up a cab to take you home."

"You'd better be sure to leave Molly with me," Tucker warned. "If a cabbie sees you with a dog, he'll flip on his 'Off Duty' sign and zip right on by."

"I'll take Molly," Jocelyn volunteered, reaching for the leash.

Tucker looked at her, but he didn't say a word. Instead he hobbled toward the memorial steps while Obediah kept a supporting hand under his arm. After some clumsy maneuvering, Tucker lowered himself into a reclining position on the steps.

"I'll be back in a minute with the cab," Obediah

said, then glanced at Jocelyn. "You stay here with Tucker and make sure he doesn't injure himself further."

Suddenly alone with Tucker, Jocelyn found herself with an awkward silence to fill.

CHAPTER 7

Adopting an attitude of cool indifference, Jocelyn led Molly to the steps and sat down a few feet to the right of Tucker. Inside, her emotions were churning. She was upset and she wasn't sure why. She did know the turmoil she felt had absolutely no basis in any fear of discovery. Tucker was definitely at the root of it, though—Tucker and the slightly heated words they had just exchanged over his refusal to see a doctor.

Why on earth did she care whether he went to a doctor or not? It certainly had nothing to do with her. She hadn't even known the man before today except through his column. All right, so she had learned this morning that he was kind of funny and warm and wise. So what?

Therein lay the problem. Tucker was the type of man she could like. *Be honest,* Jocelyn scolded herself, *you do like him; more than that, you're attracted to him and you don't want to be because it would be futile.*

The minute Tucker found out she was the president's daughter, his attitude toward her would change, and Jocelyn knew it. He'd see her differently, become blinded by the supposed status of it and not see her as an ordinary person. It had happened to her time after time, person after person.

Such a reaction was normal, Jocelyn knew. Something that was purely human nature. She herself had experienced a similar thing the first time she walked into the Oval Office and saw her father seated behind the desk. That goose-bumpy feeling had hit her then. For an instant it wasn't her father she saw, but Henry Wakefield, the president of the United States. And for that moment, Jocelyn had stared at him with awe.

Even though she fully understood how and why such a thing could happen, she still didn't like it when she was the object of it. Being the president's daughter wasn't any measure of her worth as a human being; it was simply an accident of birth and nothing more.

But would Tucker look at it that way? Deep down, Jocelyn was afraid to find out because something told her that it would hurt a lot if he didn't.

This day was supposed to be fun and carefree. Irritated that it was turning out otherwise, Jocelyn lifted her head and glared at the bright morning sun and the white spire of Washington's memorial silhouetted against it.

"Do you know . . ." Tucker began, her awareness of him tingling anew at the sound of his voice. Jocelyn stole a quick glance at him. He was scowling thoughtfully into the distance. "I find it hard to look at the Capitol building without wondering what our founding fathers would think of taxation with representation?"

The remark was so typical of his wry wit that Jocelyn had to smile. She suspected that was his intention all along.

"It would be interesting to find out, wouldn't it?" he remarked while his fingers examined the scraped palm of his hand. His attention shifted to the Washington Monument. "Do you know that if you drew a line from the Capitol to the Washington Monument, then here to the Lincoln Memorial, and followed it on across the Potomac, it would take you right to the front porch of Arlington House, Robert E. Lee's home? It's always struck me as ironic that Lincoln's memorial is located directly across from Lee's home, with a river running between them. Just about as ironic as Lee's home getting turned into our national cemetery, isn't it?"

"I suppose so." Jocelyn scratched behind Molly's ears, struggling to remain aloof and indifferent to his conversational gambit, innocent as it was.

"It feels like there's a river running between us now," Tucker said, and Jocelyn was instantly on guard. Against what, she wasn't sure. "My granddaddy always says that when you start arguing with a fool, the other guy's doing the same thing. Well, I'm feeling kinda' foolish right now for being so short with you over that doctor business and all. I'm sorry."

"Apology accepted." She continued to devote her attention to the dog.

"Good." There was a decisive nod of Tucker's head in her peripheral vision.

Nagged by her conscience, Jocelyn was obliged to say, "Obediah was right; if you don't want a doctor to look at that knee, it's your business."

"Thank you."

"You're welcome," she responded stiffly.

"Would you look at this?" he muttered in disgust. "I've got blood smeared on my jacket. From my hand, I guess."

"Don't blame Molly for that," Jocelyn stated, all her earlier irritation with him resurfacing.

"I'm not blaming Molly for it. . . . Well, maybe I did at first," Tucker conceded grudgingly while he began a search of his pockets. "But I was mad at the time. Where's my handkerchief?"

"Why were you mad? Because you fell? That isn't any reason to get mad at people."

"It wasn't that," he grumbled. "I was mad because you're from Iowa."

Dumbfounded, Jocelyn swung around on the step to stare at him. "Why would you be mad about that?"

"Because, sooner or later, you'll be going back there." Finally locating his handkerchief, Tucker pressed it against his scraped palm, blotting up the beads of fresh blood. "Chances are, I'll never see you again. And that idea doesn't sit well."

Jocelyn was certain she had never blushed in her life, but at that moment, her face felt as hot and red as a glowing log.

"That's ridiculous," she protested to cover her strange confusion. "Why should that matter to you? We don't even know each other."

"That's my point," Tucker reasoned. "There you went walking off, without me ever getting to know you better. You see, my granddaddy told me a long time ago that when I met the right woman, I'd know it." Her mouth dropped open and Tucker grinned crookedly. "Yeah, it kinda' struck me like that, too."

She stood up, ready to bolt from him and this entire conversation. The whole thing was ludicrous. Absolutely ludicrous.

"Now, don't go running off." Tucker motioned her back onto the step. "I'm going to look pretty ridiculous hopping after you with this bum knee of mine."

And he would do exactly that. Jocelyn knew it as surely as she knew day from night. She could see the whole scene unfolding in her head, including the park policeman now strolling along the bank of the Reflecting Pool. If he saw Tucker pursuing her, it was a good bet he would come to her aid. Before it was all over, the officer would probably want to see some identification—something she couldn't produce.

Jocelyn sat back down, all stiff and tense.

"You can relax," Tucker told her. "You see, my

granddaddy told me something else. He said that when you're arguing with your wife, first you have to be absolutely sure you're right, then you need to drop the subject."

"Your grandfather is a wise man," she murmured tightly.

"Yes, he is," Tucker agreed. "Unfortunately I forgot that bit of advice and tried to pick a fight with you because I was upset. All because here I'd barely met you and already you would be leaving to go back to Iowa."

"You are crazy," Jocelyn declared while struggling to convince herself of it.

"So I've been told." He nodded.

"You don't even know who or what I am," she protested.

"That's true." He considered that for a moment. "For all I know you could be an embezzler. Of course, if you are, I'm sure you had a good reason."

"I can't believe I'm listening to any of this." Jocelyn stared at the park policeman, willing him to leave the area. Or better yet, for Obediah to return with a taxi.

"What kind of music do you like?" Tucker asked, the question coming out of nowhere. "Me, I like country music, everything from Waylon Jennings and George Strait to Garth Brooks and Hank Junior. Texas swing is my favorite, though, especially when Bob Wills does it."

"I prefer jazz, rhythm and blues," Jocelyn asserted. "Everything from Fats Waller and Louis Armstrong to Miles Davis and Dizzy Gillespie. For me, though, no one can top the incomparable Billie Holiday."

Tucker grunted a noncommittal response, then asked, "What about food? What's your favorite meal?"

"Italian."

"Pizza?" he asked hopefully.

She shook her head. "Pasta. Any kind."

He sighed his regret. "Me, I like Mexican food. The more jalapeños, the better."

"Myself, I'm not very fond of dishes that are spicy hot."

"How do you feel about sports?" Tucker cocked his head at an inquiring angle, as if hoping for better luck.

"I'm a dyed-in-the-wool Redskins fan," Jocelyn blurted without thinking.

"Really?" Tucker frowned in surprise. "Coming from Iowa, I figured you would root for the Packers, or maybe the Kansas City Chiefs," he said while Jocelyn groped for a way to defend her choice of teams. But Tucker eliminated the necessity. "Basketball is my sport. Probably because I played it. I even made the winning shot at a high school tournament game once. We ended up losing the championship game, though. We got trounced by a team from a bigger school. They had a center that was six-nine. His arms seemed about that long, too," he recalled idly, then gave her a curious look. "Are you a Democrat or Republican?"

Jocelyn almost panicked at the question, then recovered. "Does it matter?" She challenged. "Isn't it obvious by now that we don't share the same likes and dislikes? When you get right down to it, we have very little in common."

Privately Jocelyn was surprised by the odd disappointment she felt.

"It does seem that way, doesn't it?" Tucker agreed with unconcern. "Which just shows that we aren't going to bore each other. Life definitely wouldn't be dull for us."

"How can you say that?" Jocelyn looked at him in amazement.

"Because it's true," he replied calmly. "My granddaddy always says the best marriage is between opposites. That way, one can balance the other."

"I have never heard anything so ridiculous." She was dumbfounded. "Do you realize how many fights that would create?"

"Only if you were trying to change the other person," he countered.

She released a small laugh of exasperation. "I would be curious to know what your grandmother thinks about that."

Tucker smiled, his eyes lighting with a genuine warmth and affection. "My grandma doesn't do a lot of thinking about such things. She's too busy enjoying life. My granddaddy is the thinker in their family."

"Whose opinion is that? Your grandfather's or yours?" Jocelyn challenged with a bit of rancor. "Obviously grandma doesn't have a brain in her pretty little head."

"Now, there you go taking this all wrong," Tucker

declared with a sad sigh. "My grandma happens to be a bright, intelligent woman, and my granddaddy would be the first one to tell you that. But by nature, she's bubbly and happy, always scatting here and there, laughing about this story or marveling over the morning dew sparkling in the wheat field, creating acres of shimmering diamonds. Which is something my granddaddy would probably never notice if she didn't grab him by the arm and drag him outside to see it. More than that, she chides him out of his thoughtful and quiet ways and makes him laugh. He probably knows the Bible by heart, but she points out the miracles. It's the balance, Jonesy," Tucker explained earnestly. "They each have something to give the other."

"It sounds beautiful." Jocelyn doubted that she had ever looked at a relationship in quite that way. Then her practical side asserted itself. "Unfortunately, people aren't normally that tolerant."

"That's the problem all over the world, isn't it?" Tucker remarked a shade glumly. "We always think other people should think the same, look the same, talk the same, and feel the same way we do. And if they don't, they're wrong, and we set out to bring them around to our way of doing it."

"And that will never happen," she murmured, sobered by the serious turn the conversation had taken.

"Let's hope not." Tucker flashed her a lopsided grin. "Can you imagine how boring this world be then—everybody running around talking the same, thinking the same, looking the same? It would be as bad as being the last human left on earth." He glanced toward the curb. "Here comes Obediah with the chariot that's going to take me home." He started to shift forward to get his weight on his right leg, then sat back and frowned. "What's he doing with two cabs?"

When Jocelyn saw the two taxis grind to a stop, one behind the other, she was as puzzled as Tucker. "Maybe one is letting out a passenger."

But Obediah Melchior was the only person to emerge from either cab. He said something to the driver of that cab, then motioned to the other, signaling him to wait there.

"What's the two cabs for?" Tucker asked when Obediah joined them.

"The first taxi won't allow dogs." Obediah tucked a shoulder under Tucker's arm, offering himself as a crutch. "The driver insists he's allergic to them."

"Allergic?" Tucker scoffed, leaning on the elderly gentleman while he headed for the curb at a hopping limp. Jocelyn followed with the dog. "More likely he doesn't want Molly drooling on the cab seat. Which is fine. We'll ride in the other one."

"May I make a suggestion?" Obediah proceeded without waiting for an answer. "It occurs to me that you will require assistance getting both in and out of the taxi. In just this short time, I can tell that your knee has already begun to stiffen. Now I would be more than happy to accompany you to your apartment. However that brings up another difficulty: the three of us—you, me, and Molly—in the same vehicle. Molly is unquestionably a fine and noble dog, but you must admit she is a bit clumsy and rambunctious at times. While she may never mean to do you further injury, the risk is definitely there."

Before Obediah ever guided Tucker all the way to the first cab, Jocelyn knew what was coming, knew exactly what he proposed. Her steps slowed in instinctive resistance to the idea while Molly tugged on the leash, anxious to keep pace with her master.

"I decided it would be best to have two taxis." Keeping a steadying hand on Tucker while he balanced himself on one foot, Obediah opened the cab's rear door. "One for you and one for Molly to travel in. That way Miss Jones can ride with you, and I can follow with Molly."

Gripping the out-swung door with one hand, Tucker looked over his shoulder at Jocelyn. "Miss Jones might have some objections to that arrangement." Mixed in with his questioning look, there was a longing that hoped she would agree.

"I am certain Miss Jones won't mind," Obediah responded, as if surprised there was any doubt.

"Somebody make up their mind," the cabbie complained. "The meter's running. Either you get in or you pay me."

Tucker remained motionless, holding her gaze. "Well, Jonesy, do I—"

Trapped and frustrated, she muttered an irritated, "Just turn around and get in there and shut up."

Calling herself every kind of fool, she passed the leash to Obediah, giving Molly into his care.

After some awkward maneuvering that involved Tucker hopping on one foot in a half circle, folding his long frame in the middle, and cracking his head against the door frame, he made it into the rear seat, his left leg slung along the edge of it and his body angled against the door. Jocelyn managed to squeeze into the space on the opposite side, banging his injured leg only once.

Armed with Tucker's address, the surly cabdriver shifted gears and pulled away from the curb. Jocelyn glanced back to make sure Obediah and Molly followed in the second cab, then squared around and faced the front again, steadfastly refusing to look at Tucker.

The silence lay thick between them, laden with strong undercurrents. At last Tucker broke it. "Thanks for coming along. I didn't think you would."

"Neither did I," she agreed stiffly.

"I guess I've messed up your holiday." There was apology in his voice.

"You don't know the half of it." Jocelyn could see all of her precious free time just slipping away, minute after minute. Even worse, she hadn't gotten to do one single thing she wanted.

"That's right; you had places to go, things to do," Tucker remembered. "I suppose I should be sorry, but it's kinda' hard because I'm too glad you're here."

"How nice that one of us is," Jocelyn murmured tightly.

"Wait a minute, now. Nobody put a gun to your head and forced you in this cab," Tucker reminded her, his tone lightly mocking. "You're here of your own free will."

She breathed out a heavy sigh. "Maybe so, but it doesn't feel like it. Right now I should be riding the elevator to the top of the Washington Monument—now, when it first opens. But you can bet by the time I can get around to doing that, I'll have to wait in line an hour. Maybe more."

"The best time to go up there is at night," Tucker informed her. "It's magical then, with all the monuments lit, the Capitol dome and the White House flooded with light and the streetlights stringing in all directions, the neon colors of the building signs and the traffic lights."

Listening to him, visualizing all the familiar landmarks in her mind, Jocelyn could easily imagine the nighttime view, right down to the navigation lights on the boats in the Potomac.

In spite of herself, she smiled. "It sounds almost as beautiful as your grandmother's wheat field of dew drops."

"I hadn't thought about it, but I guess it is a city version of it." Leaning forward, Tucker said to the cabbie, "It's that second building from the corner, that big old brick monstrosity."

It was one of those dark and heavy Victorian houses with a corner turret and a recessed porch, bereft of the airy grace of the more ornamental Queen Anne style. The four metal mailboxes near its front door revealed its conversion into apartments.

Once the driver was paid and Tucker was upright on the sidewalk, Jocelyn let her gaze travel all the way up to the peak of the three-story structure.

"Should I ask which floor your apartment's on?" She glanced sideways at him.

"Nope," he said, hopping a bit for better balance. "I think you already guessed it's on the third floor."

"You're right. I did."

Behind them, the second cab pulled up to the curb, stopping with a screech of brakes. Molly barked a greeting and tried to crawl out the window to join them. Somehow, Obediah persuaded her to change her mind.

"Shall we wait for them?" Jocelyn asked.

Both eyebrows went up at that question. "And have Molly knock me down trying to beat me up the steps? No thanks." With a hand firmly on her shoulder, Tucker motioned her forward. "Let's go. With any luck we'll get there first."

By the time they reached the front door, Molly and Obediah were just climbing out of the taxi. "I'm curious," Jocelyn said, glancing at the pair while she held the door for Tucker. "How did you convince your landlord to let you have a dog?"

"That was easy. He's blind."

"I beg your pardon?" She followed him inside the darkly paneled hall, not sure if he was speaking figuratively or literally.

"He's blind. He has a seeing-eye dog." Tucker limp-hopped to the stairs. "His name is Jake."

"Your landlord?"

"No, his dog. Jake and Molly are good buddies." He gripped the wooden railing and glanced up the stairwell. "This should be interesting."

"You'd better let me help you." Again she offered her shoulder for a crutch and went with him while he basically jumped one-footed from one step to the next.

At the landing between the second and third floors, Tucker stopped to gather himself for the last push. Jocelyn studied the glint of moisture above his upper lip, evidence of the effort that had been required to get this far.

"How would you have gotten up these steps if I hadn't been here to help?" she wondered aloud.

"Probably the same way I did when I broke my leg as a kid and my bedroom was upstairs. You sit on the steps backwards and scoot up."

From below came the sound of the front door opening, followed by the clack of claws on the hall floor. "Oh-oh, here comes Molly. We'd better get a move on." With his arm wrapped firmly around her shoulders, Tucker started up the last half flight of steps, taking them with considerably more speed than before. "I've gotta tell you," he huffed a bit, "this is a lot better than scooting up these steps. It gives me a great excuse to put my arm around you."

"I wish you wouldn't say things like that," Jocelyn protested, but without the force she would have liked.

Mainly because the sensation of his arm around her felt good.

"What am I supposed to do? Wait until you're back in Iowa?" he asked, cocking a dubious eyebrow. Rattling dog tags, clumping paws, and panting breaths echoed up the stairwell. At the top of the steps, Tucker paused and yelled down, "It's okay, Obediah. You can turn Molly loose now. We made it." Turning aside, he murmured to Jocelyn, "It's better than Molly dragging him all the way here. She'd probably give Obediah a heart attack before he got here."

There was a mad scramble of paws thundering up the steps, getting closer with each second. Tucker hopped to his apartment door, then felt his pockets with one hand while the other dipped unerringly into his right pant pocket and came out with the key.

Puzzled, Jocelyn tilted her head to the side. "Why do you do that?"

"Do what?" He unlocked the door and gave it a push.

"Pat your pockets as if you're looking for something. You knew right where the key was."

"Habit, I guess." Tucker shrugged and slipped the key back in the appropriate pocket. "People have always expected me to be a bit absentminded. I guess I've always obliged them." He hobbled into the apartment. "This is home, such as it is."

Jocelyn hadn't intended to venture into it, only to look, but Molly swept her the rest of the way through the door. It was either that or get knocked down again.

She wasn't sure what she had expected Tucker's apartment to be like—probably something masculine and on the messy side. But the living room was comfortable and inviting: clear of clutter, yet homey and inviting.

Lying neatly along the back of an overstuffed green sofa was an afghan, hand-crocheted in a zigzag pattern that incorporated broad forest green stripes with narrower bands of wine red and cream. An old platform rocker sat at an angle next to it with a combination floor lamp and end table stationed beside it. On it sat a pipe stand, complete with a humidor and three pipes in a rack. A corner of the room had been converted into a minioffice, complete with a computer work station.

Engrossed in her survey, Jocelyn was slow to notice that both Tucker and Molly had vanished. From somewhere to her right, she heard a loud thud followed by a half-smothered curse and the clatter of Molly's claws on linoleum.

"What did you do now?" she demanded and went to investigate.

She found Tucker in the small efficiency-size kitchen, trying to swing his injured leg onto the sink counter. Molly was at the opposite end, lapping up water from a large ceramic bowl.

Jocelyn stared. "What on earth are you doing?"

"What does it look like I'm doing?" Tucker flung up a hand, matching the nearly angry snap in her voice. "I'm trying to get my leg up here so I can wash my knee under the faucet and get some of the blood and grit and grime out of it."

"That is not the way to go about cleaning it. Go over there and sit down." Jocelyn pointed to an oak chair and had the satisfaction of seeing Tucker lower his leg to the floor and take the first hobbling step to do as she said. "What you need is a pan with some soapy water in it, and a clean cloth to wash it with."

Without thinking, she started opening cupboard doors and drawers to find the needed items herself. But Tucker didn't stop when he reached the chair. He kept hobbling right out of the kitchen. Jocelyn had the necessary pan in hand when she noticed him in the doorway.

"Where are you going now?" she said in confusion, letting the pan hang from her hand.

"To change clothes, of course." Tucker tossed the answer over his shoulder and continued into the small living room.

"Change clothes? Why?" She paused in the doorway, her curious frown deepening.

Tucker paused long enough to reply, "Well, you can't very well wash this scraped knee through that hole in my pants. I figured that out myself after I got the bright idea of cleaning it in the sink."

"I know, but—" Jocelyn stopped, distracted by Obediah when he stepped into the apartment, hat in hand, looking a bit winded from the climb.

Tucker, on the other hand, took no notice of him whatsoever. "For heaven's sake, Jonesy, you don't expect me to drop my pants, do you?" he asked, looking properly shocked. "We aren't even married yet."

It was the *yet* as much as the *married* part that stunned Jocelyn into silence, conscious of a burning heat that rushed into her face. Her glance raced to Obediah. He stared back at her, his dark eyes rounded with surprise, while Tucker hobbled into a back hall, as calm and unconcerned as he could be.

"Are you two engaged?" Obediah alternately pointed a gloved finger back and forth between Jocelyn and Tucker's retreating figure, his low voice dropping to a conspiratorial level.

"Good grief, no!" She was vehement in her denial even as her cheeks grew redder beneath their makeup. "I never even met Tucker before this morning. He's just talking crazy."

"Really. He sounded quite serious to me," Obediah remarked on a thoughtful and curious note, following when Jocelyn abruptly turned to reenter the kitchen.

"He's only making a bad joke." She sidestepped Molly when the dog padded off to locate her master, water dripping from her jowly lips.

"A joke," Obediah repeated on a wondering note as the click of a knob turning came from elsewhere in the apartment.

Tucker's voice filtered into the kitchen. "Decided to join me, did you, Molly? Well, come on in." The invitation was shortly followed by the sound of a door closing.

"Yes, a joke." Jocelyn went to the sink and turned

on the hot water faucet. "That's what Tucker does for a living—make jokes."

Obediah frowned. "I thought you just said that you hadn't met him before today."

"I hadn't actually met him," she confirmed. "I knew of him, though. Just about everybody in Washington does."

"Really." Obediah seemed fascinated by the information. "And he makes jokes. Is he a comedian?"

"More like a political humorist." Adjusting the water temperature, Jocelyn added some cold. "He's widely known. And his column is widely read. 'Tucker's Take,' it's called."

"Well, he certainly seems to be quite *taken* with you." His eyes twinkled at her.

She rolled hers in exasperation. "Don't remind me."

She squirted some liquid soap into the pan, then started to fill it with water. At the first blossom of bubbles, Jocelyn jerked her hands away, then hurriedly turned off the taps.

"I can't do this," she murmured.

"Do what?"

"Clean his scraped knee." She stared at the foamy water as if it had turned deadly. In one sense of the word, it had. "If I get soap and water on my hands, it will wash off the makeup on them."

"That is a problem." Obediah laid his hat and cane atop the kitchen's half table, then crossed to the cupboard area by the sink. "Perhaps he has some rubber gloves you can wear."

"A bachelor with rubber gloves?" Jocelyn was skeptical.

"It's unlikely, I know, but he does seem very domestic. We'll just look under the sink here." When he reached for the door below it, she moved out of his way. Bending low, Obediah peered inside. "Aha! I knew it!" He straightened, a pair of yellow latex gloves in his hand. "These should solve the problem very nicely."

"I hope so." Jocelyn wished she felt as sure as he did.

CHAPTER 8

The minute the bedroom door latched shut, Tucker abandoned his exaggerated limp and walked to the bed, favoring his injured leg only a little. Shrugging out of his flannel-lined jacket, he glanced at the watching dog.

"How am I doing, Molly? Jonesy bought into the sprained-knee routine, didn't she?" He grinned, giving the coat a fling onto the bed. "Hook, line, and sinker."

Molly whined softly.

"I know." Tucker held up a hand as if checking a protest, then started to unfasten his pants. "I know it's cheating, but all's fair in love and war. She was going off sightseeing, for heaven's sake. I had to think of something to stop her." He stripped off his pants, wincing a little when he had to bend his left knee to step out of them. "And I did hurt my knee, so it isn't like it's an out-and-out lie."

Molly whined again and sat down, her tail brushing the carpet.

"You're right. I never did thank you for tripping me like that. Your timing was perfect." Gimping slightly, Tucker went to the chest of drawers. "You don't happen to remember where I put those khaki walking shorts, do you?" He mumbled, half to himself and half to the dog, then began rifling through the drawers. "You know, I never really believed it could happen like this, Molly—that you could just look at someone and know she was the right one for you." Tucker looked back at the dog to make sure she was still listening. "My granddaddy always said that love was the strongest of all human passions because it could strike the head, the heart, and the senses all at the same time." He pulled the shorts out of the drawer and gestured with them to make his point. "And you know what? Granddad was right."

Molly briefly shied from the waving cloth, then stood up and whoofed at it, growling a little in her throat.

"Now, don't go getting worried," Tucker admonished, returning to sit on the bed and pull on the shorts. "I'm not going to do anything foolish like marrying in haste so I can repent at my leisure. We need to get to know each other better." Standing, he buttoned the waistband of his shorts, then pulled up the zipper. "Besides, it might take a while to get her used to the idea. First, though, I need to figure out some way to persuade her to stay for a couple hours." He crossed to the door, opened it, then motioned for Molly to go first. "I wonder what the long-distance rates are to Iowa," he mused. "It couldn't be that much different than calls to Kansas."

He started up the hall toward the kitchen. At the last moment he remembered to hobble on his 'bad' knee.

Jocelyn heard him coming and experienced that ridiculous fluttering of her heart. Hardening herself to it, she blamed it all on nerves—and the fear of discovery. With the pan of soapy water in one hand and the rubber gloves in the other, she faced the doorway. .

When he hopped into view, Jocelyn stared at the long legs that his shorts bared to her view. Even with the bloody knee, he could have passed for a serious hiker or an experienced rock climber. The muscles in his legs were hard and lean and well defined, and his skin still carried the remnants of a summer tan.

"Ready or not, here I am," Tucker announced, then paused, his glance traveling from her face to the pan she carried. "Looks like you are, too. What's that you've got in your hand? Gloves?" Frowning, he gestured at them.

"Make a note, Obediah; there is nothing wrong with his eyesight." She gave Tucker a dry look and forced her quivering legs to carry her to the table area.

"What's the matter? Have you got some phobia about germs?" Grabbing hold of the counter for support, Tucker hopped on one leg toward the kitchen chair.

"Just trying to be sanitary," she lied.

"It was my idea," Obediah explained and shrugged out of his topcoat. Beneath it he wore a bright red cardigan sweater over a plain white shirt. "In these days and times, I thought it would be wise."

Tucker nodded and carefully lowered himself onto the oak chair's wooden seat. "I'm glad to know you don't have a germ thing," he said and watched as she pushed the morning newspaper aside, making room to set the pan on the table. "You are going to take your coat off, aren't you? Even with the gloves, you could end up getting your sleeves wet."

Accepting his suggestion, Jocelyn took her coat off and hung it across the back of the second chair, convinced that it was the reason she was feeling rather warm.

"Where do you keep your first aid kit?" She began tugging on the rubber gloves, trying to be business-like. "We'll need to tape some gauze on that scrape or, at the very least, douse it with some antiseptic."

"It's in the broom closet. I'll—" Tucker started to lever himself back onto his feet.

But Obediah stopped him. "You stay right there. Just tell me where to find it."

"The closet is there by the refrigerator." Tucker

directed him to the tall door. "I keep the first aid kit on the middle shelf." He watched to make sure Obediah found it, then brought his bright glance back to Jocelyn. "The gloves are a bit big, aren't they?"

It was an observation rather than a question, but Jocelyn chose to regard it as the latter. "A little," she admitted, "but they'll work fine."

Truthfully, she felt as clumsy and awkward as a right-handed person suddenly forced to write with the left. She struggled to get her fingers around the washcloth and barely managed to dip it in the soapy water without knocking over the pan, then squished it together in an attempt to squeeze out the excess water.

Kneeling at his feet, she aimed the dripping cloth at the large patch of dried blood and scraped flesh along his kneecap.

"I will," Tucker said.

"You will what?" She drew the cloth back, glancing up in time to catch the twitching of an impish smile.

"Sorry," Tucker said, looking much too sober. "I thought for a minute that you were proposing. I mean, you are kneeling and—" Jocelyn slapped the cloth on the wound. "Ouch! Now, that wasn't necessary," he protested.

"That's a matter of opinion." But she made a genuine attempt not to inflict more discomfort. The gloves made that difficult.

"One thing is for sure: you're not a nurse," Tucker remarked and sucked in another hissing breath.

"I never claimed to be."

"What exactly do you do? For a living, I mean?" He eyed her curiously.

"I'm a teacher."

That wasn't exactly a lie. She did have her degree in education and a teaching certificate. If it weren't for her current duties, that was very likely what she would be doing.

"A teacher. Then how come you're not in school teaching?" Tucker wondered. "This is a strange time of year for a school to be having a vacation, isn't it?"

While her mind searched frantically for a plausible explanation, Jocelyn covered her hesitation by concentrating on the section of knee that she dabbed with the soapy cloth. Ultimately, she realized there was none for his question.

"Teaching is my occupation. I never said that was what I was doing now." She defended her claim, deliberately injecting a calm and reasonable tone into her voice, and privately thanked God that she had learned how to deflect difficult questions.

Unsatisfied with half an answer, Tucker persisted. "If you aren't teaching, then what are you doing?"

Obediah came to her rescue. "Have you taken a sabbatical?"

Her glance reflected the relief and gratitude she felt. "I hadn't quite looked at it that way, but yes, that's basically what this time is."

"What do you teach?" Tucker wanted to know.

Here, she was on firm ground. "American history."

"I guess that's why you chose Washington to visit," Tucker concluded.

"Yes." Jocelyn rinsed the cloth in the water.

"It makes sense. This is definitely the place to walk in the footsteps of it, corny as that might sound," Tucker said, continuing to study her every move. "After all it is our nation's capital, and a lot of our leaders have gone down in history—some farther down than others, of course."

The droll observation was typical of the kind so often found in his columns. Jocelyn found it impossible not to react with a smile at the clever wording that injected a wry humor into what was a sober truth—a humor that was not unkindly meant.

But the subject of national leaders—or the capital itself, for that matter—wasn't one she wanted to discuss.

"Did you find any antiseptic in that first aid kit, Obediah?" she asked. "I'm nearly finished here, and we'll definitely need to put something on this scrape."

"Let me check." He placed the kit on the table next to Jocelyn's pan of water and unhooked its metal latches. Opening it, Obediah paused to survey its contents. The kit was large, every inch of it crammed with tape, gauze, bandages, ointments, sprays, and assorted items. "My, but you are well prepared for almost any emergency."

"Always," Tucker confirmed with a decisive nod.

"Let me guess," Jocelyn murmured, shooting him a dryly teasing look, "you were a Boy Scout."

"I've got the badges to prove it." With an expression as serious as a Supreme Court justice, Tucker held up three fingers, signaling a Scout's pledge, but a warm, laughing light danced in his eyes. "I am loyal, helpful, and completely trustworthy."

"Something tells me Benedict told George the same thing." The scraped knee cleaned, Jocelyn dropped the cloth in the water.

Tucker's brows furrowed together in a blank look. "Benedict who? Is that your boyfriend?"

"No. Benedict Arnold, of course," she replied, not buying the dense act. "Did you find some antiseptic in there, Obediah?"

"There's some in a spray can . . ."

But Tucker talked over the top of Obediah's answer, "Oh, *that* Benedict. I wasn't sure."

". . . and a tube of antibiotic cream," Obediah finished.

"I'll bet you weren't sure." Skepticism riddled her voice as she reached for the can of antiseptic spray. "I'll use this now," she told Obediah. "We'll put the cream on the gauze before we bandage his knee."

"Do you have a boyfriend?" Tucker asked.

"Is that really any of your business?" she countered smoothly.

"It could be. It all depends on how serious it is with you two," he answered.

"And if I said it was, what would you do?" The can rattled when she shook it, reblending the mixture.

"That would probably depend on how big he is. One thing's for sure; you aren't wearing a ring." Tucker gestured at her left hand.

The rubber glove, despite all its looseness, clearly showed there was no outline of a ring on her finger.

"Maybe I took it off." The can hissed as she sprayed antiseptic over his scraped and raw flesh.

"And if you did, that's encouraging in itself," he declared, as always finding a positive side.

"Why? It could be something as simple as I was afraid of losing it." Jocelyn pushed the top back on the can.

"It could be," Tucker agreed slowly. "But my gut tells me you aren't wearing a ring 'cause you don't have one. And if you don't have one, then there's nothing serious in the offing, or you would be vacationing with him instead of wandering around Washington on your own."

The impulse was strong to make up a fictitious boyfriend just to annoy him. But the more lies she told, the harder it would be to keep them all straight.

So Jocelyn settled for the truth. "Brilliant deduction, Sherlock. There is no boyfriend."

"Elementary, my dear Jonesy, elementary," Tucker quipped.

"I wish you wouldn't call me that," she murmured, half-irritated by the alien sound of it.

She straightened, pulling off the gloves and noticing that Obediah was busy tearing off strips of adhesive tape. A large sterile gauze pad lay atop its paper package, the tube of antibiotic cream lying beside it.

"What's wrong with Jonesy?" Tucker questioned with seeming innocence. "That's your name, isn't it?"

"My name is Lynne Jones, not Jonesy." She uncapped the tube.

His eyes narrowed on her face in thoughtful scrutiny. "For some reason, Lynne doesn't seem to fit you. Now don't get me wrong. Lynne is a beautiful name," he added hastily. "But when you say it, it sorta' floats from your lips and sounds soft—kinda' dreamy and serene."

"And you think Jonesy suits me better." She regarded that as a dubious compliment.

"In a way, yes. Now, I admit Jones is a common name, but it's got a strong sound to it. And that's the way you strike me—strong and beautiful and down-to-earth, without any pretense."

That was the crux of the problem. She was all pretense. She wasn't Lynne Jones; she was Jocelyn Wakefield. Not a schoolteacher, but the president's daughter.

"A very apt description for Miss Jones." Obediah beamed at Tucker in approval. "She is clearly strong. When you fell, she reacted swiftly and exhibited no sign of panic whatsoever. Obviously she is an attractive woman, and as for being down-to-earth, what better indication of that than the way she is tending to your injuries? There certainly can be no doubt that she has a warm and caring heart."

"There, you see?" Tucker pointed to Obediah, indicating his full and absolute agreement. "I couldn't have said it better myself."

"Just stop. Both of you," Jocelyn ordered, the weight of a guilty conscience making it impossible for her to listen to any more of this. Almost angrily she squeezed a big glob of ointment on the pad, muttering, "It's embarrassing."

"And she's modest, too." Obediah's expression was benign with innocent praise, but his eyes twinkled with the secret knowledge they shared.

Jocelyn wanted to hit him. "Don't," she protested. "You are only encouraging him, Obediah."

Tucker spoke up, "Somebody needs to. I'm sure not getting any encouragement from you."

"Doesn't that give you a message?" she replied with a challenging glare.

"Yeah, it tells me I'm probably coming on too strong," he admitted glumly, then appealed for understanding: "But you gotta understand I don't have a lot of time."

"Neither do I. And I'm wasting too much of it trading remarks with you." Annoyed with herself as much as she was with him, Jocelyn snatched the gauze pad off its torn packet and knelt back down to apply it.

Tucker wisely chose to change the subject. "How does my knee look?"

"Like you skidded on concrete and scraped off a couple of layers of skin." Jocelyn paused long enough to smear the cream over the pad.

"That bad?" As Tucker leaned forward to examine it, Jocelyn bent to apply the bandage.

They bumped heads. Instantly she pressed a hand to her head, more to make sure her wig hadn't slipped than in reaction to the glancing blow.

"Did I hurt you?" Tucker asked in concern. "Let me take a look."

She brushed away the hand that reached toward her hair, realizing that he would too quickly discover she had on a wig. "I am not hurt. But one of us will be if you don't sit back in that chair and let me put this on."

"Fine, fine." Tucker made an exaggerated show of pulling back. "I was only worried about you."

"Well, don't be. I'm fine." But with each passing minute, Jocelyn became more convinced that just being around Tucker was hazardous. Gently she held the pad in place and held out a hand to Obediah. "Give me one of those tape strips, please."

"Of course."

Arms folded, Tucker watched the tape pass from Obediah to Jocelyn. Before she could affix it to the pad, he said, "I don't mean to be telling you your business, but I don't think that tape is going to stick, as damp as the skin on my leg is."

To her chagrin, Jocelyn saw he was right. The skin around the wound was wet from her washing it. "We'll need a towel."

"I'll get one." Obediah quickly shuffled toward the cupboard area.

"In that top drawer to the right of the sink, you'll find some clean dish towels," Tucker told him. "You can use one of those."

Obediah lifted out a large white cloth with a walking carrot embroidered in the corner. "Will this do?"

"Perfect," Jocelyn confirmed.

A moment later, she found herself facing a new dilemma. With one hand she was holding the pad in place while the other one had the strip of tape stuck to her finger.

Tucker solved the problem by taking the towel from Obediah himself. "Better let me do it."

Bending forward again, he slowly blotted the excess moisture from the skin along the patch's outer edge; then he shifted to the other side while she taped the first. She kept her head down, conscious of the searching touch of his eyes on her face.

From out of the blue, Tucker asked, "How come you wear so much makeup?"

Startled, Jocelyn sat back on her heels, her pulse skyrocketing in alarm. But her widened eyes saw nothing in his expression except idle curiosity.

Breathing a little easier, she took a second strip of tape from Obediah and responded with a moderately critical, "That's a bit too personal, don't you think?"

"Probably so," Tucker conceded. "But you've got such a beautiful face that I thought maybe you were covering up some scars."

"And if I were, do you really think I would tell you?" Aware that she was in an indefensible position, she went on the attack. "I'm not going to confide in you. We don't even know each other."

"But I'm trying to change all that. Don't you see? That's why I'm asking all these questions," Tucker reasoned. " 'Course, I admit it's been pretty one-sided. Maybe you should ask me some questions."

"Sorry. There's nothing about you I want to know."

As far as Jocelyn was concerned, she already knew too much—including that she liked him. More than that, she was attracted to him, which was a bit of a surprise in itself. In any other circumstances, she might have been tempted to explore that to see where it might lead.

But to do that here and now? Jocelyn thought to herself. *Not on your life.*

Tucker winced in mock hurt at her reply. "I guess I asked for that, didn't I?"

"Yes, you did." Jocelyn finished taping the gauze bandage to his knee and sat back. "There, you're all set."

"Good." He gave a satisfied nod. "Now we can get on with the rice part."

"Rice." She had an instant image of rice being thrown at a bride and groom, and her heart did a couple of quick thumps.

"Yeah, rice. R-I-C-E. That's how you treat a bad sprain: rest, ice, compression, and elevation." The explanation was delivered in an offhand manner that indicated no awareness of her literal and inadvertent interpretation. He motioned toward the first aid kit. "There should be an Ace wrap somewhere in there with all the other stuff. For the ice, you're gonna need a plastic bag. You'll find one of those kind that locks in that second drawer below the dish towels, Obediah. Make sure you use the large size."

"Yes, you will most definitely need a large one." Moving at a short-striding walk, Obediah hurried to the cupboard while Jocelyn retrieved a roll of flesh-colored elastic wrap from the kit.

"You're good at issuing orders, aren't you?" Jocelyn handed the roll's metal clasp to Tucker, then knelt once again beside his injured knee, held out straight for her to wrap.

"I wouldn't say that," Tucker corrected calmly. "I just know what needs to be done and where the things are to do them. If you two weren't here, I'd be hobbling around trying to do it all myself. I'm just glad I don't have to."

Properly chastised for her unfounded criticism, Jocelyn set to work winding the wrap around the knee area, crisscrossing it for added support and bracing. Over by the refrigerator, ice cubes rattled into the plastic bag Obediah held. When one fell onto the floor, Molly was quick to claim it and carry it over to her rug.

"Have you got any brothers or sisters?" Tucker asked, then volunteered, "I'm an only child myself."

"Me, too."

"Funny, I kinda figured you for coming from a big family. What about your folks?"

It seemed easier simply to answer the questions than make a fuss about them. Besides, the information didn't really reveal anything about her.

"My mother was killed in a driving accident several years ago," she admitted.

"I'm sorry," he said with sincerity. "Your dad's still alive, though, isn't he?"

"Yes." Here the ground turned shaky.

"What does he do?"

"He . . ." Jocelyn hesitated, trying to come up with a truthful and nonrevealing answer. "He works for the government."

Obediah coughed to cover the chuckle he choked back. Fortunately, Tucker didn't appear to notice.

"These days just about half the country works for the government. Here in Washington, if they don't work for ours, they work for somebody else's," he said.

"So I've heard. Am I wrapping this too tight?" she asked, seeking to divert him from the subject.

"No, it's fine," he assured her absently. "Do you believe in Santa Claus?"

"Are we back to Christmas again?" She was amused rather than irritated.

"Obediah'll tell you there isn't a wrong time to talk about Christmas. Besides," Tucker reasoned, "if we end up getting married and having kids, it's important for me to know what you would want to tell our children about him."

The roll slipped from her suddenly wooden fingers, the last yard of it uncurling as it fell. In the process, the last three laps around his knee came loose.

Angered by his question, her reaction to it, and the careful work that had to be redone, Jocelyn stated curtly, "We are not getting married, Tucker."

"Not for a while, that's for sure," he agreed magnanimously.

"You are absolutely incorrigible, aren't you?" she accused, jerking the wrap tight.

"Careful, now. You're gonna cut off my circulation," Tucker cautioned, then grinned crookedly. "That's what marriage does, though, doesn't it? Cuts off a man's circulation."

When Obediah chuckled, making mounds of his brown cheeks, Jocelyn flashed both men a silencing look. "Very funny."

Obediah smiled wisely. "It's better for a man to laugh about such a thing than to cry over it."

"Well said." Tucker lifted a hand in salute, then turned back to Jocelyn. "So, you haven't answered my question yet, Jonesy. Do you believe in Santa Claus?"

"I'm not a child anymore." Slowly and painstakingly, she wound the loose section of wrap back into a roll to make it easier to manage. "If I think about Santa at all, I suppose I regard the whole subject as a beautiful myth."

"Ah, but how did this myth originate?" Obediah posed the question, a knowing gleam in his eye. "To me, that story is even more beautiful."

"Story." Tucker frowned and glanced at Jocelyn to see if she knew what Obediah was talking about. But she was equally at a loss as to his meaning. "I guess I never heard it."

"I was referring to Saint Nicholas," Obediah explained.

"Saint Nicholas," Tucker repeated, unenlightened. "That's just another name for Santa Claus, isn't it?"

"True. But I was thinking specifically of Nicholas from Patara, Turkey. Until very recently, he was regarded as a saint by the Catholic Church." Obediah laid the sealed bag of ice on the table, the cubes clunking together as they settled.

"That rings a vague bell with me," Tucker admitted with an absent nod. "But I didn't happen to be raised a Catholic. How about you, Jonesy?"

"I'm not a Catholic either, but I remember reading somewhere that Saint Nicholas was the patron saint of children. Hence, his evolvement into the present-day Santa Claus." At least, that was the context Jocelyn remembered.

"There is a bit more to the story than that." Obediah pulled a second chair away from the table and sat down.

When he offered nothing further, Tucker prompted him. "Such as what?"

"Let's see. . . ." Obediah paused a minute to gather his thoughts and stared into the distance. "Back during the third century in Turkey, Nicholas was the bishop of Myra. When Emperor Constantine ordered a council to convene, then-bishop Nicholas was among those who attended. As I recall, the council was called to settle the issue of Christ's divinity. There were some in attendance who believed Jesus of Nazareth was a great prophet, but not the Son of God. Nicholas, as bishop of Myra, argued forcefully for the divinity of Christ. After months of arguing the matter, Nicholas became so exasperated with a member of the opposition that he slapped his face. So you see," his smile radiated like a glow, encompassing both of them, "Nicholas was first and foremost a defender of Christ and a protector of the Christian faith."

"Now, I didn't know that," Tucker declared in mild amazement. "How do you suppose that part got lost when he came to be Santa Claus? And how come his name was changed?"

"The events of history had a great deal to do with the name change," Obediah admitted. "During the Reformation, Martin Luther banned Saint Nicholas, who had become the most popular saint of the Middle Ages. Naturally, there was quite an outcry against that," Obediah added. "So in his place, Luther offered Kriss Kringle—which basically translates as the Christ Child."

"And how did Kriss Kringle become Santa Claus?" Jocelyn asked, intrigued as always by history.

"Ah," he said on a chuckle, "that is an answer you, as an American history teacher, should know. After the Revolutionary War, Americans were eager to get rid of anything English, which included Kriss Kringle and Saint Nicholas. They looked to New York and its Dutch past. There was Sinterklaas, essentially a Dutch variation of the name Saint Nicholas. From there, it was an easy step from Sinterklaas to Santa Claus."

"Interesting," she murmured.

"Now, how do you know all this, Obediah?" Tucker eyed him curiously. "Are you a minister or something? Should we be calling you Reverend? I can see you aren't wearing a clerical collar, but that doesn't necessarily mean you aren't a man of the cloth."

Obediah chuckled again, a throaty and deep sound that reverberated with mirth. "Ah, Tucker," he declared, "you don't have to be a man of the cloth to know God—or the ones who loved Him."

"You've got me there," Tucker admitted with an abashed nod. "And my granddaddy would agree with you on that."

"What do you do, Obediah?" Jocelyn asked curiously, and began winding the last of the elastic wrap around Tucker's knee.

"Believe it or not, I'm in the toy business," he announced with a broad smile.

"Toys! No wonder you know so much about Santa Claus," Tucker declared on a note of laughter.

She reached the end of the roll and held it tightly in place, lifting her free hand. "Do you still have that fastener I gave you?"

"Right here." Tucker offered it to her.

Carefully she hooked the free end to the rest of the wrap and pushed back from him. "You're all set."

"Now comes the ice and elevation part." Bracing one hand on the tabletop and another on the chair, Tucker levered himself upright, then gingerly put weight on his left foot. "Assuming, of course, that I can make it in to the couch."

"I'll help you." Jocelyn stepped to his side so he could lean on her.

He slipped an arm around her shoulder and slanted a smile in her direction. "I was hoping you would." Before she could even form a protest to that, he looked back at Obediah. "Bring that ice with you when you come, will you? Better grab a couple dish towels, too. My knee is kinda' bony. I'm not sure I

can balance that ice bag on it. We'll probably have
to tie it in place."

"Your knees are not bony." Jocelyn couldn't imagine where he had ever gotten the idea they were.

"You don't think so, huh?" There was something
soft in his voice. "That's good to know."

Jocelyn wished she hadn't said anything. "Are you
going to just stand there leaning on me, or are we
going into the living room?"

CHAPTER 9

With a touching awkwardness, Tucker maneuvered around the coffee table and stopped near the center of the long sofa, then stood helpless for a moment, trying to figure out how to sit down without bending his knee. Jocelyn wasn't exactly sure how best to accomplish it either.

"You need to do it at an angle, I think," she suggested finally.

"Right." He grabbed the back of the sofa for support, then shifted and twisted, trying out positions while Jocelyn hovered close by, ready to support him. He glanced sideways at her, the dryness of self-mockery in his expression. "You know what this feels like, don't you?"

"What?" It was an absent question, more automatic than curious.

"A scene out of an old Dick Van Dyke show," he told her.

Suddenly it did. Laughter gurgled in her throat. Only a small choking sound slipped out when she managed to swallow the rest of it. But there was nothing she could do about the smile that grooved the corners of her mouth.

"I'm glad somebody thinks this is funny," Tucker complained while he held his left leg out straight to the side, folded his long body in the middle, and more or less sank onto the cushions.

"You brought it up," she reminded him, still amused.

At six-four, Tucker was taller than the sofa was long. To fit on it, he scooted himself into a reclining position against one arm of it.

"You didn't have to agree." He tried to stuff the big sofa pillow behind him to give his back some support.

Watching his ungainly efforts, Jocelyn took pity on him. "Let me do that." Taking the pillow from him, she plumped it, then propped it into position.

After testing it for comfort, he nodded. "That's perfect. Now all we gotta do is get this knee elevated. You'll have to get the pillows off my bed. It's right down that hall across from the bathroom." He pointed the way, then called after her when she was halfway to the hall, "And bring my coat, will you? There are some things in my pockets I want."

Jocelyn was surprised to find his bed neatly made, the teal blue coverlet pulled smoothly over the pillows and sharply tucked beneath them. Regardless of his slightly tousled outward appearance, everything she had seen in his apartment indicated he was both tidy and well organized.

After gathering up both bed pillows, she scooped his lined jacket off the bed. Instantly her hand sank under the unexpected weight of it. She took one look at the bulging pockets and knew why it felt so heavy.

"This jacket weighs a ton." She walked into the living room carrying it, the pillows squashed inside the circle of one arm. "What on earth do you have in these pockets?"

"Now, you just stay out of my pockets. My mom was always emptying them when I was a kid. I lost more good stuff that way," Tucker complained, reaching for his coat.

Jocelyn handed it to him, grinning. "Like snips and snails and puppydog tails," she teased.

"No, little Miss Sugar and Spice, it was more like pretty rocks, butterfly wings, and pieces of what could have been arrowheads." He draped the jacket over his lap, things clunking in the pockets, and used his hands to lift his leg up so she could slide the elevating pillows under it. "Do you know one time she actually threw away my lucky four-leaf clover?"

"How awful," Jocelyn murmured in mock sympathy.

"It sure was. Why, I went through the wastebasket twice and never could find it."

"What did you do? Go out and find another one?" Turning, she took the ice bag from Obediah and jiggled the cubes around to make it flatter.

"Yup, but it was never as lucky as the one I lost," Tucker declared with regret.

"That's too bad." She draped the bag across his bandaged knee, giving the cubes another jiggle in a final, flattening adjustment. "How's that?"

"Cold." He moved his leg a little, and the bag overbalanced, slipping off to the side. "Where are those dish towels? I told you, we're gonna have to tie this thing down."

Obediah had the towels at the ready. While Tucker held the ice bag in place, Jocelyn laid both towels across it, slipped the ends under his knee, and tied them in a simple knot on top of it.

Finished, she straightened. "There you go. That's not going to go anywhere now."

"I'm surprised you didn't tie it in a bow. That way it would look as ridiculous as it feels." As complaints went, Tucker's fell in the category of wry observation.

"I still can." The hint of a smile negated any threat in her words.

"I'll tell you what you can do," Tucker began. "You can get me a glass of water and a couple aspirins. It would probably be just as well to take them now before this knee gets to throbbing too much."

"Where do you keep the aspirin? In the first aid kit?" Jocelyn started toward the kitchen.

"No, in the bathroom—in the medicine cabinet above the sink," Tucker added when she changed directions and headed toward the hall. "I keep the bottle on the second shelf. It should be right beside my can of shaving cream."

"I'll find it," she assured him, confident that it would be right where he said it was.

"I'll fetch a glass of water for him," Obediah told her, shuffling off to the kitchen.

Neither task took long, Jocelyn returning with the aspirin bottle as Obediah arrived with the water glass. She shook two pills into Tucker's upturned palm, popped the cap back on the bottle and set it on the coffee table within easy reach.

She waited until he had swallowed both pills, chasing them down with water. "Is there anything else you need?" she challenged, the suspicion growing that Tucker was coming up with all these things simply to keep her there.

He hesitated, as if going through some mental checklist, before he finally and reluctantly admitted, "No. No, I don't think so. I guess that means you and Obediah will be going now."

"That's right." Jocelyn was deliberately bright and firm.

Tucker sighed in regret and looked up at her. "I don't suppose I could talk you into staying for a while and kinda' keep me company."

"Sorry, but I can't. Obediah will have to answer for himself." Jocelyn moved away from the sofa.

"I don't know. . . ." Obediah glanced at her uncertainly when she swept past him to enter the kitchen and retrieve her coat.

"No, Jonesy's right. You've both done enough," Tucker conceded, his glance landing on Jocelyn the instant she came out of the kitchen carrying her coat. "It's just going to be boring sitting here with nothing to do, and no way to get around if I could."

"Here." She retrieved the television remote from the coffee table and handed it to him. "This will keep you company, since all you can do is sit and watch anyway."

A little disgruntled, Tucker looked at the remote, then shrugged. "I guess I could watch Saturday morning cartoons. That reminds me—what's your favorite cartoon, Jonesy?"

"I don't know." Keeping a tight hold on the cuff of her sweater, Jocelyn pushed an arm into a coat sleeve. "I've never really thought about it."

"You can think about it now, can't you?"

It was another stall tactic and she knew it. "If I had to pick one, I suppose it would be the Roadrunner and Wile E. Coyote." It was the only cartoon she could recall off the top of her head.

"Myself, I always liked the "Fractured Fairy Tale" segment on Rocky and Bullwinkle."

"That figures," Jocelyn muttered to herself.

Tucker gave no sign that he had heard her as he continued to ponder the subject. "Now, my favorite cartoon character, hands down, is the Pink Panther. I mean, just think about that, a pink panther. Do you know how brave you would have to be, to be pink *and* a panther?"

"I can't say I ever looked at it quite that way." When she struggled to get her arm in the other sleeve, Obediah, ever the gentleman, came to help her. "Thanks." She smiled, then hesitated. "Are you leaving now, too, Obediah?"

He cast a thoughtful glance at Tucker, then nodded. "Yes, just as soon as I fetch my hat and coat."

"And your cane, too," Tucker told him when Obediah quick-stepped toward the kitchen. "Don't forget that."

"It's on the table next to your hat," Jocelyn remembered.

Suddenly, Tucker started rummaging through his coat pockets. "Wait just a second here. You can't go yet, Jonesy."

Mildly exasperated with his delaying tactics, she turned back to him. "What is it now, Tucker?"

"I know, I know. You've got places to go and things to see." He pulled a scrap of paper out of one pocket and a ballpoint pen out of another, then proceeded to use the latter to scribble something on the former. When he finished, he offered it to her. "This is for you."

Curiosity made her take it. "What is it?" She turned it around to read what he had written.

"My address and phone numbers, both here and at work. In case you decide you want to reach me," Tucker added, his expression turning all boyishly innocent and hopeful. "I don't suppose you'll tell me where you're staying in town, or your address in Iowa.''

Jocelyn looked at him and said one simple word: ''No.'' But she couldn't help smiling a little at his persistence.

Molly bounded out of the kitchen with Obediah, all excited when she saw both of them with their coats. ''You think you're going with us, don't you?'' Obediah realized with a small chortle. ''Well, I'm sorry to disappoint you, young lady. But you must stay here with your master.''

The dog whipped a glance at Tucker, then once again aimed soulful eyes at Obediah and whined plaintively. Smiling, he bent and gave her head a pat. ''You take good care of him, Molly.''

''And don't get into any more trouble,'' Jocelyn admonished.

There was something forlorn in the look Molly gave her. Then the dog turned away and padded over to the sofa and Tucker. She plunked her rump on the floor and slapped a paw on his arm, then whined again.

''I know,'' Tucker told her. ''I haven't either.''

Jocelyn was by the door, ready to walk out of it. ''You haven't what?'' she said, and wanted to kick herself for asking.

''Now, it's nothing for you to be bothered about.'' Tucker waved her toward the door. She should have been suspicious right then. ''You two have done enough. Just go ahead and get about your business. Molly and I will take care of this ourselves.''

"Take care of what?" Obediah had his topcoat buttoned and his hat ready to go on his head.

"Nothing," Tucker insisted, but there was a suspicious gleam in his eyes. "It just so happens that Molly and I haven't had breakfast yet. That's all."

Jocelyn saw red. "And I suppose you expect me to take pity on you and fix it for you. Well, you can think again, because I'm leaving."

"Go. I don't recall asking you to stay," he retorted with equal force. "In fact, I don't recall asking you to come here in the first place." Tucker swung a leg to the floor, then lifted his knee off its pillow bed. "And I'm not about to ask you to fix my breakfast. With my luck, you can't even cook a frozen dinner without burning it. I'll bet you can't boil water without scorching it, either."

"For your information, I happen to be a very good cook—not that you'll ever have a chance to find out," Jocelyn stated, her hands on her hips.

"That's fine by me." Tucker stood up and immediately banged his good leg against the coffee table. "Ow!" He collapsed on the sofa, clutching his leg.

"Oh, good grief! Look what you've done now." Exasperated, she crossed the room to see how bad he'd hurt himself. "At this rate, you'll be crippled before the day is out."

"A lot you'd care," he told her. "You've got places to go, remember."

"I remember very well. Now, let me see what you've done to yourself." She tried to move his hands away.

"What I've done? I've banged it, that's what I've

done." Leaning forward, Tucker peeked through the cracks of his clutching fingers, inspecting the damage for himself. "There's gonna be a dandy bruise, I can tell you that right now. And a little knot, too." Looking up, he met her gaze, the smallest challenge in his eyes. "That should satisfy you. There's nothing serious, no broken bones or sliced flesh. You can leave without your conscience troubling you one bit."

It was true; there was no reason for her to stay. So why was she hesitating? Why didn't she simply turn and walk out the door? It was what she wanted. Wasn't it?

But she couldn't very well say any of that. "And when we leave, what will you do? Go to the kitchen and fix yourself something to eat?"

At last Molly heard the magic word, *eat*. A bark exploded from her, loud and strong, startling everyone. She tore for the kitchen, her tail rotating like a rudder out of control while she barked excitedly the whole way.

The first to recover his speech, Obediah chuckled. "I think it is safe to assume Molly is extremely hungry."

"Well, she's still growing," Tucker said in his pet's defense. "It's to be expected. And any doctor—or vet, for that matter—will tell you breakfast is the most important meal of the day."

As if on cue, Jocelyn's stomach growled softly, not satisfied with the bagel she had nervously consumed before leaving Redford Hall earlier that morning. Surprised, she glanced at her watch. It was already after ten. Where had the time gone? But she knew the answer to that: Tucker. At the moment she felt as if she had already spent a lifetime in his company.

"A good breakfast is definitely important," Obediah agreed as he began unbuttoning his topcoat.

"No." Tucker held up a hand to stop him. "Both of you just run along. I'll handle breakfast for Molly and me."

"I thought you said that knee of yours needed rest and elevation," Jocelyn reminded him.

"It'll get it. It'll just be later. It's for sure I'm not going to have much rest with my belly gnawing at my backbone."

"I can handle the hunger problem," Obediah asserted with a smile, then added with a definite gleam in his eyes, "I know it's immodest to brag, but I can fix a mean omelet."

"I'll help—" Jocelyn began, already pulling her anorak off one shoulder.

"Nope." Tucker shook his head. "I can't let you do that."

"Why not?" she demanded in astonishment, one arm half out of a coat sleeve."

"Because if I do, you'll think I tricked you into it," he told her. "And you're liable to decide I'm some devious lecher or something."

"Devious, yes. But a lecher? I don't think so." It was odd how positive she was of that.

"Why?" he countered. "Don't I do enough leering?" Tucker made a comic attempt at it, drawing a laugh from Jocelyn.

"Even with practice, you would never make a believable lecher, Tucker." She shrugged out of her coat and tossed it onto the platform rocker.

An impatient Molly bounded out of the kitchen, skidded to a halt, and barked, demanding to know why no one had come to feed her.

"I'm coming, Molly. I'm coming." Obediah laid his hat, coat, and cane on the rocker. This time Molly waited to escort him into the kitchen.

"Her food dish is there by her water bowl," Tucker called after them. "And there's dry dog food in the broom closet. You'll find a scoop in the sack. I usually give her two scoops' worth in the morning."

"Don't worry about Molly," Jocelyn ordered, once again plumping the pillow to support his back. "You just turn around here and get your knee up."

"You kinda like giving orders, too, don't you?" Tucker observed and turned sideways once again to ease the bandaged knee with its tied-on ice bag onto the sofa.

"Just about as much as you do," she countered. "Now lie back on this pillow."

She held the pillow in place while he lowered himself into a reclining position against it. The action brought their faces close. Instantly her glance became entangled with his, some invisible force holding her in place.

"You know," Tucker murmured in a soft Kansas drawl, "I may do a lousy job of leering, but I'm darn good at kissing."

The comment caught her in mid-breath, blocking

it somewhere in her throat. This close, there was a virility that she had somehow missed seeing before, a hard strength in the cut of his jawline, a smoky darkness to his hazel eyes, and a male earthiness about the firm shape of his lips. She was suddenly tantalized by the thought of kissing him, wondering how it might feel, how it might taste.

"Really," was the only word she was able to force out.

"If you don't believe me, I can prove it," Tucker promised.

Jocelyn opened her mouth to answer, but nothing came out. In the kitchen, dry kibble clattered into a metal bowl, accompanied by the sound of paws beating a rapid tattoo on the linoleum floor. The sharpness of the sounds shattered the spell.

"I'll . . . uh . . . take your word for that." She pulled herself away, moving down the sofa. "Let's get your knee back up on these pillows."

As she placed a supporting hand under his leg to lift it, Obediah poked his white head around the kitchen doorway, brown cheeks shining. "What kind of omelet would you like, Tucker? Your refrigerator has just about any choice a man could want."

"Now listen, Obediah, if you're going to cook me breakfast, then you fix enough for you and Jonesy, too. You are hungry, aren't you, Jonesy?" Tucker asked.

"As a matter of fact, I am." She saw no point in denying it.

"How about you, Obediah?"

"Thank you. That's most generous of you, Tucker."
The man beamed.

"You two are the ones who are generous, taking
your time to look after me like this. If I paid you back
proper, it would be me cooking breakfast for you,"
Tucker stated with utter sincerity.

"Another time, perhaps," Obediah suggested.

Tucker looked at Jocelyn with undisguised interest
and said, "I hope so."

She felt herself growing warm all over. "You never
did say what kind of omelet you wanted."

"Whatever you want to throw in there—ham,
tomato, bacon, cheese, onion, pepper, spinach, jala-
peno, mushrooms, potatoes, anchovies, corn. I've
eaten them all at one time or another."

"Anchovies and eggs?" Jocelyn made a face at the
thought.

"It's not my favorite combination," Tucker admitted. "But it's not bad. What's the matter? Don't you
like anchovies? You claimed Italian food was your
favorite."

"I like anchovies, but not in an omelet," she said,
giving an expressive little shudder.

"One surprise omelet coming up," Obediah
declared and ducked out of view.

"Jelly's good, too," Tucker called after him, then
said to Jocelyn, "I like grape the best. Strawberry
omelets are okay, but one with grape jelly tastes
better."

"What are you—a connoisseur of omelets?" She
frowned in amusement.

"Not really." His shoulders lifted in a dismissive shrug. "I've just experimented with different combinations. Don't try making one with pickles, though," Tucker advised with a perfectly straight face, then reconsidered. "I probably should have qualified that. A sweet-pickle omelet might be good, but you can forget dill pickles. Take my word for it."

"Believe me, I will," she promised.

His eyes narrowed briefly on her. "Something tells me you aren't a fan of omelets."

"They're all right. Omelets just aren't my first choice for breakfast," she admitted.

"What is?"

"Oatmeal with brown sugar. Sometimes with cinnamon toast on the side."

"Uh-huh, just as I thought," Tucker said with a broad and knowing nod. "You're into that healthy stuff."

"I'm not *into* anything." Jocelyn resented the implication that it was some fad thing with her. "For your information, I've liked oatmeal literally since I was a baby."

"Some people do," he agreed.

"You don't like oatmeal, do you?" Jocelyn guessed.

"To be honest, it's at the bottom of my list—just a little bit above a pickle omelet. But look at it this way," Tucker suggested. "Think of how varied the contents of our refrigerator will be."

"Oh, good grief." She swung away in exasperation. "You just won't stay off that track, will you?"

"I probably should, though," he conceded grudgingly. "I can see it bothers you."

"Of course, it bothers me. Here you are talking as if we're about to be married and we don't even know each other." She jumped on top of that sentence before Tucker had a chance. "And don't give me that love-at-first-sight, knowing-right-off, and opposites-attracting nonsense. That is a shaky basis for a marriage."

"Well, you have to admit we're quarreling like an old married couple already."

"Good grief, we are not!" she exploded, her patience lost.

"Well, what would you call it, then?" he asked with a wide-eyed look.

"The futility of trying to pound some sense into that one-track brain of yours—that's what I'd call it." Jocelyn turned and stormed off.

"Wait a minute. Where are you going?"

"To the kitchen and help Obediah." Jocelyn was surprised to discover how good, how liberating it felt to express anger, whether justified or not, instead of suppressing it as she'd done endless times during recent years, always out of concern over how others might regard her—that image thing again. It was nice to be Jonesy and not need to worry about such things.

"I thought you'd stay in here and keep me company." Tucker's voice followed her into the kitchen.

"It looks like you thought wrong, doesn't it?" Jocelyn was smiling from ear to ear, for now completely and totally delighting in her new self.

CHAPTER 10

Obediah's bright and knowing eyes noted the smile on Jocelyn's face and he guessed astutely, "You are enjoying yourself, aren't you?" His voice was pitched low, intended for her hearing only.

"I am." Her smile deepened, dimpling the corners of her mouth. Jocelyn walked over to the sink where Obediah was slicing open a green pepper, prior to seeding it. "It's been a long time since I was free to be myself and react naturally. It would be very easy to become drunk with this feeling."

"But you don't dare do that, do you?" His sideways glance was full of wisdom and understanding, mixed with a hint of sympathy.

She dragged in a deep breath and let it out in a

rush. "No. Only Jonesy can do it." Her glance strayed in the direction of the living room, regret tingeing her expression. "If Tucker finds out who I really am, it's all over. He'll start weighing everything I say or do against that light."

"You like him, don't you?" Obediah stated, certain of her answer.

Jocelyn hesitated, a little surprised to find she couldn't lie to this man. "I like him." Instantly she shot Obediah a quick warning look. "But don't you dare tell Tucker that. He'd never give me any peace about this marriage nonsense."

"But is it nonsense?" Obediah probed gently.

"Of course it is." She clung to that. "Believe me, he wouldn't be saying any of these things if he knew who I really am."

"What are you two talking about in there?" Tucker yelled from the living room. "You know, it isn't fair that all of you are out there having a good time while I'm in here twiddling my thumbs."

"You won't be alone for long," Jocelyn called back as the black Labrador gathered up another mouthful of dog food and swallowed it after a couple of crunches, wagging her tail the whole time. "Molly is almost finished with her breakfast. When she's done, she'll be in to keep you company."

"Now, that's really something to look forward to, isn't it?" Tucker mocked. "I hate to tell you this, but Molly is not the greatest conversationalist. Her vocabulary is kinda' limited to a whoof here and a bark there."

Jocelyn was quick with a comeback. "But I'll bet Molly is a good listener."

"Oh, she's real good at that," Tucker replied in a desert-dry voice.

"You should be glad about that, because you talk enough for two people." Jocelyn was surprised to find she was actually enjoying this exchange, perhaps because a room separated them. "Now, be quiet so we can get your breakfast made." With that, she turned her mind to the task at hand. "What would you like me to do, Obediah?"

"Here. You can chop this." He handed her **the** pepper half he had already washed and seeded, then searched the cupboards until he found a cutting board and an extra knife. While she began expertly slicing the pepper into thin strips, Obediah went back to ridding the other half of its seeds, now and then glancing her way in idle observation. "I can tell you have diced peppers a time or two."

"I really am a good cook," she told him. "Lately, though, I've had few opportunities to putter around in a kitchen. The kitchen staff at the White House is much too skilled, and the service is much too prompt. Most of the time it's much easier to tell them what you want to eat than to have the ingredients sent up to fix it yourself."

"I'm sure it is." Obediah laid the cleaned pepper half on a corner of her cutting board.

With the knife blade, she slid aside the first green mound of sliced peppers. "Naturally, we pay for all our own meals—not when it's an official function, of course," she inserted hastily. "Just our personal meals or when we have family or friends join us, those are charged to us. Then once a month we receive a bill from the chief usher's office for our meals, dry cleaning, and any incidentals, and we pay that."

"Interesting." Obediah cut off the top of an onion. Pungent juice oozed from its concentric rings. "I don't suppose I'd ever given much thought to how such things were handled."

"The system is very efficient," Jocelyn assured him as she began chopping the next cluster of pepper strips. Suddenly a picture of this entire scene flashed in her mind. She laughed softly and shook her head.

"Something has obviously amused you." His bright and inquiring glance skimmed her face.

"It's nothing really. I just can't believe I'm standing here chopping peppers," Jocelyn admitted. "This is not the way I planned to spend my morning. Although I'm beginning to think Gog had a premonition along this line."

"Gog?" Obediah lowered his knife.

"It's a pet name for my grandmother. Supposedly, I'm spending the weekend with her," she explained.

"Aah." He gave a nod of understanding. "Then she helped engineer your escape."

"An accessory, both before and after the fact," Jocelyn confirmed with a faint smile. It widened with the sudden thought. "Dexter would be thrilled to know I'm in a man's apartment."

"And Dexter is"—Obediah took a guess—"your grandfather?"

"No, he works for Gog and has for years. He isn't exactly a butler. I suppose you could call him 'her man Friday'."

"I see. And he would be happy you're here."

"Actually, both of them would be. You see, they had visions today would turn out to be like that old movie *Roman Holiday*."

"Yes, with Gregory Peck and Audrey Hepburn. I remember the film." His white head bobbed in fond recollection. "A beautifully romantic movie, but the ending wasn't to my liking, with each going their separate ways."

"You're a romantic, too, are you?" She realized with amusement.

"I am," Obediah confirmed, then paused to look over his shoulder before he whispered, "I'll let you in on a secret." He motioned her closer. "At heart, everyone is. Many hide it because they don't want to appear foolish. Some bury it so deep, they even succeed in convincing themselves that they have no such ridiculous tendencies."

"Really," she mused, wanting to doubt him, yet suspecting it was true.

"So, what time does Cinderella have to return from the ball?" he teased.

"You are a romantic, aren't you?" Jocelyn grinned. "Before seven tomorrow morning."

"Then you still have plenty of time to dance with Prince Charming," Obediah concluded.

She laughed at the idea. "There's not much chance

of that. Or have your forgotten that he sprained his knee?''

His dark eyes twinkled. ''Then you do see Tucker as Prince Charming.''

Suddenly flustered, Jocelyn rushed to deny the statement. ''I said no such thing.''

''No, of course, you didn't.'' He shook his head in mock agreement, then chuckled low in his throat.

''Don't you start in on me, too, Obediah,'' she declared half angrily. ''It's hard enough handling Tucker, not to mention wondering how I'm going to explain all this to Gog, short of outright lying.''

''Forgive me.'' He smiled. ''But you must know the most romantic meetings only appear that way in hindsight.''

''Nothing about this is romantic,'' Jocelyn insisted.

''Of course not. My mistake.''

Obediah was only humoring her, and Jocelyn knew it. Not for the first time, she wondered how on earth she had gotten herself into this predicament. Nothing was turning out the way she had planned back at Redford Hall. Her day was supposed to have been filled with harmless and uneventful wanderings, mixed in with some sightseeing.

On the other hand, this was the kind of adventure her grandmother would have wanted her to have. Something that would put a little spice in the day— or a lot of spice. Anything to keep it from being too tame.

This is not tame, Gog, Jocelyn thought, fully aware that somewhere she had lost control of things. And her grandmother would be clasping her hands in delight over that if she knew.

Bliss Wakefield swept into the kitchen, a scarf of emerald silk trailing from a shoulder. It settled in shimmering folds along one arm when she came to a stop, her posture as always splendidly straight. Completely ignoring the agents lounging around the table, she looked directly at Dexter.

"There you are. I have been looking everywhere for you, Dexter." Her words carried a ring of censure.

Reacting to it, Dexter wrapped himself in British aloofness. "Is there something Madam wishes?"

"Not I. But Jocelyn would like some hot tea and a slice of dry toast. You can take it up to her room when you have it prepared." The message delivered, she turned to leave.

"Tea?" Dexter questioned in skepticism, playing out his role to the letter. "Miss Jocelyn always starts her morning with coffee."

"Not always," Bliss corrected. "And certainly not this morning. She isn't feeling particularly well and would like some tea instead."

Agent Bassett was instantly all ears. "She's sick?"

After a small hesitation, Bliss faced him, adopting a pose that was her regal best. "Not sick precisely, merely feeling a bit under the weather."

"What's wrong?" His gaze narrowed in concern.

Her chin came up a fraction as she regarded him coolly. "In my day, this was not a subject a woman discussed in mixed company. You may draw the obvious conclusion from that.''

Understanding dawned in the bachelor agent's expression. He seemed suddenly just a little uncomfortable with the subject. Breaking eye contact with Bliss, he shot a look at the lone woman in the security detail. Biting back smiles, both married agents exchanged knowing looks.

''Suffice it to say,'' Bliss continued, ''a day in bed will do wonders for my granddaughter. I'm sure by tomorrow morning she'll be back to her old self.''

With another glance at Agent Donna Travers, Bassett suggested, ''Maybe you should check and see whether there's anything we can get for her.''

Under Bliss's cool eye, Agent Travers hesitated, then shook her head. ''I don't think that's necessary. Mrs. Wakefield is right—a day in bed is often the best medicine.''

After another glance at Bliss, Mike Bassett chose not to pursue the matter. Satisfied that her plan had worked to perfection, Bliss turned once again to Dexter.

''I'll tell Jocelyn you will have her tray up directly,'' she said, adding, ''Include a cup of coffee for me as well.''

''As you wish, Madam,'' Dexter replied with a faintly formal bow of his head.

Moments later he knocked at the bedroom door. Before he could identify himself, Bliss opened the door, her glance scouring the area immediately behind him in belated concern that he might not be alone.

Aware there was always the chance of listening ears, she stated, "At last. It's a wonder the tea isn't cold. Stop dawdling and come in, Dexter." The instant he cleared the door, Bliss closed it, then swung around and did an inelegant, arm-pumping victory dance. "It worked, didn't it?"

"So it would appear." Dexter stood in the center of the room, holding the tray.

"I knew it would." She paused, a little breathless with excitement and the impromptu dance. "What did they say after I left? Anything?"

"Hayes and MacElroy made a few comments about their wives and the symptoms they occasionally suffered, but not as much was said as one might suppose. Out of deference to Ms. Travers, I suspect. No doubt they feared she might consider such remarks to be sexist in nature." Dexter glanced pointedly at the items on the tray. "What would you have me do with this tea and toast, Madam?"

"Flush it down the toilet," she replied with an indifferent flip of her hand.

"Madam." Dexter looked wounded. "The tea is the very best Earl Grey."

"If it offends you to pour it in the stool, then drink it and flush the toast." She lifted her coffee cup off the tray and carried it to the window. "What do you suppose Jocelyn is doing now?"

"Let us hope she is having an organic cappuccino at the Mudd House and chatting with some handsome stranger." After setting the tray on the nightstand, he poured tea into the cup. "It is much preferable to the thought that she has been taken prisoner by some extremist."

"What on earth do you mean by that?" Bliss turned from the window, her brow puckering in bewilderment. "How can a cappuccino possibly be organic?"

"I was referring to the coffee beans with which it is made."

"Then you should have said that," Bliss informed him. "Really, Dexter, you must learn to express yourself better. Personally, I would worry more about this handsome stranger being the extremist if he's into this organic thing. People are under the false impression no chemicals are used in organic gardening."

"But they are natural chemicals, Madam," he pointed out.

Her glance rolled toward the ceiling in disgust. "That makes all the difference, of course. How foolish of me."

"How refreshing that you recognize it, Madam," Dexter observed dryly.

"Recognize what?" she demanded.

"How foolish your attitude is." He picked up the cup, leaving the saucer on the tray next to the bed.

"Foolish. I'll tell you what is foolish: putting up with you. Now, either drink that tea or throw it out. But not all of it," she admonished. "Leave a little in the cup for the sake of appearances."

The cup was halfway to his mouth when Dexter

paused, looking somewhat stricken. "Is it necessary for me to put on lipstick first?"

"Lipstick?" She repeated in disbelief.

"Yes. So it would appear Miss Jocelyn drank it," he explained, then his expression became troubled. "Although if the Secret Service should compare the lip print—"

"Lipstick won't be necessary, Dexter." Amusement riddled her voice and her expression. "As much as I would love to see you in it. A woman who is too ill to get out of bed would also be too ill to put on lipstick."

Dexter sighed, his expression clearing. "I am very relieved to hear that, Madam." He took a sip of tea.

"Hand me the toast. I'll get rid of it while you finish the tea."

With vague regret, Dexter held out the plate to her. "Will this continue all day? Preparing food to be thrown away?"

"We'll keep the menu simple," Bliss promised and sailed to the bathroom, toast in hand. Seconds later came the distinctive sound of a toilet flushing.

Sugar-cured bacon sizzled in the skillet, filling the kitchen with the scent of sweet salted pork. In the corner Molly nosed her empty bowl around the floor, searching for any stray kibbles that might have fallen out. Convinced there was no more to be found, the dog lapped up more water from the dish, then watched as Obediah cracked an egg against the side of a glass bowl, broke it open, and dumped the contents on top of two other raw eggs. When it became clear no handouts were being offered, Molly trotted into the living room.

"You finally decided to check on me, did you? You sure took your time about it," Tucker accused when she sat down beside the sofa. "I figured you had deserted me, too."

Molly swung her head toward the kitchen, then pricked her floppy ears at him and whined softly.

"I know. The knee wasn't such a great idea." He cast a disgruntled glance at the ice bag that crowned his bandaged knee. "Now I'm stuck in here and she's out there." Lifting his head, he yelled to the kitchen, "Hey! How much longer before the food is ready?"

"It will be a little while yet," came the answer. "Obediah is just whisking the eggs now."

"A while," Tucker muttered to the dog, then yelled again, "I hope you don't expect me to eat in here by myself while you two stay in there and have your breakfast at the table."

"We haven't figured out the eating arrangements yet," was the reply.

"This is my apartment, you know," he hollered. "It's only proper that I eat with my guests. In case you haven't noticed, Jonesy, it's kinda' hard to carry on a conversation with someone when they're in the next room."

"I've noticed. My advice is to give it up."

"And what would you suggest I do instead?" Tucker challenged, pleased to have her talking to him.

"Watch television. You can reach the remote."

It lay on the coffee table. Tucker briefly glared at it, then smiled with an idea. "Instead of doing that, why don't you bring me that newspaper lying on the table? I didn't manage to get it all read before I left this morning." Molly cringed a little and whined. "All right," he whispered in concession, "as excuses go, it isn't the best, but it will get her in the room."

In exasperation, Jocelyn shoved the tongs onto the spoon rest and stalked over to the table, scooped up the various sections of the morning paper, and marched into the living room. Ignoring the big smile of welcome Tucker wore, she crossed to the sofa and dumped them on his chest.

"There. Now read that and leave us alone," she ordered.

"My, aren't we touchy?" He gave her a big-eyed and innocent look. "Are you always like this when you're working in the kitchen?"

"Only when I'm constantly interrupted." Her smile was deliberately sweet. "Now, unless you like your bacon charred, you'll read your paper and stop bothering us."

"You know, that's the worst thing about accidents in the kitchen—you usually have to eat them." Tucker picked up a section of paper and shook it open.

The humorous and unexpected quip shattered all her carefully nurtured irritation. It was, she was discovering, impossible to stay mad at someone who could make you laugh. Jocelyn was still smiling over his comment when she walked back into the kitchen. She went directly to the stove to check the bacon.

"Did you just take him the newspaper?" Obediah whispered.

"Yes." She glanced at him curiously.

"All of it?"

"Yes."

He sighed heavily. "I'm afraid that wasn't a good idea."

"Why not?" She had the feeling there was a shoe hanging somewhere in the air, about to drop.

"Because," Obediah whispered back, "there was a large article in the feature section about the president's daughter, complete with an excellent color photograph."

"Oh, no," Jocelyn murmured and threw a worried look toward the living room.

"Oh, yes." Obediah nodded sadly.

"Maybe he won't read it. Maybe he won't see any resemblance. Maybe—"

"Maybe you better not take any chances," Obediah suggested.

"But how—" Then she thought of a way and again laid the tongs on the spoon rest. "Watch the bacon, Obediah."

Back into the living room she went.

Tucker lowered the sports section in surprise, then grinned. "I have to admit I didn't expect to see you back so soon."

"I didn't expect to be back." She plucked the newspaper from his hands and stacked it with the rest, then laid them on the coffee table.

"Wait, I was reading that." He made a groping reach for the sports page.

"You can read it later. Obediah just poured your omelet in the skillet. By the time we get you settled in the kitchen, it should be ready." She removed the pillows from under his knee.

"In the kitchen?"

"You said you didn't want to eat in here by yourself," Jocelyn reminded him.

"I know that's what I said." Sitting up, Tucker put one foot on the floor and laid a protective hand on his injured knee. "But how am I going to keep my leg up in there?"

"We can prop it on another chair. It will make eating at the table a little awkward, but no more than it would be trying to eat from a plate balanced on your lap." Jocelyn tucked a supporting hand under his arm, lifting and steadying when he rose to his feet.

Using her as a crutch again, he wrapped a long arm around her shoulders and hopped a little to adjust his balance, then paused as if gathering himself to make the short trek into the kitchen.

"You know, I should have thought of resting my leg on a chair, but I didn't." He glanced sideways at her, a disturbing warmth in his eyes. "I'm glad you did, though."

"That's nice." She attempted to slough off his comment and pretend that she wasn't in the least affected by his closeness and this contact with him. Contact that had her nestled snugly against his side, hip to hip.

Tall as she was, Jocelyn wasn't used to looking up to meet someone's eyes, certainly not this far up. Oddly enough, it made her feel softer and more feminine.

"You're pretty wonderful, Jonesy." There was a quiet rumble to his voice as feeling vibrated through it and right into her, making Jocelyn much too aware of him as a man rather than as Grady Tucker, political columnist. Which was something she was finding harder and harder to remember about him.

"I am absolutely fabulous." She feigned an airiness while fighting an inner breathlessness.

Tucker gazed at her for a long, heart-tripping second, then sighed and shook his head, a wry resignation tugging at his mouth corners. "It's no use," he murmured. "I've got to find out."

"Find out what?" Jocelyn murmured, conscious of the downward dip of his head.

"If there's fireworks ... or bells." His breath fanned her lips, briefly heating them before his mouth slanted onto them.

It was more as if the earth had moved. Jocelyn was certain the floor tilted beneath her feet at the contact. His lips were softer than she had expected, softer and deftly persuasive. She responded without thinking, lured by the natural ease of the kiss, an ease that carried a sense of rightness, a kind of homecoming that was at once both satisfying and thrilling.

The pressure deepened a notch, bringing the kiss to a new level of intimacy. She trembled with it, half afraid of the next step, afraid she wouldn't want to back away from it. Yet she had always wondered if a man's kiss could evoke this sensation in her—all liquid and shimmery like molten gold.

When his lips untangled from their mating with hers, Jocelyn felt positively heady, aglow with the magic of it. For a moment, she didn't move at all as an awareness slowly stole into her that he had both arms folded around her. Beneath the hand she had flattened to his chest, she could feel the hard and uneven thudding of his heart, an echo of the disturbed beat of her own.

Slowly she raised her lashes, and the strong lines of his face filled her vision. Tucker looked as dazzled by the wonder of the kiss as she felt, his hazel eyes all warm and glimmering with bright gold flecks.

"Wow." The word was as soft and breathy as a whisper. "You pack quite a punch, Jonesy."

At that instant, Jocelyn wanted to hit him for real, mostly because she was angry with herself for letting that kiss happen. Instead, she drew back and reached behind her to remove his encircling arm.

"I believe we were on our way to the kitchen," she reminded him, hotly conscious of the husky tremor in her voice.

To her relief, Tucker nodded agreeably and withdrew his arm, his body shifting in place to resume their former side-by-side position. "So we were." He took a step forward, carefully putting his weight on his left foot. "You wouldn't reconsider giving me your address in Waterloo, would you?"

"I won't."

The line of his mouth thinned in resignation. "You're determined to make it hard for me to find you again, aren't you?"

"As hard as I possibly can." Little did he know how easy it would be if he knew who she really was.

Leaning on her, he limped forward a second step. "Give me one good reason why you won't."

"Because you're crazy."

He stopped sharply. Judging from the stunned look on his face, she must have sounded more sincere than she realized. "You don't think I'm one of those lunatics who fixate on some woman and stalk her wherever she goes."

Jocelyn seized the excuse. "How do I know you're not? I hope you don't expect me to take your word for it."

"You'd be pretty foolish if you did," Tucker replied and sighed heavily, moving toward the kitchen again. "I guess that means the next move has to be yours. You aren't one of those old-fashioned kind of girls who don't believe in calling up a guy, are you?"

Truthfully, no such occasion had ever arisen; she wasn't sure what she would do. She settled for a different kind of truth. "I have always considered myself to be a liberated woman."

"I have to be honest, Jonesy," Tucker said with a wry grimace. "I have never understood what that meant."

Taken aback by his candor, Jocelyn faltered and searched frantically for an answer. "You know what?" she said on a note of amused surprise. "I don't think I do either, except I know it's all tied up somehow with respect. You don't use or take for granted someone you respect; you don't disregard their desires or dreams."

"What are your desires and dreams?" he inquired softly, his gaze turning a little too probing, a little too intent.

She had never intended the conversation to take such a serious turn when she answered him. "That's easy," she said quickly. "To get you into the kitchen."

"I am serious," Tucker protested.

"So am I. Let's go."

CHAPTER 11

By the time Jocelyn had Tucker comfortably settled in the kitchen with his leg up and the table set for three, breakfast was ready to be served. She helped Obediah carry the food to the table, then took her own seat. All the delicious aromas whetted an appetite already sharp from hunger. Removing her napkin from the table, she opened it and draped it across her lap.

"Obediah, would you offer the blessing for us?" Tucker asked, spreading his own napkin.

When her mother was alive, every meal was preceded by a word of grace. Lately it had been a custom observed only on special occasions or official functions. She wasn't sure she wanted to regard this as a special occasion.

A little awkwardly, Jocelyn copied Obediah's pose and bowed her head, closing her eyes as his richly deep voice intoned the words: "O Lord, Thou didst create the earth for man, and gave him the fruits of the earth and of the flocks and herds for his support, and hast said that our food is to be sanctified by prayer. Sanctify this food to us, and us to Thy service for Jesus' sake. Amen."

"Amen," she echoed in chorus with Tucker, then carefully avoided looking at him when she took a slice of toast from the plate before passing the plate to Obediah.

During those first few bites of food, silence reigned at the table, broken only by the clink of silverware or the satisfying crunch of crisp bacon.

"This omelet is delicious, Obediah," Jocelyn stated. "Some woman will be very lucky to have you for a husband."

He chuckled softly. "I'll tell my wife you said that."

"You're married?" For some reason, she had assumed he was single, or at least a widower.

"Nearly all of my adult life," he confirmed, then added with a teasing grin, "And all those years to the same woman. Very happily, too."

"If you can say that, you must share my granddaddy's philosophy," Tucker remarked. "He claims that making a marriage work is like operating a farm; every morning you have to start all over again."

Obediah chuckled again. "How very true."

"Do you live here in the capital?" Jocelyn asked curiously.

"No, I'm just passing through on business."

"The toy business." Tucker sliced off another bite of omelet with his fork.

"That's right." Nodding, Obediah spooned strawberry jam onto his toast.

Letting the bite of omelet lie on his plate, Tucker frowned thoughtfully at Obediah. "You seem to know a lot about Santa Claus. I'm curious about something. How come he always wears red?"

"If I'm not mistaken, I believe the traditional robe of a bishop is red. And, as you recall, St Nicholas was a bishop in the early church." He glanced at Tucker, a sudden sparkle in his eyes. "There's an interesting sidebar to that. The bishop wears a tall hat that comes to a point. And he also carries a staff, which some believe is the origin of the traditional Christmas treat, a candy cane."

"You're kidding. Well, isn't that something?" There was a kind of boyish delight in Tucker's expression. "The bishop's staff became a candy cane. Then how did this gift business come about?"

"I want to know how we got back on the subject of Christmas," Jocelyn inserted, amazed at the way it kept cropping up.

"We can talk about something else if you like." There was something in the way Tucker looked at her that led Jocelyn to suspect marriage would be the topic. *Their* marriage.

Rather than take him up on his offer, she answered

his initial question. "For your information, the custom of gift-giving goes back to the Magi and the gifts they brought to the Christ Child."

"No doubt that was a very strong influence," Obediah agreed, but not completely. "However, the giving of anonymous gifts—like the kind Santa leaves for children—can again be traced back to Saint Nicholas."

"Really?" Jocelyn couldn't check her amazement.

"Very definitely." Obediah nodded, a gentle smile curving his mouth and lifting the corners of his white mustache. "According to stories handed down over the centuries, Saint Nicholas often placed himself in the role of an anonymous benefactor to the needy. In fact, one of the stories also explains Santa's practice of putting presents in a stocking 'hung by the chimney with care.' "

"That goes back to Saint Nick, too!" Tucker drew his head back in surprise. "I never would have guessed that. I thought that was something Clemens came up with to make his rhyme, or parents did, so they wouldn't have to give their children so much."

"Tell us the story," Jocelyn urged, partly out of curiosity and partly to keep the conversation away from less comfortable topics.

"Very well." Obediah paused, gathering his thoughts. "First of all, I should explain that back in the third century, it was the custom for parents to provide dowries for their daughters. Without one a girl couldn't marry. Which virtually sentenced her to a life of prostitution. A sad commentary, but a fact," he stated.

"Now, as I mentioned earlier, Nicholas, the bishop of Myra, was the son of wealthy parents, which meant he had considerable money at his disposal. Now, as the story goes, the bishop of Myra learned about these two daughters who were about to be sold into prostitution because their father had no money to provide a dowry for them. Taking pity on them, Nicholas took some gold coins, tied them in a little bundle, and tossed it through a window in the family's dwelling. Legend has it that the bundle fell into one of the girls' stockings hanging by the chimney."

"Ah, but how did she know to hang her stocking there?" Tucker challenged.

Smiling broadly, Obediah replied, "One must suppose that her stockings were wet and she hung them by the fireplace to dry. You must remember that in those days, they had no such modern conveniences as washers and dryers. They also didn't possess a vast wardrobe, especially those of the poor and working class. Some were not even fortunate enough to have a change of clothes. And nothing makes you feel colder than to have wet feet. To remedy that, logically you would remove your wet stockings and hang them up to dry near a heat source—like a fireplace."

"But how do we know the money came from Bishop Nicholas if the gift was anonymous, as you say? Did someone see him toss it through the window?" Jocelyn broke a slice of bacon in half and nibbled at one end, turning a curious gaze on Obediah.

"Possibly. Or he might have been seen on the street by a neighbor. And I think it's safe to assume that the wealth of his family would be widely known in the community. No doubt there was a great deal of rejoicing when the family discovered the coins. And when a person has a stroke of good fortune like that, the typical human response is to run and share the news with family and friends. I'm sure word spread quickly. And when it did, I'm sure there was a great deal of guessing going on about who the anonymous benefactor was. I doubt there were a great number of choices. Of course, that's all conjecture on my part," Obediah conceded.

"But it makes sense," Tucker agreed thoughtfully as he speared another bite of omelet with his fork.

"And over time, others in need received similar monetary gifts, which no doubt shortened the list even more. Invariably the welfare of a child was at the heart of such cases." Again Obediah's smile was like a glow that reached his dark eyes, giving them a sparkle and shine. "When you think about it, who better to know the private needs and sufferings of families than the man who has the task of ministering to them? And who would be in a better position to intercede, not only through prayer?"

"Why do you suppose he did it anonymously?" Jocelyn wondered aloud. "Why didn't he just give the money outright?"

"He probably didn't want a lot of people showing up at his door begging for money, whether they needed it or not," Tucker reasoned with a heavy dose of cynicism. "Look what happens today. If you donate some money to one charity, within a week your mailbox will be filled with requests from a hundred others. Sometimes I think we were better off in the old days when charity was a virtue instead of an industry.''

Obediah chortled softly at that and nodded. ''Perhaps we were.''

''And you know when we really get inundated with requests,'' Tucker challenged, gesturing with his fork. ''Christmas, that's when.'' He jabbed the air to emphasize the point.

''And we resent that,'' Jocelyn murmured, recalling the observation Obediah had made when they were at the Lincoln Memorial. ''Christmas is the time of year when we're urged to think of others—and we would much rather dwell on ourselves. It's that whole 'me' thing, isn't it?'' She sighed as another thought occurred to her. ''Maybe that's why we're so quick to want the government to handle anything like that. That way, we won't have to think about it. But you know what's really sad?'' She glanced at both of them. ''Charity is a deduction, a kind of reward for giving to others. It makes you wonder how many people would give at all if it weren't the case. If they did, it would probably be to enhance their own public image.''

''You know?'' Tucker cocked his head to one side, a thoughtful frown darkening his expression. ''I'd like to disagree with you about that, Jonesy, but I'm kinda' afraid you're right. Most of the time our motives for giving aren't very altruistic. Probably half the time we do it just to buy off our guilty conscience. And we really like others to think well of us. Sometimes it's just plain old good business—you scratch somebody else's back through their pet charity in hopes they'll scratch yours."

"Now do you understand the true beauty of an anonymous gift?" Obediah inserted.

Jocelyn hesitated, then shook her head uncertainly. "I'm not sure I follow you."

"When you give anonymously, you don't seek the other person's undying gratitude or praise from the community or a tax write-off. In other words, you don't get anything for it except the inner satisfaction of knowing you were able to help someone in need. Not because you had to, but because you wanted to. Sometimes you don't even get to see the joy on that person's face when they receive it."

"Which may be why 'it is more blessed to give than receive,' " Jocelyn mused.

"Parents get the joy of seeing their children's faces on Christmas morning," Tucker pointed out.

"But they get no praise for the gifts," Obediah reminded him. "If anything, a child usually declares how wonderful *Santa* is."

Tucker mulled that over and nodded. "That's true."

"Now do you see?" Obediah asked gently, his warm glance inspecting each of them. "That long-ago bishop of Myra didn't give to receive any personal glory, to have praises heaped upon him, or for the world to know how generous and good he was. He gave because he could, and because he cared. A very godly trait, you must admit. And isn't that when we feel best about ourselves—when we are doing as God would have us do, unselfishly, with absolutely no expectation of return?"

"Now there's a thought to make you sit up and take inventory of yourself," Tucker admitted soberly.

"It reminds me of that person a few years back who mailed a winning lottery ticket to some charitable organization," Jocelyn recalled. "There was no return address on the envelope, nothing to identify the original holder of the ticket."

"Don't be fooled by all the bad news reported by the media," Obediah advised, eyes twinkling and a smile lurking at the corners of his mouth. "There are a great many good people out there whose deeds of kindness never make the headlines."

"I'd like to believe that," Jocelyn murmured and took another bite of omelet.

"You can," Obediah replied simply.

As far as Jocelyn was concerned, believing wasn't as easy as Obediah made it sound. "How?" Her skepticism showed in her voice.

"You're sitting here, aren't you?"

"Yes, but—" She didn't see what that had to do with anything, but Obediah didn't give her a chance to say that.

"Why?" he interrupted.

"Why what?" she asked in confusion.

"Why are you sitting here?"

"Because . . ." Hesitating, she glanced across the table at Tucker. His eyes were on her, something disturbingly soft lighting their depths and scrambling her pulse. She dredged up annoyance to smother her reaction. "I have no idea why I'm here. I must have been out of my mind at the time."

A low and hearty chuckle came from Obediah, rich with genuine amusement. "No doubt it seems that way now. After all, you had your day planned—"

"Until Molly knocked me down. After that, everything went from bad to worse." Jocelyn stabbed at the last bite of omelet.

Hearing her name mentioned, the dog trotted up to the table and sat down facing Jocelyn, panting happily.

"That's right. Molly had a major role in all this, didn't you, girl?" Obediah gave her head an affectionate pat, and the dog cast an adoring look his direction. "Perhaps Tucker should have named you Dolly instead."

"Dolly?" Tucker arched a puzzled eyebrow. "Molly is a lot of things, but Dolly Parton, she isn't."

"By that I didn't mean Dolly Parton. I was referring to the matchmaker in that Broadway musical, *Hello, Dolly,*" Obediah explained. "After all, she did instigate your first meeting."

"That was a sheer accident," Jocelyn insisted. "My mistake was in agreeing to have coffee with Tucker instead of just walking off and forgetting the whole thing."

"Which was exactly what you were going to do when Molly tripped me," Tucker reminded her.

"It's a pity I didn't." She jammed the bite of omelet in her mouth and chewed on it fiercely.

"Ahh, but why didn't you?" Again there was that knowing gleam in Obediah's eyes.

She hurriedly swallowed the partially chewed bite. "Because Tucker was hurt. I couldn't very well walk off and leave him lying there."

"Of course you couldn't," Obediah agreed. "And it was this same concern for his well-being that made you see to it that Tucker arrived home safely, that his injuries were treated, and that he had something to eat. You are here because you unselfishly put aside your own plans and placed his needs first. You are here . . . because you cared."

"And I regret every minute of it." She glared at Tucker, irritated by the smugly happy expression on his face.

"Only because you're worried about the way things might turn out." Obediah's glance was filled with the secret knowledge of her true identity.

Tucker raised his hand. "Hold it right there a second, Obediah. Up to now, you've been making a lot of sense, but you just lost me with that one. What does Jonesy have to be worried about?"

"The same thing I've been worried about all along," she answered truthfully, then tacked on a half lie: "How much of this day I'll be able to salvage."

"I guess I have done a good job of messing up your day." Tucker turned a little glum and grim.

"That's a bit of an understatement, don't you think?" The observation was close to an accusation, but she managed to keep her irritation in check and gathered up her silverware, dumping it on her plate before rising from her chair. "You two go ahead and finish your breakfast while I start clearing things up."

Like a flash, Molly whipped around and trotted out of the kitchen, a dog on a mission. Plate and water glass in hand, Jocelyn crossed to the sink counter, then paused, her glance raking under the cabinet area.

"Where's your dishwasher, Tucker?"

"Right here." She turned to see where he was pointing. He had both hands in the air, turning them front to back. "My dishwasher is an old-fashioned one, the manual kind. Just rinse those off and stack them in the sink," he told her, motioning at the items in her hand. "I'll take care of them later myself."

Obediah didn't give her a chance to agree to his suggestion.

"Nonsense. Jo—" He caught himself at the last second. "—onesy and I are perfectly capable of washing these few dishes. Why, with the two of us working together, we'll have them done in no time. Isn't that right?" He looked to her for agreement.

She was trapped again, this time by the way Obediah had so glowingly praised her unselfishness only minutes ago. And ridiculously, Jocelyn wanted him to think well of her. She hoped it wasn't because he knew who she really was.

"Of course we'll do them," she agreed with leaden enthusiasm and turned to the sink, for now setting her dirty dishes on the counter.

As Jocelyn busied herself gathering up the bowls, utensils, and skillets used in preparing and cooking the meal, Molly trotted back into the kitchen dragging her leash. She went straight to Obediah's chair and jumped, planting both front paws on his leg and dangling the leash in front of his face.

After an initial start of surprise, Obediah recovered. "Well, what do we have here?" he asked with a definite smile in his voice.

"Good golly, Molly, you get off of him right now," Tucker ordered with a trace of embarrassment. "Don't you know you're not supposed to go around jumping on people? Get down now."

Molly ignored him and swung the leash closer to Obediah. The instant his hand closed around it, the dog let go of it and pushed off his leg to stand on all fours, then barked once, a sharp, demanding sound.

"I believe she wants me to take her somewhere." Obediah looked at Tucker for an explanation.

"I know. You see, I usually take her for a short walk after she eats. I guess she knows I can't get around so good. Just ignore her," he said. "She can wait until later this afternoon."

"Why should she?" Obediah countered in perfect innocence. "I am more than able to take her. Aren't I, Molly?"

The dog gave a happy little *whoof* of agreement and flailed the air with her tail, setting her whole rear end to wagging. Leaning down, Obediah snapped the leash to her collar.

"I'll do it," Jocelyn volunteered quickly, unwilling to be left alone with Tucker, especially with visions of that last kiss still fresh in her mind.

"There's no need." Obediah rose from the chair, leash in hand. "I am perfectly capable of taking Molly for a short walk."

"Of course, you are, but . . . you haven't finished your breakfast," she pointed out hurriedly.

"I assure you I'm quite full. I really couldn't eat another bite," Obediah insisted as Molly bounced anxiously beside him. "Be patient, girl. We're going. First, I have to fetch my hat and coat."

"I really think I should take her," Jocelyn tried again. "Molly can be a little rambunctious at times, and I wouldn't want her dragging you down the steps."

Obediah brushed aside her concern. "You needn't concern yourself about that. During our ride in the taxi, Molly and I came to an understanding about such things. Didn't we, girl? I won't go too slow, and you won't go too fast."

Molly barked again, prancing in place.

Obediah laughed. "You see? She thinks I'm moving too slow now."

Together man and dog set off for the living room. Jocelyn watched them for a minute, then sensed Tucker's gaze on her and turned back to the sink, determined to ignore him. Which was an impossibility when the table had to be cleared. But she made short work of stacking the dirty plates and flatware.

"We'll be back shortly," Obediah called from the living room. Then came the click of the apartment door closing behind them.

"I feel pretty useless just sitting here, watching you

work," Tucker said as she carried the dirty dishes from the table to the sink.

"Don't watch," Jocelyn countered.

"That's too easy, You'll find a plastic dishpan and drainboard under the sink," he told her.

"I know." She had noticed them when she put the rubber gloves away.

With a sinking heart, Jocelyn realized she would need the gloves again. For now, she set the drainboard on the counter and the dishpan in the sink, turned the faucet on to fill it, and added a squirt of dish soap. As the bubbles billowed, she retrieved the gloves and pulled them on.

"You sure are germ-conscious, aren't you?" Tucker marveled.

"My hands are sensitive to certain brands of soaps," Jocelyn lied.

"In that case," a chair leg scraped the floor, "I'll wash and you dry."

She turned to see Tucker lumber to his feet. "You're supposed to be resting that knee," she accused.

"I'll rest it. I'll just do it standing up for a while." He hobbled to the sink. "Now before you go getting all upset, look at it this way. By the time Obediah gets back, we can have these dishes washed and dried and put away. Of course, if you insist on waiting until he gets back, we will. But that will mean you'll have to hang around here that much longer."

"Perish the thought," Jocelyn muttered.

"I was pretty sure that was the way you would look at it." Leaning against the counter, his weight balanced mainly on one foot, Tucker slid the stack of dishes and flatware into the soapy water. "And let's be honest; trying to wash dishes with those cumbersome gloves on, you're liable to drop something and break it and get yourself cut in the process. Then I'll be the one bandaging you up."

He had a point there, as reluctant as Jocelyn was to admit it. Dragging off the gloves, she laid them aside and searched through the drawer to find a clean towel for drying.

"Besides," Tucker continued, "I think you should know I'm not the kind of guy who considers it unmanly to have his hands in dishwater. I don't do a bad job at housework either—cleaning, dusting, mopping floors, that sort of thing."

"How very domestic of you." Jocelyn reached for the plate he stood upright in the rack.

"My mom always said housework is one thing nobody notices unless you don't do it."

As always, his tidbit of wisdom, couched in dryly humorous phrases, drew a smile from Jocelyn. "Your mother said that?" she questioned in a lightly teasing tone. "I'm surprised it wasn't your granddaddy."

"Oh, he probably would have said it if he had thought of it, but this time it was my mom. She's a wise woman, too." His expression was completely guileless, but there was a gleam of shared humor in the look he sent her.

"I'm glad to hear that." Her smile widened a little.

When Tucker was like this, it was easy for Jocelyn to relax and simply enjoy his company and the light banter of his talk. He had a way of looking things squarely in the eye, without taking them too seriously.

In the White House, just about everything was serious: the problems, the responsibilities, the issues, and the duties, with few opportunities for relief that weren't shadowed by the looming office of the presidency.

"By the way . . ." Tucker held a plate under the faucet and rinsed off the soap before passing it to Jocelyn. "Breakfast was good. Thanks."

She shrugged off the compliment. "Obediah did most of the cooking."

"He's quite a guy, isn't he?" Tucker remarked, then suddenly chuckled to himself.

"What are you laughing about?" She paused in the act of drying the plate to study him curiously.

"I was just remembering something I read somewhere," he replied, a small smile turning up the corners of his mouth. "It was something to the effect that a man goes through three stages in his life: he believes in Santa Claus; he doesn't believe in Santa Claus; then he *is* Santa Claus. Until I met Obediah, I think I was at stage two."

"And now?" Jocelyn grinned.

"I think I moved back to stage one."

"I know what you mean." She slid the dried plate onto the stack in the cupboard.

"You, too, huh?"

"Yup." She reached for the last plate.

"Do you know you're the only one who's ever helped me with the dishes other than my mom? It kinda' makes me feel like we're an old married couple already who just had a friend over for breakfast, and here we are cleaning up afterwards, me washing and rinsing while you do the drying and putting away.''

Her fingers froze on the rim of the plate at the shock she felt. Shock that it felt exactly the way he described, right down to the bone. She felt at home in his kitchen, at home with him. Which was completely illogical. How could it possibly feel like she had known Tucker half her life when they had met only a few hours ago? How could she feel so certain inside that, despite their many differences, they shared the same basic values? It made no sense at all.

Even worse, there was no future in it. It was all a lie. She was a lie.

''That's it.'' In one motion, Jocelyn let go of the plate and hurled the towel into the corner. ''I can't handle anymore of this!''

Ignoring Tucker's dumbfounded look, she bolted for the living room. He turned from the sink, drops of water and froth dripping from his wet hands.

''Can't take anymore of what?'' he asked.

She swung around and jabbed an accusing finger at him. ''You, that's what. You and all your talk about marriage.'' The tears were close. Too close. ''It isn't going to happen. Not today. Not tomorrow. Not ever. Is that clear?''

For an instant, her gaze clashed with his, her eyes all hot and stormy with temper. But in their darkness, Tucker glimpsed a shimmer of pain. Stunned by it, he was slow to react when she spun away and charged into the living room.

"Wait a minute, Jonesy." In his haste to follow, he forgot to limp, but the constricting wrap around his knee hampered his range of movement, slowing him. "Where are you going?"

"Isn't it obvious?" She hurled the words over her shoulder as she snatched her coat off the platform rocker. "I'm leaving."

"But . . ." He stopped in the kitchen doorway and pressed a hand to his thigh.

This time, however, she wasn't moved by his play for sympathy. "If you can stand and wash dishes, you are obviously well enough to look after yourself, Tucker."

She raked him with a scathing glance, jerked the door open, and stalked out of it. Tucker winced when she slammed it shut behind her. He took a step after her, then stopped and punched a hand against the kitchen jamb in frustration and regret.

The stairwell echoed with the rapid pound of her footsteps as Jocelyn ran down all three floors. Without checking her pace, she barreled out the door and nearly collided with Obediah on the sidewalk.

"Jocelyn." His hands came up automatically to catch her arms and check her headlong rush, his expression one of astonishment and concern. "What happened? What's wrong?"

He glanced past her, half expecting to see Tucker come out of the building after her. But the front door remained closed.

"The man is crazy. That's what's wrong." She pushed his hands away so she could go on by him, but Molly leaped up to greet her, creating a new obstacle.

"Crazy?" Obediah showed his disbelief.

"The way he goes on and on about marriage, what else would you call it? It's sheer idiocy and we both know it." Her voice wavered with a hundred different emotions, all warring for supremacy.

Obediah looked at her with sudden understanding. "And you feel like a fraud."

"I—" Jocelyn opened her mouth to deny that, but nothing came out. Instead, she shoved the dog's paws off her. "For heaven's sake, Molly, get down."

The minute she was free of the dog, she took off blindly up the street. Molly barked and lunged after her, but stopped when Obediah pulled sharply on the leash. Looking back at him, Molly whined anxiously.

"I know, girl. I know." Reaching down, he gave the dog an absently reassuring pat. "I'm worried, too. Things were going so well and . . ." Obediah checked the rest of the sentence and glanced up to the old mansion's third floor. "I think we'd better see what we can do about this, Molly."

CHAPTER 12

Tucker stood in the doorway to the apartment, waiting for them when Obediah and Molly came up the last flight of steps.

"You saw her, didn't you?" Tucker guessed, looking forlorn and a little lost. He paid no attention to the dog when Molly shouldered her way past him into the apartment.

"Yes, we saw her," Obediah confirmed, a little breathless from the long climb.

"She charged out of here madder than a hornet." Shoulders slumping, Tucker turned out of the doorway and walked over to the sofa. "I blew it this time, Obediah. I really blew it." He sank onto the cushion, slouching forward to rest his elbows on his knees and staring dejectedly at the floor. "I knew she was getting touchy about the marriage business. I told myself I wasn't going to say any more about it. And what do you think I start blabbing about? Marriage. But it's what I was thinking."

Tucker lifted his head in a further protestation of innocence, a hand waving in a vague gesture. "There we were washing dishes together and getting along like an old married couple. The minute it struck me that's the way we were, out it popped." He sighed in disgust. "I thought about going after her. Except I figured she'd probably call a cop and have me arrested."

"I don't think she would do that." Obediah deposited his hat and coat on the chair again.

A short, explosive laugh came from Tucker. "You don't know how mad she was when she left."

"I have a fair idea," he murmured.

"That's right, you saw her, didn't you," Tucker remembered. "I'll tell you one thing—there isn't much chance I'll ever see her again."

"I wouldn't be too sure about that." On his way to the sofa, Obediah deliberately knocked the newspaper off the coffee table, scattering the pages onto the floor. He clicked his tongue in mock reproach and stooped to gather them up. "How clumsy of me."

"Just leave them. It doesn't matter anyway," Tucker said dejectedly.

"Nonsense." He shuffled noisily through them until he found the page he wanted. "Isn't this a lovely picture of the president's daughter? Have you seen it, Tucker?''

"No." He cast a disinterested glance at the paper and turned away.

"You should take a look at it. It's really quite good." Obediah held it out to him.

"Maybe later." Tucker waved him off.

"Suit yourself." Obediah shrugged and laid the newspaper on the coffee table, the photograph facing up within easy range of Tucker's vision. "But I think you would find it very interesting."

"Look," Tucker said with thinning patience, "I have seen Wakefield's daughter before. She's a beautiful woman." In irritation, he snatched up the paper, looked at the photograph, and nodded. "Yup, she's beautiful, all right."

As he started to lay it back down, Obediah tapped a finger on the picture, redirecting Tucker's attention to it. "Especially her eyes. They are such an amazing shade of brown, so dark and rich like Swiss chocolate, don't you think?''

"Yup, they're beautiful eyes. And brown, too." He studied them a second longer, his mouth crooking in a wistful line. "They kinda' remind me of Jonesy's."

"Do they?" Obediah peered over Tucker's shoulder.

"She even has Jonesy's nose and mouth," he commented.

"Really? Isn't that remarkable?"

"Yeah, remarkable," Tucker echoed glumly and dropped the newspaper on the coffee table, releasing a heavy sigh. "I suppose that will start happening now. Every time I look at another woman, I'll see something that reminds me of Jonesy."

"Do you think so?" Obediah said with a convincing show of concern.

"I know so. Just look at that picture of Jocelyn Wakefield." Tucker gestured to it with a flinging wave of his hand.

"You see a resemblance?"

"Resemblance?!" Tucker scoffed. "To me, she's practically the spitting image of Jonesy. Ignore the red hair for a minute." Bending forward, he made a frame of his hands, placing them on the color photograph and blocking out Jocelyn's trademark strawberry blond hair, leaving only her face to be seen. "Imagine that she had on a brown wig and darker makeup and—"

Abruptly he broke off the sentence, lifted his hands, then laid them down again, then repeated the process a second time before pulling his hands away and resting them on his knees.

"It isn't possible," he murmured, staring at the likeness. "It couldn't be."

"What?"

Not immediately answering, Tucker stood up and paced away from the table, then turned back and raked fingers through his hair, creating furrows in it.

"I really am losing my mind," he said at last.

"Why do you say that?" Obediah asked innocently.

"Because . . ." Tucker laughed shortly, his glance running again to the photograph, ". . . for a second there, I almost convinced myself that Jonesy is Jocelyn Wakefield.''

"Really?" Obediah marveled.

"Well, they both are about the same height and build. And their faces—they're virtually twins.'' Again Tucker motioned to the picture with an upraised palm. "And politics—every time I brought up anything about it, she was darned quick to change the subject. Do you remember how she said her father worked for the government? She sure didn't say in what capacity either, did she? Like maybe the president? And everybody knows Wakefield's wife died several years ago. So did Jonesy's mother. Then there's that business about Iowa. Jocelyn Wakefield practically lived there during those months before the Iowa primaries. There were even jokes going around that the governor was going to make her an honorary resident.'' With a snap of his fingers, Tucker remembered something else. "Teaching, that's the other thing. Wakefield's daughter has a degree in education, too, and always claimed she wants to make teaching her career.''

"My, that is quite a string of coincidences.'' Obediah sat back on the sofa, all wide-eyed at the list.

"A few too many coincidences, if you ask me.'' Long, angry strides carried Tucker back to the table, where he scooped up the feature section with its large color photograph of Jocelyn Wakefield. He slapped the picture with the back of his fingers. "I knew Jonesy looked familiar the minute I saw her face. But I talked myself into believing it was because she was the girl meant for me." Grimly furious, Tucker threw the paper at the coffee table. "I'll bet she got a good laugh out of that. Grady Tucker falls for Jocelyn Wakefield in disguise. Of all the dirty rotten tricks—"

"Careful," Obediah admonished.

"Well, what would you call it?" Tucker challenged hotly. "I was up-front with her from the start. She knew exactly who I was; don't kid yourself. But did I know who she was? No sirree Bob. She feeds me this Jonesy tale. No matter how you cut it, that is deliberate deceit."

A white eyebrow went up. "Is her deceit any worse than yours?"

"Mine?!" Tucker drew his head back in an attitude of indignant denial.

"Yes, yours," Obediah repeated, a hint of mockery in the faint smile he wore. He glanced at Tucker's elaborately wrapped leg. "Your knee is no more sprained than mine. If Miss Wakefield had been thinking clearly, she would have noticed there was almost no swelling at all."

"All right, so maybe I did pretend to be hurt worse than I was," Tucker grudgingly conceded that point. "But it's pretty darn harmless when you put it up against the way she played me for a fool. Wait a minute here." He pointed an accusing finger at Obediah. "You just called her Miss Wakefield. You're convinced that's who she is, too, and you don't look very surprised about it. You'd already figured out who she was, hadn't you? That's why you made such a point of showing me her picture, isn't it?"

"Regretfully," Obediah sighed, a knowing sparkle in his eyes, "that's a question I can't answer without breaking a solemn promise."

"And you swore not to tell who she was," Tucker guessed.

"Not a single word of the kind has ever passed my lips." He folded his hands across his stomach.

"No, no, it sure hasn't," Tucker nodded with sly amusement. "You just pointed me in the right direction, confident I had enough brains to figure it out."

"I suppose it could look that way."

"It does more than look that way," Tucker declared, then sighed grimly. "Unfortunately, I didn't figure it out before I made a complete fool of myself." He paused and fired a sharp glance at Obediah. "What was she doing in that getup anyway?"

"Why does anybody wear a disguise?" Obediah countered with a question of his own.

"We both know the answer to that," Tucker retorted. "So they won't be recognized."

"I suppose that would be the logical conclusion, wouldn't it?"

"There's something else I'd like to know." A frown creased the troubled lines in Tucker's forehead. "Where were the Secret Service agents assigned to protect her?"

"Good question." Obediah sat Buddha-like, pondering the possibilities.

"They should have jumped on Molly and me the second after Molly knocked her down. The little fool slipped away from them, didn't she?" Tucker said, then threw up his hands. "Of all the stupid, hare-brained stunts to pull! She's out there wandering around by herself—the president's daughter! Doesn't she realize she could be kidnapped by some lunatic?"

"You don't think such a thing could really happen, do you?" There was a flicker of worry in Obediah's expression, so brief that Tucker wasn't sure whether it was an act.

"Why not?" he argued. "If *you* recognized her and *I* recognized her, then it's for sure somebody else could."

Obediah sat forward, appearing gravely concerned. "What do you think we should do?"

On that, Tucker hesitated. "I don't know. We should call somebody.

"I suppose we could always call the police," Obediah agreed. "But what would we tell them? That the president's daughter just left your apartment wearing a wig and heavy makeup? If no alert has gone out that she's missing, we could have a difficult time convincing them of that, don't you think?"

"Maybe," he conceded.

"I think it's more than likely that a lot of precious time would be wasted simply confirming that she is gone," Obediah reasoned. "Under those circumstances, perhaps you should go look for her."

"Me?" Tucker frowned.

"Somebody needs to keep an eye on her," he pointed out. "And I don't think Miss Wakefield would be surprised if you popped up again. She might even be pleased."

Tucker expelled a short, dry laugh of disbelief. "I doubt that very much."

"I think there is a distinct possibility you are wrong," Obediah told him. "Speaking strictly as an observer, I think she was beginning to like you—perhaps more than was comfortable. Have you considered why she left so abruptly? Is it possible that her conscience was bothering her because she wasn't the person you believed her to be?"

"It's possible." Tucker was stunned to realize how much he wanted to believe that. And even more stunned when he carried Obediah's suggestion to its logical conclusion. "Good grief, you aren't saying that Jocelyn Wakefield is interested in me. She's the president's daughter, for heaven's sake."

"But first she is a woman with feelings and desires no different than anyone else's. In fact," Obediah added with a smile, "no different than Jonesy's."

"You've got me there, Obediah." Tucker ducked his head in sheepish self-disgust. "I've gotta be honest, I never thought my attitude toward someone was influenced by status or fame. But I never would have spoken so openly about my feelings if I had known she was Jocelyn Wakefield. And it's for darned sure I would have moved a lot slower."

"Don't you think she guessed that, too?"

"Probably." He nodded.

"Well? What are you standing around here for? Shouldn't you be out looking for her?" Obediah prompted.

"Right." Tucker turned toward the door.

"You might want to consider changing clothes first." An amused smile played across Obediah's lips, twitching his mustache. "It might get chilly in those shorts come nightfall."

Tucker looked down at his bare legs and changed directions. "Right." He headed for the bedroom.

Two minutes later he walked out of it, giving a final hitch to the faded jeans he now wore before pulling his sweater hem over their waistband. He spared Obediah a brief glance as he picked up his coat.

"Which way did she go? Did you notice?" Tucker started going through the pockets, muttering to himself, "My car keys are in here somewhere."

"The last time I saw her she headed east, toward the corner," Obediah replied. "But which direction she went after that, I couldn't say."

"That's the problem. Where would she go?" Troubled by the long list of possibilities, Tucker sighed, his hand diving into still more pockets in search of the car keys.

"I suspect that a person who has one day to sightsee would spend it in the Mall area," Obediah said. "It is, after all, where we met her."

"And for that very reason, she might not go back there." Yet the more Tucker thought, the more logical it seemed.

"Perhaps. But I believe she will be drawn there, regardless," Obediah stated with confidence. "Remember, she enjoys American history, and there is no better place in the capital to find it on display than the Mall area with all its museums and monuments. No doubt she believes she can lose herself in the crowds.''

"It's for sure it will take luck to find her there. If she decides to go through one of the museums, she could be in there for hours and I'd never find her. And I certainly couldn't go through all of them looking for her. It would be worse than finding a needle in a haystack." Tucker dipped his hand in another pocket, muttering, "I know I had the keys in here."

"Something tells me that, no matter where she might go in the meantime, sooner or later she will show up at the memorial to Thomas Jefferson. That's strictly a guess, mind you," Obediah added.

"It's a good one, though," Tucker agreed. "And there's a place to park right nearby, assuming I can ever find my keys."

"Check the right inside pocket," he suggested.

Tucker plunged a hand into the pocket and came out with a set of keys on a chain. "How did you know where they were?" He stared at Obediah in surprise.

"I heard them rattling, and your last pass over it was a cursory one."

"Oh." Tucker clinked them together in his hand, as if verifying the sound they made, then took a step toward the door, halted, and looked back. "You are coming along, aren't you? Two pairs of eyes are better than one."

"No. I'll stay here and keep Molly company." Obediah stroked the dog's glistening black head.

Tucker hesitated. "Are you sure?"

"I'm positive. Give me a call when you find her."

"You'd better cross your fingers that I do find her," he advised, opening the door.

"You will. And Tucker . . ." Obediah checked him before he went out the door. "While you're looking for her, you might consider why she slipped away in the first place. She wanted to spend a day as an ordinary person, without dragging along all the baggage that goes with being Jocelyn Wakefield. It may not seem like much to you and me, but to her it's something precious. You might even call it an early Christmas gift."

After a thoughtful pause, Tucker nodded and continued out the door, calling over his shoulder, "I'll be talking to you—with good news, I hope."

He clippety-clumped down the stairs, his long legs bending at jutting angles. Outside the old Victorian manor house, he circled around to the back, where he kept his car parked. Keys in hand, he unlocked the door to an ancient Volkswagen that sported a spiffy new coat of flame red paint and a fake raccoon's tail tied to its antenna. With the deftness that can only come from years of practice, Tucker folded his tall frame into the small space behind the wheel.

He went through the ritual he always followed after inserting the key in the ignition switch. Before turning it, he gave the dashboard a love tap.

"Wake up, Betsy," he murmured, then pumped the accelerator twice and twice only. "It's time to rise and shine, Bets." He turned the key. There was a groan, a grind, and a sputtering cough. He pumped the accelerator the third time. "Come on, Betsy. You can do it."

After one more cough, the engine chugged to life, all four cylinders rattling happily away. Smiling, Tucker gripped the floor-mounted gear lever, stepped on the clutch, and shifted into reverse. He backed out of the reserved parking space, cranked the wheel, shifted into first gear, and turned into the narrow alley. Seconds later the bright red bug was tootling along the street.

Tucker spent well over an hour cruising the area between his apartment and the Mall, scanning the sidewalks and the entrances to the Metro. Finally giving that up as a lost cause, he swung onto Ohio Drive and used up another twenty minutes searching for a place to park. From the lot, he walked to the round-topped memorial honoring the nation's third president.

Once there, Tucker circled it a couple times, then planted himself beside one of the Ionic columns that ringed it. A half-dozen times during the next hour he thought he spotted her and took off in pursuit. But each time, when he got within hailing distance, Tucker realized it wasn't her.

On his way back from the last false sighting, he noticed a brunette in a plaid anorak standing in the interior shadows of the monument's coffered dome. She faced the nineteen-foot-tall statue of Jefferson, dressed in knee breeches and a fur-collared greatcoat. Something about the way she stood, the tilt of her head, confirmed what his instincts shouted.

Janet Dailey

With an effort, Tucker kept his pace casual and crossed the pink-and-gray floor of Tennessee marble, making his approach to her at an angle. All his senses were at a high pitch of awareness, but inside there was only this strong and solid feeling of rightness that had him drinking in the sight of her.

Initially, she appeared wholly engrossed by the majestic bronze statue. But as he drew closer, Tucker observed the vacancy of her stare and the vaguely dissatisfied look on her face, the kind that hinted she wasn't as interested in it as she wanted to be.

When she heard the squeak of his rubber-soled shoes on the marble, she darted a quick, wary glance his way, then shot him a second look. Something that strongly resembled gladness leaped into her eyes, but she made a visible attempt to contain it when she turned fully to face him.

"What are you doing here?" The question was half demand and half surprise.

"Looking for you." Hands in his pockets, Tucker walked the last two steps with an ease of movement she immediately noted.

"It appears you have made a miraculous recovery, Tucker. Your knee doesn't seem to be bothering you at all," she observed with a challenging lift of her chin. "Which is amazing when you consider that two hours ago you could hardly put your weight on it."

He ducked his head, smiling with sheepish regret. "I'm afraid I kinda' stretched the truth a little about that."

"More than a little, I would say." Jocelyn folded

her arms in front of her as if provoked with him, but there was a tiny glint of amusement in her eyes. "That was a dirty trick, Tucker."

The impulse was there to echo Obediah's words and suggest that his faked injury was no worse than her deceit. He briefly skipped his glance over the wig and dark makeup, surprised to see how obvious the disguise seemed to him now that he knew her true identity.

And he could strip it from her by simply speaking her name. But something told him that as Jonesy, she was comfortable with him, if a little wary; Jocelyn Wakefield, on the other hand, would undoubtedly run for cover.

"It was a dirty trick," he admitted. "But you know the old saying: confession is good for the soul. 'Course in Washington, it can also be a best-seller."

Her smile was quick and wry. "You have an uncanny ability to joke your way out of awkward situations, don't you?"

Tucker smiled back. "I try."

Her eyes narrowed on him. "How did you know I'd come here anyway?"

"I can't take the credit for figuring that out. It properly goes to Obediah. With you being interested in American history, he said you'd definitely pay a visit to Jefferson's memorial." His attention shifted to the bronze figure. "Probably because Jefferson was more than just this country's third president; he was also the author of our Declaration of Independence, the first proponent for the separation of church and state, and the purchaser of the Louisiana Territory. A man of endless contradictions: eloquent with a pen, but poor as a speaker; in favor of abolishing slavery, yet never freed his own slaves." Tucker paused, his glance flicking back to her. "But I guess you know all that."

"Yes," she acknowledged and scanned the area behind him. "Where is Obediah? Didn't he come with you?"

"No, he's back at the apartment, Molly-sitting. He was worried about you being by yourself."

"When you see him, you can tell him for me that he didn't need to worry. I'm fine." Without warning, she started walking away.

"Wait a minute, Jonesy." Tucker hurried after her.

"What is it now?" She continued walking.

"I came looking for you so I could apologize for the way I behaved—"

"Apology accepted."

Tucker ignored her interruption. "After you left, it got to bothering me that you'd be going back to Iowa, your trip ruined by memories of this crazy guy who kept going on about marrying you."

"It's a pity that didn't occur to you before." Side by side, they passed between two columns and descended onto the first step.

"That's true, but I found it hard to think clearly around you." Which was the truth. It was still hard.

"Save the flattery, Tucker." Her glance was dry and faintly mocking.

"The truth isn't flattery," he insisted. "Anyway, I

swear I won't say one more word about it the rest of the day."

Jocelyn stopped on the third step. "That promise assumes you'll be spending the rest of the day in my company."

"It does, doesn't it?" He scratched the back of his head, covertly watching the amused smile that toyed with her lips. "I guess that's because I thought I could make up for ruining your morning by showing you around my town. You see, to most people, Washington, D.C. is a city full of monuments and government buildings. They don't usually get to see the other side of it—the side that doesn't have anything to do with politics."

"And you actually believe I'll agree to that?" she said in amazement.

"Admit it, Jonesy." Tucker tried out his most winsome smile on her. "You're just a little bit curious, aren't you?"

"Being curious is not the same as agreeing," she reminded him.

"No, but it's a start. Think about it, Jonesy," Tucker reasoned. "Do you want the standard guidebook tour of Washington—the kind that tells you that the Jefferson Memorial anchors the southern end of L'Enfant's north-south axis, that from its steps you have the best view of the White House at the north end?" He pointed to the mansion, clearly visible in the distance. When he saw the sudden tension that claimed her, he regretted his choice of examples. He knew only one way out of it. "You do know what the favorite pastime is in Washington, don't you?"

"What?" She grabbed at the question, betraying an eagerness to change the subject.

"Riding the president." His grin was on the wicked and naughty side.

Amid the shock and discomfort that flickered in her expression, there was laughter, too. Jocelyn went with the latter.

"Something tells me there are times when the president would agree with that," she said.

"Probably." Privately Tucker admired both the quickness of her recovery and the tactful expression of support for her father. "So, what's it going to be, Jonesy? Do you want to spend more time rubbing elbows with tourists, or do you want to do things that ordinary, everyday people do on the weekend?"

"Like what, for instance?"

He shook his head, refusing to be specific. "You'll have to trust me."

She looked him straight in the eye. "I am not going back to your apartment, Tucker."

He feigned shock. "No guide would dream of taking a client to his apartment unless it was a specific request."

"As long as that's clear," she said and hesitated.

"Clear as a Kansas sky in August," he promised.

Jocelyn studied him for another long second. "I must be crazy to agree to this. I wouldn't, but I have the feeling you'll keep hounding me until I do."

"Somewhere in there, I think I heard an affirmative. Let's go.'' He tucked a hand under her elbow to guide her down the steps.

"Wait a minute.'' She pulled away from his touch. "Where are we going first?''

"*First,* we're going to my car. It's parked in the lot off Ohio Drive.'' He saw her follow-up question forming and moved to sidetrack her. "Did you know that in Washington, driving schools don't teach students how to park anymore?''

"You're kidding, of course.'' She decided.

"No, I'm serious.'' He started down the steps, smiling when she automatically followed. "They consider it a waste of time. If you don't believe me, ask anyone who's tried to find a place to park in this town.''

"Obviously you managed to find one,'' she countered dryly.

"Which only proves there are such things as miracles.'' He flashed her a grin.

"You are hopeless, Tucker.'' In spite of herself, she smiled.

Looking at her, at the shine of amusement in her eyes and the soft curve of her lips, Tucker knew she was right. He was hopeless—hopelessly in love with her. Maybe it was all one-sided, but he didn't think so.

Right now, he had time on his side—totally confident that Jocelyn Wakefield wouldn't be going to Iowa any time soon.

CHAPTER 13

As they approached the parking lot, Jocelyn watched with amusement while Tucker went through the ridiculous ritual of searching his pockets for the car keys. She was stunned to discover how light-hearted she felt in his company.

Every ounce of common sense told her she should never have agreed to go with him. But she had only to remember how dull and boring everything had seemed to her *after* she had left his apartment.

Even worse, she had been so certain it was what she had wanted—to wander about completely on her own. She had spent an hour trying to convince herself that she was enjoying every minute, when the truth was the exact opposite.

Then Tucker had shown up, and she knew what had been missing.

"Found them." He rattled the set of keys on their chain.

"The next question is, where's your car?" Every space in the lot had a vehicle in it, with more cruising around searching for a place to park.

"That's easy," Tucker told her, pointing. "It's the one with the raccoon's tail on the antenna."

She spotted it instantly, hanging above the car roofs. "It's fake, I hope."

"Of course." He looked at her askance. "You don't think I want to invite the wrath of the animal rights activists down on me, do you?"

"I wouldn't think so." She smiled. "Are you a closet Davy Crockett fan?"

"No, my mom is." He smiled. "She gave me the tail off her old coonskin cap when I went off to college."

Jocelyn wasn't sure whether to believe him or not. "That's a slightly unusual thing to give your son. Was it supposed to be a good-luck charm or what?"

"An 'or what,' " he replied, grinning. "She was worried that I would forget where I parked my car and I wouldn't be able to find it. I have to admit, that raccoon's tail saved me from wearing out a lot of shoe leather. It still does."

"I can believe that," she said, then stopped, her mouth dropping open when she saw the distinctive beetle-shaped car that the antenna sprouted from. She turned disbelieving eyes on the tall, lanky man. "You can't be serious. You drive a Volkswagen?!"

"Yup." He bent low to unlock the passenger-side door for her.

"I'm surprised you can even get into it." She stared at the bucket seats and cramped interior.

"It took some practice." Opening the door, he held it for her.

Hesitantly she approached the car, her glance running over its shiny red paint. "I didn't realize they were making these things again."

"Actually, they are, but this isn't one of the new, improved models."

Jocelyn paused with one foot inside the car and a hand resting on its curved top. "You mean . . . this is . . ." She stopped to search for the right word.

Tucker supplied it. "One of the originals. Watch it that you don't bump your head when you get in."

Wisely Jocelyn took his suggestion and devoted her attention to getting into the passenger seat. It didn't prove to be as awkward as she thought it would be. Tucker waited until she was all the way in, then closed the door and went around to the driver's side.

"What year is this car?" she asked after he closed his own door.

"Nineteen sixty-three." He patted the dashboard, mumbled something, then pumped the foot feed.

"It's a wonder it still runs," Jocelyn murmured in amazement when the engine turned over and caught with the first switch of the key.

"I'll have you know, Betsy not only looks like a top, she still runs like one."

"Betsy?"

Tucker reached for the floor shift, sliding her a twinkling glance. "Yup, that's what I call her."

"Betsy. As in 'Heavens to'?" Jocelyn guessed.

"You've got it." His grin was wide and infectious, eliciting a soft laugh from her. She felt oddly pleased with herself that she had guessed accurately.

"How long have you had Betsy?" Jocelyn asked when he backed the car out of its space.

"Since my junior year in high school. I bought her used off this old guy that lived down the road from us." Simultaneously working the clutch and the gear shift, Tucker pointed the car forward.

"You mean Betsy is your first car?"

Tucker dipped his head in confirmation. "I'm a loyal man."

"Or else you're very cheap," she mocked teasingly.

"I admit Betsy is economical to operate. And she can squeeze into spaces where only a bug can fit." He smiled when Jocelyn groaned at the pun. "Better yet, she hasn't needed any major repairs. Which is good for a car that's close to being a classic. That isn't to say Betsy doesn't have her drawbacks."

"Such as?"

"For one thing, it's darn hard to make out with a girl in Betsy's back seat—especially for me. Once I get back there, there is no room for the girl." He waited for a break in the traffic, then pulled onto the street.

Jocelyn laughed. "Talk about putting a cramp in your social life."

Wincing, Tucker lightly accused, "Now who's making the bad puns?"

"You'll just have to blame it on the company I've been keeping," Jocelyn countered, surprising herself with the ease of it; then she sobered with another thought. "Wait a minute. Are you saying that you drove this car all the way from Kansas?"

"I didn't have much choice," he replied. "They wouldn't sell me a plane seat for her, and it was too expensive to put her in the cargo hold."

"Very funny."

"Actually, it didn't take as long as you might think to drive here." He glanced sideways at Jocelyn. "Betsy can scoot right along when she has a tailwind." As if to prove his point, the little car zipped along the street at a good clip. " 'Course, in Washington traffic, speed isn't as essential as reliability," Tucker added.

"And Betsy is clearly reliable," Jocelyn murmured, just a little bit tongue-in-cheek.

"Now, that isn't to say Betsy doesn't have her bad moments," he inserted, his drawl thickening. "On cold mornings, she can be hard to start. But I don't hold that against her," he stated, sliding a smile at Jocelyn. "On cold mornings, I sometimes have trouble getting started, too."

"Don't we all." She settled back in the seat, determined to relax and enjoy herself. Which, in some ways, was remarkably easy to do, so long as she didn't spend too much time looking at Tucker. And that was difficult to avoid. Her glance kept being drawn to the clean, angular lines of his profile, fascinated by the innate strength in them and the earthy quality of his features, fresh and open and all male.

Jocelyn barely noticed when Tucker bypassed a freeway entrance. "Betsy and I are a backroads pair," he said, as if in explanation. "We aren't much for freeways and fast lanes."

Jocelyn could have argued with that, but it would have meant bringing up all his marriage talk—something she was loath to do. Mostly because she didn't want to think about tomorrow. She wanted to enjoy this day, this moment.

"Do you ever travel the backroads, Jonesy?"

"Some." But not in a long while. "Usually I don't have time to dawdle when I'm going somewhere. Which means I have to go the fastest way possible."

"Most of the world's in a hurry," he agreed. "They may not know where they're going, but you can be darned sure they aren't going to be late."

"Life can get hectic." Hers certainly had.

"But when it does, that's all the more reason to stop a minute and smell the flowers." Tucker paused and flashed her another glinting smile. " 'Course, there are some who'll tell you that our national flower is the concrete cloverleaf."

She laughed at that, a warm, throaty sound that tunneled into him. He could see that she was becoming at ease with him. Determined to keep it that way, Tucker kept up a steady run of chatter, punctuating it here and there with light quips. Never once did he attempt to seek any personal information about her, allowing her to volunteer it instead if she chose.

When they crossed the bridge over Rock Creek and entered Georgetown, Jocelyn's glance cut to him, bright with speculation. "Don't tell me you plan on showing me around old, historic Georgetown?"

"Nope. Though I'll admit Betsy negotiates its narrow streets with ease. But I've got something a bit more adventurous in mind than wandering past a bunch of quaint shops and trendy restaurants," he told her. "For a lot of folks, that's their idea of a leisure activity, but it isn't mine."

"Where are we going, then?"

"You'll see." He maintained a westerly course through the popular business district. "You know, you never have asked what I do for a living."

"There wasn't any need. Within minutes after we met, I put two and two together and figured out you were *the* Grady Tucker of 'Tucker's Take'." There was a hint of knowing smugness in her expression.

"You've read my column?" He looked both pleased and surprised.

"We do have newspapers in Iowa," Jocelyn chided, a suppressed smile grooving the corners of her mouth.

He winced at the light reproof. "Touché." For a moment he was silent, then cast her a dry sideways glance. "It isn't really fair to tell a person that you've read their column without also saying what you thought of it."

"You're right. It isn't fair." Her smile widened, her glance turning warm. "I find the column to be a reflection of its author: funny at times, invariably thought-provoking, but never mean-spirited.''

His sigh had a disappointed ring to it. "Too bad you couldn't have thrown in 'handsome' and 'charming.' '' Unfortunately, I've never heard the written word called either of those things.''

"Neither have I.'' She noticed the campus of Georgetown University on the right side. "But there is such a thing as exceeding the limit when you're fishing for compliments.''

It was Tucker's turn to grin. "I opened myself up wide to that, didn't I? It's one of those cases that proves if the truth hurts, it's because it should.''

As the campus fell behind them, Jocelyn studied the road ahead. "Are you taking me to Great Falls Park?'' She couldn't think of any other destination that lay in this direction.

"Have you been there before?'' Tucker countered.

"As a matter of fact, I have,'' she admitted.

In her mind, Jocelyn had a vivid picture of the spectacular falls created by the Potomac River plunging some seventy-six feet into a steep, jagged gorge strewn with massive boulders. During spring floods, the volume of water had been known to exceed that of the more famous Niagara Falls.

"Stunning, isn't it?''

"Definitely.''

A mile farther along the road, Tucker suddenly slapped the steering wheel in self-disgust. "I forgot to call Obediah.'' Leaning forward, he peered ahead. "Aha, they should have a pay phone up there.''

Before Jocelyn had fully taken in what was happening, he flipped on the turn signal and whipped the red Volkswagen into the driveway of a boat rental place. He parked near an outside pay telephone and switched off the motor.

"It shouldn't take more than a minute." He opened the door and started to climb out, then looked back at her. "Want to come along? More than likely Obediah will want to talk to you himself."

"Okay." She fumbled briefly with her seat belt, searching for its release catch.

By the time she joined Tucker, he had Obediah on the phone. "Yup, she was right where you said she'd be, at the Jefferson Memorial." He turned to her while he listened to Obediah's response. "Yeah, she's fine." A car with a faulty muffler roared past, and Tucker pressed the phone closer to his ear, covering the other one. "What did you say? Where are we?" He looked around. "At some boat rental place." There was another short pause. "That's a good idea. Maybe we will. Just a minute." He lowered the receiver, cupping a hand over the mouthpiece. "How about all three of us meeting somewhere for dinner tonight?"

When she considered the alternatives—dining alone or only with Tucker—Jocelyn shrugged. "Why not?"

Removing his hand, Tucker raised the phone to his ear again. "Do you want to meet Jonesy and me for dinner, say, around seven o'clock?" The reply was obviously affirmative. "You pick the restaurant and we'll be there." He nodded at the choice. "I know where it is. Do you want to talk to Jonesy?" . . . "Here she is."

Jocelyn took the phone from him, conscious of the warm tingle that traveled through her when their fingers brushed. It turned her voice just a little breathless. "Hello."

"I hope you are not too upset with me for suggesting to Tucker where he might find you, Jocelyn," Obediah said in lieu of a greeting.

"I probably should be, but I'm not," she assured him.

"Good. I'm quite sure you two have plans for the afternoon, so I won't keep you from them. I'll see you both at seven."

"We'll be there." After an exchange of good-byes, she hung up and turned to Tucker.

"Have you ever been canoeing?" he asked, startling her with the unexpected question.

"Not in years."

"What do you say—shall we paddle a ways down the canal?" Tucker waved a hand toward the racks of rental canoes. "The weather is perfect, the water is smooth, and they definitely have plenty of canoes available."

She looked at the canoes, then back at Tucker. "This is what you had in mind all along, isn't it?" she guessed.

"Can you think of a more idyllic way to spend an afternoon?" he reasoned. "A quiet setting, beautiful scenery, a piece of history—and all without a horde of tourists?'' Tucker watched the smile form on her lips and knew the answer to his question before he asked it. ''Are you game?''

Idyllic was the perfect description, Jocelyn decided as the canoe glided silently along the old stretch of the Chesapeake and Ohio Canal. Ahead of them, the narrow slice of water sparkled in the sunlight with a blanket of diamonds. Here and there, a fallen leaf floated, the wetness of it turning its autumn hue a vivid shade that created a jewel-like mix of rubies and gold against a diamond setting.

''I guess you probably know this canal was the brainchild of George Washington himself.'' Tucker dipped his paddle in the water, again with a reaching stroke.

Jocelyn nodded, dredging up the facts from her memory banks. ''He was one of the investors in it, and even supervised some of its construction. He had visions of it running all the way from Chesapeake Bay to the Ohio River, but it only made it as far as Cumberland, Maryland.''

''By then, the B and O Railroad was already completed, making the canal virtually obsolete before it was finished,'' Tucker filled in the parts she left out. ''Now, there's just this twenty-two-mile stretch of it left. Unless you count the towpath that still runs all the way to Cumberland.''

A jogger in headphones and designer gear loped into view along the canal's towpath, the crunch of his footsteps on its graveled surface intruding on the silence. He seemed out of place against the backdrop of ancient oaks and giant sycamores.

"It's easy to imagine how it must have been back then, though," Jocelyn mused.

"During warmer months, there are rides you can take on one of the old restored canal boats, complete with guides in period costume and mules hauling the boat from the towpath." Tucker raised his paddle out of the water and rested it on his leg, letting the canoe drift.

"I've heard about that," she admitted while drinking in the dank smells that swirled off the water. "It must be like stepping back into the past."

Tucker studied the profile she showed him, noting the faraway look in her expression. Smiling to himself, he swept his paddle forward again.

"Are you going to just sit up there enjoying the view, or are you going to use that paddle in your lap?" he challenged.

She threw a lightly mocking look over her shoulder, lifting her paddle. "Whip-cracker."

In retaliation, he began to sing, "Row, row, row your boat."

Laughing, Jocelyn joined in. After two rousing—if slightly off-key—renditions of the old song, they tried it as a round. Halfway through it, Jocelyn lost her place, tried to find it, and managed to confuse Tucker in the process. The singing quickly dissolved into laughter.

But it set the mood for the rest of the afternoon. They never talked seriously for more than two minutes without something striking one of them funny.

The laughter seemed to make the other shared moments that much more special.

Like the quiet moments when they watched in silence while a half-dozen mallard ducks swooped low to skim the canal's surface before settling gracefully onto it. Dazzling moments when the water mirrored the scarlet coat of a towering maple that grew along its bank. Precious moments when perfect understanding was exchanged with a simple meeting of glances.

A salmon-colored sun sat halfway below the horizon, watching as they returned to their starting point at the boathouse. Hues of orange and peach pink painted the scattering of clouds in the western sky.

Contented and completely carefree, Jocelyn climbed into the Volkswagen and buckled her seat belt. Neither said a single word during the drive back to the city. This, Jocelyn decided, was what was meant by a companionable silence, the kind that found conversation unnecessary.

"Hungry?" Tucker asked when he pulled into the public parking lot.

"Starved," Jocelyn admitted. "I don't know whether to blame it on all the fresh air or paddling the canoe, or both."

"You forgot to mention how long it's been since we ate last," he said.

The "we" came out naturally, the familiarity of it evoking a sense of easy intimacy—as comfortable to Jocelyn as their previous silence had been. She ignored all the voices in her head that warned against getting used to it, and instead chose to accept it as a fact.

"It has been a while, hasn't it?" she admitted.

"My stomach says it's been a lot longer than a while." Tucker swung the Volkswagen into a spot reserved for compact cars. The beetle-shaped car qualified and then some. With the engine off, he pushed open the driver's door. "The restaurant's about a block from here. I hope you don't mind walking. I never thought to ask."

"I don't mind at all," she told him.

After what felt like years of being picked up at the door and dropped at another door where a security detail waited to usher her inside, walking a block sounded wonderfully ordinary and normal. Jocelyn discovered an equal sense of freedom in opening her own car door and stepping out of the vehicle unaided, even though Tucker had come halfway around the Volkswagen to perform just that same courtesy.

After locking both doors, they set off together toward the attended parking booth. Jocelyn waited while Tucker dug out his money and paid the set fee. He rejoined her, shaking his head and wearing a wry look.

"Do you know it costs almost as much to park Betsy for an evening as it does to operate her?" There was marvel in his voice.

"In Washington that doesn't surprise me at all." She laughed softly.

Tucking a hand under her elbow, Tucker guided her toward the sidewalk. "You know, the next politician that promises two cars in every garage needs to make sure there's an economical place to park them."

"Now, there's a line that belongs in 'Tucker's Take,'" she teased.

"I'll have to remember that." His face was angled toward her, his smile warm and admiring. She felt that instant quickening of her heartbeat, that sudden kindling of heat. Struggling to counteract it, she looked away. "Which way is the restaurant?"

"That way." He pointed to the right.

His hand fell away from her arm as they both swung that direction, but he remained at her side, shortening his stride to keep pace with her.

Without the sun's rays to warm it, the night air had a definite bite of winter to it. The chill of it turned their breath into vaporous clouds of steam that went before them.

Jocelyn scanned the street directly in front, noting the number of darkened shop windows. Three separate neon signs identified the entrances to restaurants across the street, but there were only two on this side. Judging by the steady flow of people entering and leaving, Saturday night business appeared to be brisk.

"We aren't late, are we?" she wondered.

Tucker held his watch up to the light of a nearby street lamp. "According to this, we have two minutes to go before it's straight up seven o'clock. I think you'll like Donnie Frank's."

"At this point I'll like any restaurant." Jocelyn spotted the green neon letters that spelled out the name Donnie Frank's on the sign above the far corner building.

"I think Obediah picked it as a compromise, knowing I liked Mexican and you prefer Italian. The cuisine at Donnie Frank's is strictly American."

"That sounds like Obediah." The mere mention of the elderly gentleman was enough to bring a smile to her lips.

"I'm a little surprised he knew about Donnie Frank's, though," Tucker remarked thoughtfully. "They cater pretty much to the local crowd. You rarely ever see people from out of town in there. It's one of those small hole-in-the-wall places that are short on decor and long on good food."

"I hope they don't have a dress code," she murmured, suddenly conscious of the thrift-shop clothes she was wearing.

By no stretch of the imagination were they any kind of fashion statement, and definitely not the kind of statement she was used to making the rare times she and her father had ventured out of the White House for dinner.

"If they did, we'd both be out of luck." Tucker grinned. "Fortunately, it's one of those come-as-you-are kind of restaurants. Which is probably why the locals like it after a week of suit and ties. In case you haven't noticed, that's standard dress in official Washington."

"I've noticed." She waited while he stepped ahead

to open the heavy oak-and-leaded-glass door to the restaurant.

Warm air enveloped her when she walked inside. On it wafted a host of mouth-watering smells to stimulate appetites. Inhaling them, her sharp nose quickly separated the yeasty aroma of fresh-baked bread from the cinnamon-spiced scent of apple pie, sagey baked chicken from rosemaryed roast beef.

Pressing a hand to her ravenously hungry stomach, Jocelyn ran an inspecting glance over the restaurant's interior. For a place that was supposed to be short on decor, she was charmed by Old World touches she found in its darkly stained woodwork, soft lighting, and the nonintrusive shade of pale antique gold in the patterned fabric on its walls.

"Want me to hang that up for you?" Tucker offered, nodding toward her jacket. His own was already slung over his arm.

"Please."

With token assistance from him, Jocelyn shed the anorak and waited in the paneled entry area while he hung both garments on the coatrack in a side alcove. He tapped the black homburg sitting on the shelf above it, drawing her attention to the item.

"Looks like Obediah got here ahead of us," Tucker remarked, rejoining her.

"Something tells me he is always punctual." She smiled at Tucker, realizing that they shared an affection for the elderly man.

"Look, Mom." A young voice, high with excite-

ment, spoke from some point close to Jocelyn. "Do
you see who that is?"

She froze in place, going white beneath her
makeup. Her heart pounded like a cornered rabbit,
certain that her unmasking was imminent.

CHAPTER 14

"Where, darling?" the child's mother inquired with mild interest, her voice warm and softly cultured.

"Right there."

Jocelyn refused to turn, as if by not looking it was somehow easier to believe the child wasn't pointing at her. Her glance skipped to Tucker's face. His attention was obviously focused on the child, his expression faintly amused by what he saw.

The child's voice dropped to a fervent whisper. "It's Santa Claus, Mom. I know it is!"

The wave of relief Jocelyn felt was so great that her knees nearly buckled. Nerves brought a bubble of laughter to her throat. She barely managed to choke it back when she finally turned to look.

A young African-American couple stood in the archway to the dining area, exchanging warmly indulgent looks over the head of the six-year-old boy fairly dancing with excitement between them.

The woman bent slightly. "Honey, I'm sorry, but I don't think that's Santa."

"Yes, it is. See?" The boy pointed into the dining room. "He's got white hair and a beard. And he's even got a red sweater on, Mom."

Tucker leaned closer, murmuring near her ear. "It must be Obediah."

Jocelyn nodded, feeling foolish and a little embarrassed over leaping to such a wrong conclusion. Even now, when there was no more threat of discovery, her nerves were still on the jumpy side.

"Just because he has white hair and a red sweater, that doesn't mean he's Santa Claus, Brian," the father reasoned patiently.

"But it *is* him, Dad," the boy insisted. "I know it is. Can I go talk to him? Santa won't mind. Honest."

"We'll talk about this at the table," the father replied and held up three fingers, signaling to a jacketed waiter the number in his party.

When the boy started to protest the decision, his mother shushed him and laid a firm hand between his shoulders, guiding him forward into the dining area.

With the way open to them, Tucker escorted her to the archway, commenting, "Personally, I can't imagine anyone who would make a better Santa Claus than Obediah."

"He's definitely a natural," Jocelyn agreed, her glance instantly lighting on the man under discussion.

In his bright red sweater and snow-white hair, Obediah was impossible to miss. Seated at a table set for three along a side wall, he immediately noticed Jocelyn and Tucker and waved, rising to his feet, a smile beaming from his shiny brown face.

It was all the invitation the young boy Brian needed. In a flash, he broke away from his mother and dashed over to Obediah's table, then stopped a foot short of it to stare at him with wide-eyed uncertainty.

"Well, hello there, young man." Obediah switched his smile to the boy as Jocelyn and Tucker made their way toward him.

The instant the boy heard Obediah's rich and warm bass voice, his face lit up. "I knew it," he declared breathlessly. "You are—"

His mother grabbed him by the shoulders and briefly clamped a silencing hand over his mouth. "I'm so sorry," she rushed in embarrassment. "You'll have to excuse my son. Brian isn't normally this ill-mannered, but—he thinks you're Santa Claus."

"Ahh." Obediah lifted his head in an exaggerated nod of comprehension, then turned his darkly bright eyes on the boy. "So you think I'm Santa Claus, do you, Brian?"

Suddenly speechless, the boy nodded slowly and stared at Obediah with awe.

"It was the beard, wasn't it?" Obediah stroked the long and neatly trimmed whiskers on his face.

"And your red sweater." Brian discreetly pointed to it.

"The sweater, too. Dear, dear, dear," he murmured and sighed in mock regret, his twinkling glance running to Jocelyn when she slid into one of the empty chairs. "Young Brian here believes me to be Santa Claus."

Jocelyn feigned a look of alarm and whispered quickly, "Has he told anyone?" She sent her glance scurrying over the amused faces of customers looking on from nearby tables.

"I don't know. Have you, Brian?" Obediah asked.

"Just my mom and my dad." Brian darted a glance in his father's direction, then leaned closer to whisper, "Don't you want anybody to know who you are, Santa? Is that how come you don't have your fur suit on?"

"You are a very clever boy, Brian."

He nodded importantly. "I got all *satisfactory*s on my report card."

"That's wonderful," Obediah said, quick to praise the achievement.

But school was the least of Brian's interests at the moment. "Did you park your reindeer and sleigh outside? Can I go pet them?" he asked eagerly.

"Brian," his mother murmured helplessly.

"No, I left my reindeer and sleigh at home this trip," Obediah replied quite seriously.

Disappointment pulled at the corners of the boy's mouth. "Even Rudolph?"

"Yes, even Rudolph," Obediah admitted with regret.

Young Brian cocked his head, a wondering curiosity rounding his dark eyes. "Then how did you get here?"

"I can't tell you that." After a slow shake of his head, his eyebrows lifted in a white arc. "It's a secret," Obediah whispered.

The boy's mouth formed a big O before closing in a wide smile. For the first time he took note of Jocelyn seated at the table and the tall and lanky Tucker standing near her chair.

"Are they your friends?" he wondered.

"They certainly are. Miss Jones, Mr. Tucker, I would like you to meet Brian and his mother . . ." He glanced expectantly at the slim young woman.

"Barnes. Dienne Barnes." She turned to include the man now approaching the table. "And this is my husband, Anthony Barnes," she said and repeated Obediah's introductions of Jocelyn and Tucker to her husband, then hesitated over identifying Obediah.

But Brian had no such difficulty. "This is Santa Claus, Dad," he stated proudly, then added a smug, "I told you it was him."

"How do you do, Mr. Barnes." Obediah extended a hand in greeting. "It is a pleasure to meet you. This is quite a bright young boy you have here."

"Thank you." In gold-rimmed glasses, a dark pullover, and a button-down shirt, Anthony Barnes had the scholarly look of a young professor much more comfortable dealing with calculus problems than he was with a small boy's fantasies. Mixed in with genuine affection for his son, there was a touch of both embarrassment and gratitude for Obediah's indulgence with him. After a brief acknowledging nod to Jocelyn and Tucker, he attempted an awkward apology. "I hope all of you will forgive my son for intruding on you this way."

"It's quite all right, Mr. Barnes," Obediah assured him. "Don't give it another thought."

"That's very understanding of you." Aware they were making a scene, Anthony Barnes sought to bring it to a quick end. "I think it's time we were returning to our own table. Brian, thank Mr.... uh ... Claus"— he stumbled self-consciously over the name—"for his time."

Craning his head back, Brian cast an appealing look at his father. "Can I ask Santa one more thing first?"

"May I," his mother corrected automatically.

"May I? Please," Brian added for good measure.

After bouncing an uncertain glance off Obediah, Anthony Barnes attempted to sound stern, "I think you have bothered him enough with your questions for one night, Brian." But that initial hesitancy betrayed his lack of conviction.

Brian was quick to take note of it, protesting with the typical, "But, Dad—"

Obediah settled the issue. "What is it you wanted to ask me, Brian?"

The boy turned suddenly shy, dipping his chin down and touching a finger to his mouth, his glance darting about to note the number of people watching him. "Can I whisper it to you?" he asked in a voice barely above one.

"Of course." Obediah bent low, turning his head to offer an ear to the boy.

Rising on his tiptoes, Brian cupped a hand to the side of his mouth and whispered something directly into Obediah's ear. Only the sibilant tones in his speech could be heard in the unexpectedly hushed restaurant. The request was a short one, over almost as soon as it began.

As Obediah straightened, his smile grew wider and wider. "I think I can manage that." He winked at Brian, his dark eyes sparkling with the same bright light that danced in the boy's.

A chuckle started deep in his chest, growing in resonance and merriment. When he clamped both hands to the sides of his barrel-round stomach, Jocelyn watched with dawning comprehension. Then it came—that rich and hearty—and remarkably genuine-sounding—"Ho! Ho! Ho!"

But Obediah didn't stop with the customary three ho-ho-ho's. He kept it up for a good ten seconds, filling the room with the deep ring of his laughter. By the time it faded, others had joined in, softly, some of them self-consciously. But it was as if something magical had happened; there wasn't an unsmiling face in the room, and all had a wistful little twinkle in their eyes. Jocelyn felt the sting of tears, and she wasn't sure why.

"Wow," Brian breathed the word, totally awestruck.

"Was that good enough?" Obediah stood with his

hands on his hips and his smile running from ear to ear, every inch the jolly Santa.

"Yeah." Again the answer was all breath.

"Tell Santa thank you." This time Anthony Barnes had no trouble at all with the name.

"Thank you, Santa." Brian still sounded a bit dazed and dazzled.

"You're welcome," Obediah replied. "And you remember to be good—for goodness' sake," he said, then paused, arching an eyebrow in an infinitely wise look. "Do you know what that means, Brian?"

The boy chewed at his lower lip, seriously pondering the question. "I'm not sure," he admitted with regret.

"It means"—Obediah again bent down to the boy's level—"that you should be good, not because somebody might give you a toy or let you stay up past your bedtime. You should be good because it's the *right* thing to do."

A troubled frown puckered his forehead. "I'm only a kid, though. How will I know what's right?"

"You'll know," Obediah assured him, then tapped his chest. "Right here. Deep down in our hearts, we always know when we are being naughty or nice. Don't we?"

There was a trace of guilt in the way Brian buried his chin in his neck. "Yeah," he sighed.

"That's what I thought." Smiling warmly, Obediah straightened to his full diminutive height. "So don't forget: you be good for goodness' sake."

"I will," Brian promised as murmurs of approval circled the room.

"Thank you, Santa." Anthony Barnes smiled.

Prompted by sound of his father's words, Brian echoed them. "Yes, thank you, Santa." When his parents attempted to herd him away from the table, Brian turned back. "Tell Rudolph 'hi' for me, Santa. And Dasher and Dancer and Prancer and Blitzen and all the rest of the reindeer, too."

"I'll do that," Obediah promised with a farewell wave. Then, chuckling, he took his seat while Tucker pulled out the chair beside Jocelyn and sat down.

"If you ever decide to take up a new occupation, Obediah, you would make a perfect Santa Claus," Tucker declared, opening the menu before him, a lazy smile tugging at one side of his mouth.

Obediah grinned in response. "I'll keep that in mind."

"It's true, though," Jocelyn insisted with a smile. "By the time you were done, you not only had convinced Brian that you were Santa Claus; you had his parents believing it as well. In fact, this whole place was absolutely full of the Christmas spirit." She still felt the glow of it inside. "You could see it on everyone's face."

"The Christmas spirit," Obediah repeated thoughtfully. "It's a phrase you hear a lot." He paused and glanced at the pair of them, lightly challenging, "What do you think it means?"

As Tucker said, "Happiness," Jocelyn simultaneously answered, "Joy."

"Both of which mean a person is filled with a lot of warm and good feelings," Obediah pointed out with an approving nod, then went on to elaborate: "You feel good not just about yourself, but about others, life, and the world in general. In fact, there's a kind of beautiful contentment in the moment."

"Peace on earth, goodwill toward men," Tucker murmured, smiling to himself.

"Yes. You have followed my thinking." Obediah's smile widened in approval. "Peace and joy. Joy and peace. Whatever the order, one automatically follows the other. After all"—again his expression took on a wise and knowing quality—"in the Scriptures, Jesus says, 'I came that you might have and enjoy life.' He didn't say that He came so you could worry about tomorrow or fret over yesterday. I am reminded of an epigram I once heard. It went: 'Yesterday is history; tomorrow is a mystery; today is a gift; that's why we call it the present!' "

"True," Jocelyn murmured thoughtfully. "Most of us are all too often guilty of not enjoying the moment."

"Then let us resolve to enjoy this one," Tucker suggested and nudged Jocelyn with his elbow. "What are you going to have to eat tonight?"

"I don't know. What looks good?" She reached for her menu.

"Everything."

"That narrows the choice a lot," she mocked lightly.

While they good-naturedly bickered back and forth

over the selections, the waiter came to take their drink order. When he returned, each had settled on their final choice: baked chicken for Jocelyn; Yankee pot roast for Tucker; and stuffed pork chops for Obediah. Both Tucker and Obediah chose a green salad for starters, but Jocelyn opted for a cup of black bean soup.

Tucker watched her take the first spoonful. When she dipped her spoon in the second time, he sighed in envy. "I never have been able to master that."

"Master what?" she asked, not following him.

"Soup." He nodded at her cup. "My mom always told me soup should be seen and not heard. No matter how I tried, I always managed to slurp mine."

"So do I, when it's too hot," she admitted and idly glanced at the couple being escorted to an empty table. A chill ran up her spine when she recognized Maude Farnsworth and her husband, the staid and stalwart Judge Davis Osgood Farnsworth.

Her first impulse was to sink a little lower in her chair. The desire strengthened when Maude sat in a chair directly facing their table.

"Is something wrong?" Obediah inquired, his inspecting glance running over her.

"No." Jocelyn rushed the answer, then tried to cover the haste of it. "I was just thinking about . . ." She scrambled to find a safe topic. There was only one that came to mind. After all, what was safer than "Santa Claus and some of the things you've said"?

"That's funny." Tucker's glance was warm with surprise. "I was just thinking about that, too."

"You were?" Jocelyn practically trembled with relief, eager to have him do the talking and take any focus from her. "What was bothering you?"

"I don't know if *bothering* is the right word, but . . ." Tucker stopped and started again, his brow furrowed by thought. "I remember all that you told us about the original St. Nick, Obediah, but I have trouble making this leap from Santa to God. Yet you seem to do it without any effort at all." As always, his words were accompanied by an expansive gesturing of his hands.

"Perhaps you should ask yourself why the so-called myth of Santa Claus has managed to survive for some fifteen centuries," Obediah suggested instead.

"That's a darned good question," Tucker stated, his frown deepening. "I'm not sure I know the answer to it, though."

"Then maybe you need to ask yourself instead, who has kept it alive?" The soft inflection held a note of wisdom. It shone in his eyes like a warm and comforting light in the darkness.

"You're right." Tucker lowered his fork. "Children only know what they're told by their parents. Which means it's the parents who have perpetuated the legend of Santa Claus. Not just the parents, either," he added on further thought. "But adults in general."

"Why do you suppose they would do that?" Obediah prompted with a marvelous innocence in his expression, as always, leading them in the direction he wanted them to go.

"I can think of one good reason. Santa is the best

marketing gimmick to come along in this century,"
Tucker stated cynically and dug into his salad. "During the holidays, he pitches more products than
Michael Jordan."

"But it isn't Santa the salesman we love," Jocelyn
protested, a little louder than she planned.

She darted a quick, furtive glance at the Farnsworths' table and instantly jerked it away when she
caught Maude staring in her direction, looking
slightly puzzled and uncertain. Tension gripped the
muscles around her heart, her anxiety level
increasing.

"You know, that's true, Jonesy." Tucker emphasized his argument by waving his fork at her. "Even
while we're sitting in front of the television, smiling
at some commercial where a fella in a Santa suit sells
us razors or perfumes, a part of us knows the real
Santa Claus wouldn't do that." He paused and
laughed at himself. "Did you hear what I just said?
The *real* Santa Claus. Like he actually exists."

"Perhaps in your heart, he still does." Somewhere
in Obediah's words there was a hint of challenge.

"I don't know if I'd go that far," Tucker countered
dryly and used his knife to cut a wedge of tomato
into bite-sized pieces. "Still, I can't help remembering
that only a minute ago I could have spoken up and
told that little boy Brian who you really were. But
when you started pretending to be Santa, I just stood
by and watched. In fact, I got a real kick out of the
way he reacted. Which doesn't make sense because

when you think about it, it was kind of a dirty trick to pull on him."

"Why would you think that?" Jocelyn frowned. "It wasn't a dirty trick."

"What else would you call it?" Tucker speared the bite of tomato on his fork. "Sooner or later the kid will find it's really his parents who have been playing Santa Claus all these years. And he's gonna be pretty darned disillusioned when he does, too," he stated emphatically.

"Were you?" Obediah wondered.

"In my case, by the time my folks got around to telling me the truth, I had pretty well figured it out on my own." Tucker glanced at Jocelyn in silent question.

"It was the same for me, too," she admitted, remembering the sadness and regret she had felt.

"Were you upset? Angry? Hurt?" Obediah prompted.

Tucker thought about that before answering. "I guess I was sorry more than anything."

Jocelyn only half listened to his answer, her thoughts backtracking to Tucker's previous comments. "If you think it's wrong for a child to believe in Santa Claus, why didn't you tell Brian the truth?"

"I never said it was wrong." Tucker gave her an indignant look.

"You don't seem to think it was right, either," she reminded him. "So why didn't you tell him?"

He shifted uneasily in his chair. "I don't know. It didn't seem like it would do any harm if he believed in Santa a little longer."

Another rich chuckle vibrated from Obediah's throat, the amused and deep sound drawing glances from the surrounding diners, including Maude Farnsworth. Jocelyn ducked her head and concentrated on finishing the last two spoonfuls of soup.

"I believe I detected a note of envy, Tucker," Obediah accused lightly.

"I wouldn't go so far as to say that," he protested, but he didn't deny it.

It was as if a light suddenly flashed on in Jocelyn's head, surprising a small, exultant laugh from her and blinding her to any thought of her grandmother's friend.

"That's it, isn't it?" Jocelyn looked at Obediah in amazement. "No matter how grown-up we might be or how much we know better, a part of us still longs to believe in Santa Claus. No, it's more than that," she realized. "In our hearts, we still believe in the goodness of Santa Claus. That's what he symbolizes, isn't it? Goodness—for goodness' sake. That's why we are so determined to keep his spirit alive, isn't it?"

"Well, I'll be darned," Tucker murmured. "That is it."

There was something beatific in the smile that beamed from Obediah's face. "If you take that thought a step farther, then you have to wonder where it originated. Did it begin with that long-ago bishop from Myra called Nicholas? Or was he emulating the One he served? Is it possible that God put this desire in our hearts?"

Eyes widening, Tucker laid down his fork and sat back in his chair. "Now, that's a profound thought."

"If He did do that," Obediah went on, "then it would be perfectly natural to wonder why He would want us to keep alive the child inside us."

Out of nowhere, Jocelyn pulled a verse from the Scriptures. "And Jesus said, 'Truly, I say unto you, unless you turn and become like children, you will never enter the kingdom of heaven.'"

There was both amusement and amazement in the breath Tucker expelled. "My granddaddy always said there was nothing as powerful as the simple faith of a child."

Jocelyn smiled absently, distracted by her thoughts. "Maybe believing in Santa isn't so foolish after all."

"God often chooses the weak and foolish things of the world to confound the wise." With that, Obediah turned to the waiter approaching their table, a glass pot of steaming, freshly brewed coffee in his hand.

He stopped at their table. "Would any of you care for a refill?"

"I would." Obediah pushed his cup closer.

"Yes, please." Jocelyn held out her cup as well.

There, directly in her line of vision, sat Maude Farnsworth. Jocelyn was careful not to look at her, but she noticed the instant Maude touched her husband's arm, murmuring something to him. She couldn't hear what was said, but she could tell by the woman's body language that Maude was pointing her out to him.

With a vaguely bored swing of his head, Judge Davis

Farnsworth turned, stared, made some brief comment to Maude, and went back to eating his appetizer. Maude didn't appear entirely pleased with his response. Finally, she sighed and shrugged her thick shoulders, as if dismissing the whole thing from her mind.

It was an easy leap for Jocelyn to conclude that Maude thought she looked familiar. Unable to place her, she had asked the judge if he recognized her. Obviously he hadn't.

Mentally Jocelyn crossed her fingers, hoping her luck would hold a little longer.

Unfortunately, as a conversationalist, Judge Farnsworth left a great deal to be desired. Usually Maude's loquacity more than made up for his natural reticence. But not this night.

A half-dozen times during the meal, Jocelyn felt the scrutiny of Maude's eyes on her. There was absolutely no escape from it, short of moving to the opposite side of the table. She had to force herself to eat slowly and not rush through her food. Even then, she finished her dinner before Tucker and Obediah had eaten theirs.

When the waiter brought the dessert tray to the table, Jocelyn refused, eager for the meal to end. "Nothing for me, thanks."

Obediah patted his round stomach and sighed. "I couldn't eat another bite either."

"Are you sure?" Tucker gazed longingly at the slice of pecan pie on the dessert tray.

"Very," Jocelyn stated. Besides, it's getting late."

He looked at his watch and blinked in surprise. "It is, isn't it?"

"Anything for you, sir?" The waiter directed the question at Tucker. "Pie? A slice of cake?"

With a look of regret, Tucker shook his head. "Just the check, thanks."

"Right away, sir."

True to his word, the waiter returned promptly with it. When he placed it before Tucker, Obediah immediately objected. "I'll take that."

"Nope." Tucker scooped it up and dug through his pockets, searching for his wallet. "After all these years, it's high time I treated you to something more substantial than cookies and milk."

Flashing Obediah a quick grin, he extracted a credit card from his wallet and handed it to the waiter.

Jocelyn chafed inwardly at this additional delay, a delay made worse when she saw Maude rise from her chair and head toward the powder room. The seconds crawled along as slowly as the traffic around the Beltway during rush hour.

At last, Tucker signed the credit card slip, pocketed his copy, and stood when she pushed her chair back. Maude had yet to return to her table. Jocelyn wasn't sure if that was a good sign or a bad one.

"Merry Christmas, Mr. Santa," the young boy Brian called from his table.

"Merry Christmas, Brian." Obediah waved to him.

Anxious to leave before Maude came back, Jocelyn didn't take the time to glance at the young family. As swiftly as decency allowed, she crossed the dining area and went straight to the coatrack. Too late, she noticed the entrance to the powder room was directly to her left.

"Let me help you with that." Tucker took the plaid jacket from her fumbling fingers and held it for her.

As Jocelyn slid an arm into the second sleeve, Maude came out of the powder room. For an instant they were face to face. After no more than a split second's hesitation, Jocelyn turned away, straining for an air of nonchalance as she adjusted the front of her jacket.

"Gracious!" Maude exclaimed in open astonishment. "I almost didn't recognize you in that wig. What are you doing here? I—"

"I beg your pardon." Calling on whatever gram of acting skill she possessed, Jocelyn gave her a blank look.

From behind her shoulder, Tucker said, "Don't tell me you know Jonesy? Talk about a small world; this is definitely it."

"Jonesy?" Startled by the name, Maude jerked her glance to Tucker when he moved to stand beside Jocelyn while casually shrugging into his coat.

"Are you from Iowa as well?" Obediah inquired, a model of innocent interest.

"Of course not!" Maude looked aghast at the thought.

"If you're not from Iowa, then how do you know Jonesy?" Tucker wore an exaggerated frown of bewilderment.

"I think she's mistaken me for someone else." Jocelyn strove to change the texture of her voice, altering its pitch and adding an edge to it. "It's this face of mine. Somebody's always telling me I look like their cousin or their niece or somebody." On impulse, she reached out and patted Maude's arm. It was an alien gesture, one Jocelyn Wakefield would never do. "Don't let it bother you, honey. It happens all the time," Jocelyn declared, then glanced at her companions. "Are we ready?"

"If you are." Donning his homburg, Obediah stepped to the door, opening it for Jocelyn.

Maude's mouth worked, but no sound came from it when Jocelyn crossed to the door with Tucker right on her heels. She didn't draw an easy breath until she was outside and the door had closed solidly behind her. She paused, her legs momentarily turning rubbery with relief. That call had been a little too close. Even worse were the suspicions it could have aroused in Tucker.

Up the block, a yellow taxi pulled away from the curb after depositing its passengers at the entrance to another restaurant. When Obediah hailed it with an overhead wave of his arm, the cab swung toward him, the twin beams of its headlights punching holes in the night's shadows.

To Jocelyn, the cab offered immediate escape— escape from any comments or questions Tucker might ask, ones she might find awkward to answer.

"Would you mind if I shared that taxi with you, Obediah?"

"I would be delighted—"

"Taxi? But my car's just up the street." A surprised and confused Tucker jerked a hand toward the parking lot.

"I know—" Jocelyn began.

Tucker interrupted before she could voice a refusal. "I thought we'd go see the Mall by night, with all the lights shining and—"

She shook her head. "It's late, Tucker."

"It's the shank of the night," he insisted with a coaxing smile.

"Not for an Iowa girl used to going to bed with the chickens," she lied and felt guilty about it.

On the verge of arguing that point, Tucker appeared to change his mind. "How about tomorrow? We could—"

"I'm going home tomorrow," Jocelyn told him, then added, "Early."

"Too early for breakfast?" His smile was quick and hopeful, the kind difficult to resist.

"Yes." She had trouble meeting his eyes.

There was an instant of silence that Jocelyn found painfully awkward. She was half-afraid Tucker would try to talk her into changing her mind. She was wrong.

"I guess . . . this is good-bye, then." He held her gaze, a longing in his eyes tinged with sadness and regret.

"Yes." This was harder than she had expected it to be. Almost painful. Jocelyn had the awful feeling that she really would never see him again.

His mouth quirked in that familiar wry smile. "I'm going to remember this day the rest of my life, Jonesy.

You're one in a million. Make that a zillion." He held out his hand.

"So are you," she murmured through the lump in her throat and started to take his hand.

At the last second, she stepped closer, lifting a hand to his cheek and rising up those few inches to lightly press her lips against his in a warm but fleeting kiss.

When she started to pull away, Tucker hooked a hand behind her waist. "Oh, no, you don't. If you're gonna kiss me good-bye, it's gonna be for real."

He folded her into his arms, his mouth coming down to claim hers in a kiss full of need and desire. There was no coaxing, no persuasion—just raw, honest emotion—on his part and on hers. She was shaken by it, shaken by both the power of it and the glory. There was a feeling of completeness and rightness that Jocelyn knew she would never find again.

"Jonesy, don't go." He rubbed his mouth over her lips, her cheek, and the lobe of her ear.

For a moment, she was tempted. "I have to."

Blindly she twisted out of his arms and bolted for the cab. Obediah held the door open for her. She ducked into the rear seat and slid to the far side, a hand already reaching up to wipe at a tear trickling down her cheek.

CHAPTER 15

After Obediah had bundled himself into the cab, the driver slid open the dividing glass window. "Where to, please?" he inquired, his English carrying the thick accent of Pakistan.

Before Jocelyn could supply the address of her hotel, Obediah spoke up, "We'll settle that in a moment. For now, just drive away, please."

"Drive away," the driver repeated, startled by this unusual request. "But which way, my friend."

"Straight ahead for now."

"If that is what you wish." With a high shrug of his shoulders, the driver squared around to face the front.

As the taxi pulled onto the street, Jocelyn stole a

quick glance out the rear window. Tucker stood at the curb, watching them, his hands thrust deep in his pockets, giving his shoulders a slight droop. His face was in shadow, but she had no trouble at all imagining the pain that would have been in his eyes, the same heart-squeezing kind she felt.

"It hurts to leave him, doesn't it?" Obediah observed gently.

Because it was true, Jocelyn had to discount the effect of it. "I'll get over it." She dragged her gaze back to the front, avoiding Obediah's astute eyes.

"Of course you will." But he didn't sound any more convinced of that than she felt. "You do realize that Tucker is very sincere about his feelings for you."

"You mean his feelings for Jonesy," she corrected stiffly.

"Then you don't think he would feel the same if he found out who you really are," Obediah surmised.

"Do you?" she challenged, conscious of the ache that had crept into her voice.

"It doesn't matter what I think," he replied softly.

"You're right," she admitted and released a weighty sigh.

"I believe there is a more important question that you need to consider, though," Obediah ventured.

"What's that?" Jocelyn asked with disinterest, her attention turned inward on the emptiness she felt.

"Whether you want to spend the rest of your life wondering if Tucker could care as much for you as he does Jonesy."

The question was like a knife slicing her open to

a whole host of new hurts. "Are you saying you think I should go back there and tell him who I am?" Jocelyn demanded in near anger.

"I merely believe it's something you should consider," Obediah replied. "Would it be so difficult to tell him the truth?"

"You don't understand, Obediah," Jocelyn murmured, her anger dissolving in weary resignation. "Tucker writes a column. A *political* column."

"You mean, he's a member of the press—therefore not someone to be trusted," he said, taking her comment to its logical conclusion.

"Not if you have an ounce of sense, you wouldn't," she countered.

"And you are, of course, very sensible."

Jocelyn detected a dry note of mockery in his voice and refused to be baited by it. Most of the time she was extremely sensible. This ridiculous masquerade had been the one completely senseless thing she had done in years. She wasn't about to compound that mistake with another.

When the cab stopped at an intersection to wait for the traffic light to change, she searched for street signs. "My hotel is downtown," she told Obediah, determined to direct the conversation to a topic other than Tucker. "Why don't you drop me off first?

"Do you think it's wise for you to spend a night alone in a hotel?"

"If that's a backhanded way of inviting me to spend the night at your hotel, the answer is thanks, but no thanks.'' She began digging through her pouch purse for the money to pay the cab fare.

"Actually I was going to suggest that it might be best if you returned to your grandmother's tonight," Obediah replied.

It sounded infinitely preferable to being alone in a sterile hotel room where everything was either bolted to the wall or wrapped in plastic. There was only one problem with that.

"Unfortunately, they aren't expecting me until tomorrow morning." Her fingers closed around the paper currency.

"That's easily remedied." Leaning forward, Obediah tapped the head of his cane on the glass partition.

"There's a pay phone at the next corner," he told the driver. "Would you pull over to it so the young lady can make a quick phone call?"

"I will pull over, but then you must tell me where it is you wish me to take you," the man replied.

"Of course." Obediah sat back in his seat, both hands once again resting atop his cane.

A cozy fire blazed cheerily in the parlor's hearth at Redford Hall, its flames dancing to the music that filled the room. The state-of-the-art entertainment system in the corner sat silent, but the lid to an old console cabinet was raised. Inside it, an ancient 78-rpm record went round and round on an equally ancient turntable while a lone speaker blared a scratchy but original rendition of Glenn Miller's "String of Pearls."

Bliss Wakefield sat at the room's cherry-wood game table, tapping a toe to the music while surveying the solitaire game spread out before her. After going through the deck a second time without finding a play, she pursed her lips in irritation and started through it again, this time reversing the order of the cards.

Dexter saw what she was doing the instant he entered the room. He carried the small serving tray with its two empty cups and a carafe of hot chocolate to the table. Removing one cup from the tray, he set it on a coaster conveniently located to her right.

"*That* is cheating, Madam." He poured cocoa from the carafe into her cup.

"I'm winning, aren't I?" She countered with unconcern.

"Cheating is not winning," he informed her.

"Oh, mind your own business," she grumbled. "Better yet," Bliss said on second thought, "find 'Tangerine' and put it on the record player."

"Must we listen to that wretched song *again?*" Dexter murmured in disdain, but he was already changing directions to do as she asked.

Before he had taken two steps, the telephone rang, the shrillness of it striking a discordant note with the orchestra's trombone and saxophone blend.

"Good heavens, who could be calling at this hour on Saturday night?" Bliss frowned, then flashed a worried look at Dexter. "You don't think something's happened to—"

Abandoning his usual slow and measured pace, Dexter crossed to the parlor extension and snatched up the receiver. Simultaneously Bliss rose from her chair, one hand at her throat and the other on the table, while she mentally braced herself for the worst.

"Redford Hall," Dexter declared, his delivery a bit quicker than normal. Two seconds later, the tension went out of him. "Yes, Mrs. Farnsworth."

Bliss mouthed the word *Maude* and sighed a relieved laugh, then thought better of it when Dexter went on the alert again.

"I'm sorry, Mrs. Farnsworth, but she has already retired for the evening," he said into the receiver, then cupped a hand over the mouthpiece and whispered loudly, "She wants to talk to Jocelyn." Just as quickly, he lifted his hand to reply, "Yes, it is a bit earlier than usual. May I take a message?" he inquired, then saw Bliss signaling to give her the phone. "Or would you care to speak to Madam?" Obtaining an affirmative response, he held out the phone to Bliss.

Leaving the solitaire deck on the table, she walked over to him, took the phone, then paused to draw in a deep, calming breath, then lifted the receiver to her ear.

"Hello, Maude. How are you?" she said smoothly.

"Fine." The woman's answer was as automatic as Bliss's question. "I was calling in hopes of speaking to Jocelyn, but Dexter tells me she has already gone to bed."

"That's hardly surprising after the incredible schedule she's had these last two weeks. The poor girl pushes herself much too hard."

"Of course. I hadn't considered that," Maude admitted, then laughed a bit self-consciously. "I probably shouldn't have called at all, but the strangest thing happened tonight. I knew Jocelyn would find it amusing."

"Maude, you cannot tell me that the strangest thing happened without also telling me what it is," Bliss declared with a strong sense of foreboding.

"The judge and I went out to dinner tonight and there was this woman in the restaurant. She looked so familiar—it bothered me that I couldn't place who she was. Then just as she was leaving, it hit me." She paused deliberately to build the suspense. "She looked exactly like Jocelyn. When I realized that she was wearing a wig, I was certain she was Jocelyn."

"Why on earth would you think Jocelyn would be dining alone in some restaurant when you knew she was spending the weekend with me?" Attack seemed a much wiser course of action to Bliss than a mere weak denial, but she exchanged a worried look with Dexter.

"Oh, she wasn't alone," Maude replied with utter conviction.

"She wasn't?" Bliss echoed in surprise, her concern escalating. "Who was she with, then?"

"Two men. I admit they didn't really look like Secret

Service types." At this new revelation from Maude, Bliss held the phone slightly away from her ear so Dexter could listen in. "In fact, one of them was about as far as you could get from that."

"What do you mean?" In her mind, Bliss was picturing various photographs of terrorists she'd seen in the newspapers and on television.

"He was an elderly man, an African-American with snow-white hair and a beard. He even pretended to be Santa Claus for some little boy who was there with his parents, so I'm told."

"Wait a minute. You thought you saw Jocelyn with some elderly black gentleman who was pretending to be Santa Claus? Maude, have you been drinking?" She wanted to laugh in relief.

"Don't be ridiculous," Maude protested indignantly. "I had one glass of wine with dinner and that is all."

"It doesn't sound like it to me."

"This is not the kind of thing I would make up," Maude insisted. Bliss had to agree with that; the woman had very little imagination. "And that woman I saw—her resemblance to Jocelyn was positively uncanny."

"I'll have to take your word for that, obviously." But Bliss had the uneasy feeling Maude had actually seen Jocelyn. However, it was the two men her granddaughter was seen with that troubled her the most. "You said she was with two men. What was the other one like?" she asked, then couldn't resist adding impishly, "One of Santa's elves?"

"Hardly. He was tall, and a bit on the scrawny side. He looked like a basketball player from the Midwest. Come to think of it, maybe he was."

"Why do you say that?"

"Because this girl—the one who looked so much like Jocelyn—was from Iowa," Maude explained.

"How do you know that?" Bliss clutched the phone a little closer. "Did you speak with her?"

"Of course I did," Maude declared, sounding faintly annoyed by the question.

"How embarrassing it must have been for you when you realized you made a mistake," Bliss inserted quickly, determined to put the woman off her stride.

"In a way, it was. Unfortunately I didn't get to talk to her all that long."

"Which is probably just as well. But I am so glad you called, Maude," Bliss stated airily. "You're right. Jocelyn will find this most amusing when I tell her about it tomorrow morning."

"Yes, well, it is getting late. I won't keep you," Maude murmured as if it had suddenly occurred to her that she would be the butt of their humor.

"Give my regards to the judge," Bliss said and echoed Maude's good-bye, then hung up.

"She saw Jocelyn," Dexter guessed.

"Yes. But that isn't what worries me." Bliss nibbled at a fingertip.

Dexter nodded in solemn agreement. "It's the two men."

"Neither one sounded like Gregory Peck to me."

Sighing in concern, she clasped both hands tightly together. "What if they kidnapped her, Dexter?"

"I told you this whole thing was dangerous."

"I don't need to hear that, Dexter," Bliss flared in irritation. "If Gregory Peck were standing here, he would be assuring me that everything was fine, that I was worrying without any cause."

He pulled himself up to his full height. "If things had gone according to plan, Madam, Gregory Peck would not be standing here with you. He would be with Miss Jocelyn," he informed her coolly.

"Shut up and go lift that needle off the record," she ordered, impatient with his irrefutable logic. "That scratch-scratching is driving me crazy."

With a head-high pose of wounded dignity, Dexter went to the console, picked up the player's arm, and swung it over to its stand. The telephone rang again, and they both jumped.

"They wouldn't call here to make their ransom demand, would they?" Bliss stared at the phone, the tips of her fingers pressed to her lip.

"I doubt that very much, Madam." Dexter calmly lifted the receiver. "Redford Hall." He swung back to Bliss, a smile transforming his face. "It's Miss Jocelyn," he whispered in utter relief.

Bliss snatched the phone from him. "Are you all right, Jocelyn? We have been so worried sick about you. Where are you?" The questions rushed from her unchecked.

"I'm fine, Gog," came the quiet reply. Unusually quiet, to Bliss's ears.

"Are you sure?" She wasn't convinced. "You sound upset."

"I'm just in a hurry. The cab's waiting and—I'm calling to let you know I'm on my way back. Ask Dexter to unlock the gate for me."

"Now?" She repeated in surprise. "But I thought you weren't planning to come back until morning."

"I've changed my mind, Gog, and I don't have time to explain everything now."

"All right." Bliss accepted that for the moment. "What time will you be here?"

"I'm not sure. Soon."

"But Dexter will have to distract—"

"Obediah is going to take care of that," Jocelyn inserted. "Dexter just needs to unlock the gate."

"Who is Obediah?" Bliss frowned at the strange name.

"A friend. Look, I'll explain everything when I get there, Gog. I've got to go now."

There was the click on the line; the connection was broken. Bliss lowered the phone and turned to Dexter. "She's coming back tonight instead of in the morning. You'll need to unlock the gate right away."

"Of course. But who is Obediah?"

"I have no idea," she said and sighed in bewilderment. "A friend, she said. I hope she's right."

Two blocks from Redford Hall, Jocelyn signaled the driver to pull over to the side. "I'll get out here," she told Obediah. "Give me about a five-minute head start before you come."

"Five minutes." He pushed back his coat sleeve to check the time on his watch, then grinned at her. "This is very exciting. I feel like a commando."

"Are you sure you can handle this, Obediah?" she asked in concern. "I don't want you to do anything that might get you arrested."

"Not to worry." The amusement in his voice matched the big smile he wore. "There are advantages to both my age and my color. They will be quick to notice an old and bewildered black man wondering about the street in front of your grandmother's house. And they will be equally quick, regardless of how well dressed I might appear, to point me in the right direction. I will simply seem to be a bit slow and addled in understanding the location of the address I am supposedly seeking. There won't be any trouble, I assure you of that."

"I hope not." Jocelyn wished she felt that confident, but too many things had already gone wrong. In fact, her escape from Redford Hall had been about the only thing that had gone precisely as planned. She stepped out of the taxi, then swung back to peer inside. "Be careful, Obediah."

His smile became one of gentle reproof. "You need to stop being so fearful."

"I can't help being worried for you," she replied, aware that he wouldn't be in this situation if it weren't for her.

"Oh, I wasn't referring to myself."

"Then who?" Jocelyn frowned. "I'm not afraid for myself, if that's what you think."

"I'm sorry to disagree with you, but it's very apparent you are afraid," he informed her.

"Of what?" The challenge in her voice was the equivalent of a denial.

"You're afraid if Tucker finds out who you are, his feelings toward you will change. That's why you won't tell him, isn't it? It doesn't really have anything to do with how he makes his living."

He saw way too much, definitely more than Jocelyn wanted to face. Again she chose the coward's way out.

"This isn't a good time to discuss this, Obediah," she said and glanced at her watch. "Remember, I need five minutes."

With that, she closed the door and moved quickly into the street's deepest shadows. But the darkness couldn't hide the truth in his words. It nagged at her all the way to Redford Hall.

Concealed near some bushes, Jocelyn waited until Obediah occupied the attention of both agents on duty. Another time, she might have admired the laudable acting job he did, convincing the agents that his taxi driver had taken him to the wrong address and he now required directions to the correct one, directions he had great difficulty getting straight. But she was too distracted by her own thoughts and the necessity of getting through the gate without being seen.

Hugging the shadows, Jocelyn reached the gate and offered up a silent prayer that Dexter had managed to slip outside and unlock it. The gate swung silently inward at the touch of her hand. She slipped through the opening and closed the gate behind her. From there it was a quick dash to the carriage house and the safety of the underground passage.

When she reached the secret stairwell, her steps slowed considerably. Jocelyn made the long climb with a leadenness of spirit she was reluctant to examine. On the top step, she paused to gather herself for the barrage of questions she knew would be waiting for her.

In that, Jocelyn wasn't wrong. Her grandmother barely gave her a chance to step into the room before she started in.

"Thank heavens, you are all right." Bliss clutched at Jocelyn's hands, squeezing them in a mixture of relief and concern. "You have no idea how worried we've been about you, Jocelyn."

"There was really no need. I'm fine." Her smile was quick and forced.

Dexter's eyebrow went up when he took note of her attire. "Where is your jogging suit?"

"At the hotel, along with everything else." Pulling her hands free, she turned away from both of them and began searching out the pins that secured her wig in place. "There didn't seem any point in going back for them. People don't go jogging this late at night."

"But someone at the hotel is bound to wonder what happened to you," he protested.

"Let them wonder," her grandmother declared, an upflung hand dismissing such concerns as inconsequential. "They'll never be able to trace any of the items to Jocelyn. This Obediah person is another matter. Who is he?"

"Obediah is a wonderfully kind gentleman I met at the Lincoln Memorial." With all the pins removed, Jocelyn lifted off the wig and discarded it on the dresser top.

"He doesn't know who you are, does he?" Bliss hurriedly picked up the wig and stuffed it in a pink plastic bag.

"He recognized me right away. You should remember him, Gog." Jocelyn unclipped her own hair and shook it free. "He was that elderly black man with the white beard who was part of that group you guided through the White House last week."

"The one who asked you all those questions about the Christmas tree and this year's theme?" she said in surprise.

"The same."

"Good heavens," Bliss murmured, then stared at Jocelyn again. "Then who was the other man with you?"

Jocelyn tensed. "What other man?"

"The one Maude saw you with at the restaurant."

"Maude called you?" she asked, stalling for time while she decided whether to tell her grandmother about Tucker. And if she did, what?

"Right before you phoned."

Jocelyn released a defeated sigh. "I thought we had convinced her that she had made a mistake."

"You did. That's beside the point, though. You still haven't told me who that man from Iowa was."

"He's from Kansas, not Iowa," she corrected automatically.

"Kansas, shmansas, I don't care where he's from," Bliss declared in exasperation. "I want to know who he is."

After all the lies she had told already today, Jocelyn realized she didn't want to tell anymore. "Grady Tucker."

The name drew the reaction she expected. "Grady Tucker. *The* Grady Tucker?" Bliss looked aghast.

"The same," Jocelyn admitted, then whirled on Dexter and pointed a quick finger at him. "He was not Gregory Peck, so don't even think it."

He looked profoundly wounded. "It never crossed my mind."

"Don't tell me *he* recognized you, too." Bliss stared, a hand pressed to her breastbone, as if preparing herself for another blow.

"No. No, he didn't." For some crazy reason, Jocelyn was sorry about that.

"Oh, dear," Bliss murmured in sympathy. "Your day didn't go very well, did it?"

"Sometimes it was more fun than I expected. And sometimes it was miserable. But I did learn one thing, Gog." Her mouth curved in a sad smile. "There is no freedom in pretending to be somebody else. I thought there would be, but there isn't."

"You poor dear." Bliss wrapped a comforting arm around her. "I'm so sorry."

"So am I," she admitted and managed a smile. "If you don't mind, I'd really rather not talk about it now. It's been a long day, and I'm really tired."

"Of course you are. And you'll be surprised how amusing this will all seem tomorrow morning after a good night's sleep."

"Sure." But Jocelyn knew better.

CHAPTER 16

A sharp November wind sent a dozen tattered leaves scuttling along the sidewalk before trapping them against the black iron fence that surrounded the North Lawn of the White House. Beyond the bars, bright yellow mums circled the fountain in the lawn's center, but their cheery color paled beneath the gray gloom of the sky's thick cloud cover.

Tucker turned up his collar to ward off the cold bite of winter's breath on his neck, then stuffed his hands back in his pockets and stared glumly at the second-floor windows of the presidential mansion, the first family's living quarters.

Footsteps approached his position, their measured cadence accompanied by the tap-tapping of a cane on the concrete walk. They stopped about a yard away. The white-bearded figure of a short, stout man in a homburg, dark topcoat, and a red wool muffler filled the left side of his vision. Glancing at the man, Tucker couldn't have explained why, but he wasn't at all surprised to see Obediah.

Obediah returned his look with an expression of warm understanding. "I thought I would find you somewhere around here," he stated by way of a greeting.

"Corny, isn't it? Wanting to be on the street where she lives."

Tucker turned back to gaze at the White House, but without the sense of elation Lerner and Loewe had written about in their song.

Obediah smiled in understanding. "I wouldn't call it crazy."

"She hasn't called me." Tucker continued to gaze at the second-floor windows, his mouth turned down at the corners. "She has my phone number, both at home and at the paper, and she hasn't called. When I didn't hear from her Sunday, I wasn't surprised. Monday I didn't expect a call either. Not even Tuesday. But yesterday . . ." He broke off the sentence with a forlorn sigh and hunched his shoulders a little deeper in the coat. "I guess she isn't going to call. I really thought she would, Obediah."

"Perhaps she needs a little more time." The wind snatched at the breath cloud that came from Obediah's mouth when he spoke.

Tucker shook his head at that possibility. "The

more days that go by, the colder her feet will get, and she'll talk herself out of calling at all.''

"In a way, it's understandable that she hasn't called.'' Obediah glanced idly at the White House. "She truly believes that when you learn who she is, your feelings toward her will change.''

"Well, she's wrong,'' Tucker stated half angrily.

"What are you going to do about it?'' Obediah countered, studying Tucker with an inspecting side glance, a glint of amusement lurking in his coal dark eyes.

"What can I do?'' Tucker lifted his shoulders in a bewildered shrug, then pulled a hand out of his pocket and gestured in the direction of the White House. "That isn't the kind of house where you can just walk up and ring the doorbell and ask to have a word with the man's daughter. I thought about calling her, but this isn't something you want to talk about over a telephone. It would be awkward enough face to face.''

"In other words, unless she contacts you, you're giving up. Is that what you're saying?''

His head came up at that, his glance slashing to Obediah. Then he realized what the old man was up to and smiled crookedly. "You know better than that. Trouble is, I can't figure out how to see her. You have to go through so many layers just to get an appointment with her—operators, secretaries, assistants. She could block me anywhere along the line, and there wouldn't be anything I could do about it, either.''

"I see the problem," Obediah murmured with a thoughtful nod.

"So do I." Sighing, Tucker once again focused his attention on the mansion's imposing north facade. "She's better insulated than most houses. There's only one place where she isn't surrounded by staff and security, and that's right up there." He nodded toward the second-floor windows as a gust of wind whipped through his hair, raising tufts of it. He slanted a grin at Obediah. "It's too bad you aren't Santa Claus. If you were, you could stuff me in your bag, take me down the chimney, and leave me there."

"But if I were, I could only do that on Christmas Eve. Do you really want to wait that long?" Obediah countered, an impish gleam dancing in his eyes.

"Not hardly," Tucker admitted and released another sigh. "But I don't know any other way to get from here to there."

"Instead of trying to make a frontal assault, perhaps you need to think of a way to outflank her," Obediah suggested.

"You're looking at a writer, not a military tactician, Obediah. If you have something in mind, you'll have to speak plainer than that," Tucker told him.

"All right. How well do you know the president?"

"Not as well as some of the reporters in the White House press corps, but I have spoken to him a few times. I guess you could say we have a nodding acquaintance." Pausing, he cocked his head to one side, his gaze narrowing on Obediah in sharp suspicion. "I hope you aren't suggesting that I go to the president and ask for his daughter's hand in marriage. It's bad enough that *she* thinks I'm Mr. Looney Tunes without—"

Obediah's hearty laugh broke across his words. "No, something a bit more subtle might be more effective," he replied. "After all, your desire for the time being is simply to gain access to the second floor in order to speak privately with Jocelyn. Isn't that correct?"

"Yes." Tucker's frown deepened as he tried to guess what Obediah had in mind.

"Then you merely have to find a way to accomplish that."

"Which is easier said than done."

"True," Obediah agreed. "Members of the public aren't allowed into the upper floors of the White House—only invited guests of the president and his family. Which is a pity when you consider how many people would love to see some of its historical areas, such as the Treaty Room and, most especially, Lincoln's Bedroom."

"Yeah, I wouldn't mind seeing it myself." It was an offhand response, made without a lot of conscious thought.

"Really? Have you ever asked anyone if they would show it to you?"

The question surprised him. "No."

"Maybe you should." Obediah turned back the cuff of his coat sleeve, glancing at the face of his wristwatch. "Gracious, look at the time. I'll have to be going or I'll be late for my appointment. Good luck to you, Tucker." He touched his fingers to his hat brim in a farewell gesture. "And give my regards to Jocelyn when you see her."

"You talk as though you think I will see her." It was almost an accusation.

Obediah's smile widened a notch. "You are a very resourceful man, Tucker. I have every confidence in you. Good day." He walked off with a short, brisk stride, swinging his cane to land ahead of him.

Tucker watched him for a run of several seconds, then broke into a smile, remembering that day on the South Lawn when he had learned that certain members of the president's staff regarded him as a good-luck charm. Maybe this one time the rabbit's foot could get lucky.

"You know," he murmured to himself, "Obediah not only would make a good Santa Claus, but he'd be a darned good farmer, too. After he plants a seed, he gives it just enough water to germinate."

Still smiling, Tucker set off in the direction of the mansion's famous West Wing, where both the president's Oval Office and the Press Room were located.

By White House standards, the press facility was relatively new, built during the Nixon administration, in space that had formerly been the site of President Franklin Roosevelt's swimming pool. As always, when there was no crisis on the horizon, there were a couple of dozen reporters lounging about the room waiting for a story, preferably the kind that garnered headlines. When Tucker wandered into the Press Room, they were quick to note the relative stranger in their midst.

"Hey, Tucker, what's going on here?" one of them chided.

"Yeah, Tucker," Cleve Barnes of the *Post* chimed in. "This is the second time in less than two weeks that you've showed up here. What's the deal?"

"Running low on ideas for your column, are you?" another jibed.

"If I was, this is the last place I'd come to look for any new ones," Tucker countered and let his glance sweep the room. "I don't even see any good old ones."

"That should shut you up, Fisher," Cleve joked, then turned back to Tucker. "Seriously, what brings you here?"

"Some personal business," he replied, deliberately vague in his answer. "Maybe you can help me. Who's the best person to ask if you need a favor? On the staff, I mean."

"How big a favor?" The reporter studied him with heightened interest.

"Big," Tucker admitted ruefully.

"Let me guess," Cleve grinned suddenly. "Your parents are coming from Kansas and they want to meet the president."

Tucker rubbed the back of his neck and grinned. "It's just about as bad as that. Might be even worse."

"Lots of luck, Tucker." Cleve shook his head in amusement.

"Seriously, who should I talk to?" he persisted.

"Paula Landry, I guess," he replied with a shrug. "At least she'll hear you out before she starts laughing."

"I can't ask for more than that. Where do I find her?"

"I'll show you."

Twenty minutes later Tucker was ushered into Paula Landry's small office. By then, he had learned she was one of many deputy assistants to the press secretary, but one with intelligence, ambition, and political savvy—a combination guaranteed to carry her higher.

"Hello, Tucker. It's a pleasure to meet you." Tall and a little on the chunky side, the dark-rooted blonde woman greeted him with a firm handshake before motioning him toward the chair in front of her desk. "I know you've heard this before, but I enjoy your column."

"Thanks. And thanks for taking the time to see me, too." He lowered himself into the chair.

"No trouble." Her smile was warm and automatic, the right blend of friendliness and courtesy. "What can I do for you?"

"This is kind of embarrassing, Ms. Landry—" Tucker began.

"Paula, please," she inserted.

"Paula," he echoed. "I don't know quite how to say this, so I'll just blurt it out and hope for the best."

Her smile deepened, producing attractive dimples n her cheeks. "You do that, Tucker."

"It's like this, Paula," he began, then changed course and started over. "The simple truth of the matter is that I'd like to see the Lincoln Bedroom. Not just see it. Stand in it." Brief as it was, Tucker observed the flicker of surprise in her expression. Actually it was closer to astonishment. But Paula Landry was quick to mask it. "Now, I know it's off limits to the public, but . . . I was hoping you might be able to arrange to get me the necessary permission. I know it's the kind of request that has to go through channels. And if it can't be done, I understand that, too. But I figured if I never asked, I'd never know whether it could be done or not. And let's face it; the worst that can happen is that you will tell me no'."

There was silent laughter in the burst of air that came from her. "I have to be honest, Tucker," she confessed. I thought you were going to ask me for something simple like an autographed picture of the president, personalized for your aunt Sally. Lincoln's Bedroom."

"It's kind of a wild request, isn't it?" he admitted with a crooked, self-conscious smile.

"Let's put it this way: if anyone other than you had asked me this, I would be giving a flat 'no' right now. But . . . considering it is you, I'll make a couple calls and get back to you."

"I appreciate that, Paula. I mean that." Tucker dug through his pockets and finally came up with a

business card. Rising, he passed it to her. "That's g⟨
my apartment number on it, too. I do most of m⟨
writing at home, so you can reach me there just abou⟨
any time."

"I'll let you know when I have an answer," sh⟨
promised.

"No hurry," he lied.

Molly greeted Tucker with a whining howl of jo⟨
when he entered the apartment. She was a one-do⟨
motion machine, twisting and winding about his leg⟨
all dancing feet and whipping tail. When he took th⟨
leash off the wall hook, the dog leaped in ecstasy an⟨
yelped some more.

"Good golly, Molly, will you sit down?" Tucker pus⟨
ed her forepaws off his chest. "I'm never gonna ge⟨
this thing hooked to your collar if you keep bouncin⟨
around like some pogo stick with a tail."

Whining, the dog went down on all fours an⟨
plopped her rump on the floor, quivering with eage⟨
ness. As he snapped the leash to her collar, the tel⟨
phone rang. Even though Tucker knew the answerin⟨
machine would intercept the call after a specifie⟨
interval, the ringing of a phone was something h⟨
had never been able to ignore. And Molly knew i⟨
She galloped to the phone, barking with impatience⟨

"I'm not going to be able to hear myself talk if yo⟨
don't stop that noise," Tucker warned. With an effor⟨
the dog brought the barking down to an anxiou⟨

whine when he picked up the receiver. "Tucker here."

"Tucker. It's Wally Hamilton."

The president's deputy chief of staff. Torn between hooting with laughter and sitting down in surprise, Tucker opted for a strangled, "Wally. What can I do for you?" he added carefully, just in case this wasn't about his request.

"You have that backwards. It's what I can do for you," the man countered with smug satisfaction. "I spoke with Paula Landry a few minutes ago. Have you got a minute?"

"A minute? I've got a whole slew of them." This time Tucker did sit down.

"The president would like to speak with you. Can you hang on?"

"Sure." He settled back in the chair. When Molly saw that, she lay down with a groan and rested her nose between her paws to gaze at him with sad eyes.

The line went silent for a long stretch of seconds. Then the strong, confident voice of the president was speaking in his ear. "Tucker, it's Hank Wakefield. How are you?"

"Fine, Mr. President. Just fine, thank you." At that moment, Tucker was certain he would get to see the Lincoln Bedroom. But somehow he had to also finagle a way to see Jocelyn in the process.

"I understand you are an admirer of Lincoln," the president said.

"That's one way of putting it, sir." Tucker was suddenly struck by the thought that, with any luck, he

was talking to his future father-in-law. It was enough
to tongue-tie anyone.

"You're right. Who isn't an admirer of Abe?" The
president agreed. "The man cast a long shadow—
and left big shoes to fill along the way. Wally tells me
you're interested in seeing the Lincoln Bedroom."

"I certainly am," he stated, then added quickly. "I
know it's an imposition—"

"Not at all." The president smoothly dismissed
that. "I'd be happy to show it to you. How would early
this evening work for you? I'll probably be wrapped up
here around six-thirty."

"Six-thirty will suit me just fine, sir."

In her combination sitting room and office, Jocelyn
sat at the Eleanor Roosevelt desk. Before her lay an
untouched stack of messages marked to her attention.
But she stared instead at a slip of paper that lay separately from them. A slip of paper with Tucker's
address and phone number written on it, in his own
hand.

She twisted her fingers together in her lap, trying
to work up the nerve to call him. Darkness welled
outside the room's windows. At this hour, Jocelyn
knew he'd be home. All she had to do was pick up
the phone and dial his number.

And say what?

That was the problem. She had rehearsed a dozen
different speeches and imagined a dozen different
reactions from Tucker, few of them positive. It was

those possible reactions that made her hesitate yet again.

Coward, she thought. The taunt was the goad she needed to reach for the telephone. It rang before her fingers touched it, and she nearly jumped out of her skin. Almost guiltily, she grabbed the receiver and carried it to her ear, hurriedly removing the pearl earring clipped to her lobe.

"Hello." Her voice sounded as strained as her nerves felt.

"Is that you, Jocelyn?"

"Yes. Hi, Dad," she said, instantly recognizing his voice.

"For a minute it didn't sound like you. Did you get my message?" he asked.

"It's probably here in this stack." She glanced at the pile. "I haven't gone through them yet. I only walked in a few minutes ago. Why? What's the problem?"

"No problem. I called earlier to let you know I'll be bringing someone over for drinks and a tour of the Lincoln Bedroom. You'll need to push dinner back an hour, maybe an hour and a half. But I forgot to mention that you need to make sure we have some Black Label on hand. While you're at it, call down and have the kitchen fix an appetizer tray. Nothing fancy."

"Will do." Jocelyn scratched a quick note to that effect on the pad next to the telephone. "What time?"

"Six-thirty, give or take."

"Consider it done," she promised. "By the way who—"

"Saunders is holding on the other line for me Jocelyn. I've got to run." The line went dead, the conversation cut short by the press of business as had happened countless other times—too many for her to regard this time as anything unusual.

Jocelyn started to sift through the messages to ascertain the identity of this guest, then noticed the time. It was already three minutes after six. There was the bar to check, the appetizers to be ordered, and a quick freshening up to do for herself.

In truth, Jocelyn couldn't summon any real curiosity about the person her father was bringing back to the White House with him. From experience, she knew it could be anyone from some top corporate executive to a party faithful, a senior adviser to a junior congressman. Whatever the case, her role was the same: meet and greet and make the necessary small talk. Part of her welcomed the distraction of a guest, knowing it would mean less time to think about Tucker.

Precisely at six-thirty-five, Jocelyn heard the distinctive sound of her father's voice coming from the stair case to the second floor. He rarely used the elevator eschewing it in favor of climbing the red-carpeted steps, insisting the exercise was good for him.

She cast a last inspecting glance over the Yellow Oval Room, always her father's choice for entertaining first-time guests to the family quarters. For all its formality, the drawing room was bright and cheery

and its access to the Truman Balcony offered a pan-
oramic view of the Mall with all its lighted monuments.

Assured that all was in readiness, Jocelyn turned
toward the door and ran a smoothing hand down the
front of her navy wool slacks, briefly concerned that
her attire might be too casual. That thought had
barely registered when she heard a second voice. It
zinged through her like a paralyzing electric shock.

Tucker. It sounded just like Tucker.

"It can't be," she whispered, certain it had been
wishful thinking on her part.

Then he walked through the doorway to the drawing room, all gorgeous six feet, four inches of him.
At the sight of this long and lanky man, it was as if
a pair of fists had seized her, choking off the air to
her lungs and squeezing her heart, silencing its beat.
She wanted to run—either from him or to him, she
wasn't sure. But it didn't matter. Her feet were rooted
to the floor.

Tieless, he was dressed casually but well in a camel
blazer and dark slacks, both tailored to enhance his
lean build. And his pockets didn't bulge with the
usual collection of oddities, giving a neatness to his
appearance.

She felt the touch of his glance and searched for
that initial flicker of recognition in his eyes. But there
was none. Impossible as it seemed, that hurt.

Her father greeted her with a warm, "I hope we
haven't kept you waiting long, Jocelyn."

"Not at all." Her voice was husky with the control she placed in it.

"I don't believe you two have met," he said, glancing at Tucker.

"Not formally," Tucker admitted with an easy smile. "But I don't imagine there's anyone in the country who wouldn't recognize you on sight, Miss Wakefield."

Jocelyn had the urge to lash out that *he* hadn't, but she managed to bite her tongue while her father made the needless introductions. When Tucker extended a hand in formal greeting, she coolly gave him only her fingers. But even that small contact ignited a heat that traveled all the way up her arm.

"I hope you don't mind me saying this, Miss Wakefield, but you're even more beautiful in the flesh. Your pictures don't do you justice," Tucker said with an artless smile.

She forced a laugh, working to keep the hurt out of it. "I remember in your column one time, that you said flattery was like chewing gum—something to be enjoyed but not swallowed."

His smile took on that familiar sheepish quality. "Now I'm the one who's flattered that you've read my column."

"It's become quite popular." As a compliment, hers had a sting of indifference to it. But Tucker didn't seem to notice.

"Amazing, isn't it?" he said, rubbing the back of his neck with that familiar self-conscious gesture of his.

What Jocelyn found amazing was his failure to recognize her. This from a man who had endlessly talked about marrying her. She had been a fool to think he had meant a single word of it. It made her furious. It was the kind of fury born out of the depths of pain.

The telephone rang. Jocelyn laid a restraining hand on her father's arm when he turned to answer it. "I'll get that," she told him, eager to escape from Tucker's presence before she did something really foolish—like hitting him smack in the face.

Again she unclipped her earring and lifted the receiver. "This is Jocelyn," she said into the mouthpiece.

"Jocelyn, it's Wally. I apologize for the interruption, but I need to talk to the president. He's there, isn't he?"

"Yes. Just a minute." Lowering the phone, she swung back toward her father. "Wally needs to speak with you."

"I'll be right there." He nodded, then smiled an apology to Tucker. "This shouldn't take long." He crossed to the extension and took the phone from Jocelyn. As he raised it to his ear, he covered the mouthpiece. "Jocelyn, why don't you go ahead and show Tucker the Lincoln Bedroom. I'll catch up with the two of you there."

Short of creating a scene, she had little choice but to agree. With teeth gritted behind her smile, she held out her hand, directing Tucker to the doorway.

"It's this way," she murmured.

With brisk, long strides, Jocelyn traversed the expansive hall, a pace designed to keep chitchat at the minimum. But Tucker wasn't so easily deterred as he loped effortlessly alongside her.

"Wasn't it Lady Bird Johnson who said, 'History thunders down the corridor at you'?" he remarked, looking around with interest. "Living here has to be a bit daunting at times."

"You get used to it after a while," she said with feigned indifference.

"Maybe," he conceded. "But I'll bet there are still times when it steps out and hits you where you are and who else has walked these halls."

There were, but Jocelyn wasn't about to admit it to Tucker. She crossed the East Sitting Hall, its lemon yellow rug absorbing the sound of their footsteps. With any other guest, she would have provided tidbits of information about the room and pointed out particular items of interest. But with Tucker, she had to work at merely appearing civil.

She opened the door to the Lincoln Suite, then stepped back to admit him. He walked by without so much as a glance in her direction, infuriating Jocelyn even more. She had half a notion to walk off and leave him to explore the room on his own, but the knowledge that her father would be joining them shortly sent her after him.

Light gleamed from the chandelier's frosted globes and sparkled onto the crystals that dripped from its curved arms. Around the spacious room, more Victorian-era lamps were lit, spreading a soft glow to every corner.

Tucker paused briefly in the room's center, his gaze

sweeping over the period furnishings and the framed portraits on the walls. Then he crossed to the massive rosewood bed adorned with lavish rococo carvings of birds, grape clusters, and flowers.

With a trace of awkwardness, he ran a hand over a curved arm that jutted from its ornate headboard. "So this is where Lincoln slept."

"As a matter of fact, there is no record that Lincoln ever slept in this bed, although both Presidents Theodore Roosevelt and Woodrow Wilson did, along with a host of other notables over the ensuing years," Jocelyn informed him coolly. "According to a newspaper article of Lincoln's time, this bed was actually in one of the mansion's guest rooms. It's believed to be part of the furniture Mary Todd Lincoln purchased for use in the White House."

"But Lincoln never slept here," Tucker repeated, staring at her as if to make certain he had heard correctly.

"No." Jocelyn took perverse delight in disabusing him of the notion. But truth forced her to add, "It's possible, I suppose, that he might have taken a nap in this room, since this was officially his office while he was president."

"This was his office and not his bedroom." He cocked his head, as if this was all news to him.

For a brief moment, Jocelyn had trouble believing that, then dismissed the entire thought. "You have to remember that until nineteen-oh-two, when the West Wing was built, the offices for the president and his staff were located here on the second floor."

"This is where he worked, then." Tucker looked about the room with new eyes.

"Yes." In spite of her irritation with him, Jocelyn warmed a little to the subject. "During the Civil War, maps covered the walls, charting the course of the war. The place was littered with dispatches, newspapers, mail, and endless requests from office-seekers and the like. Here, the first reading of the famous Emancipation Proclamation took place, as depicted in the engraving there by the mantel." She gestured to it, then crossed to one of the windows that overlooked the South Lawn, the Ellipse beyond it, and the floodlit obelisk of the Washington Monument. "From these windows, he could see the hills of secessionist Virginia and the partially finished monument to Washington."

Hands in his pant pockets, Tucker strolled over to gaze out the window at the Washington nightscape. After a moment, he turned back to survey the room again.

"This is all a big sham, isn't it?" he concluded flatly.

Jocelyn stiffened at his tone. "I beg your pardon."

"That's what it is—a sham." He pulled a hand from his pocket and gestured broadly to encompass their surroundings. "You call this the Lincoln Bedroom, but it was never his bedroom. And he never even slept in the bed."

"But it was a room used by Lincoln, one in which he spent a great deal of his time—probably more than in the room where he actually slept. Decisions of historical significance took place here. Simply because it has been converted to a guest bedroom doesn't change that," she argued. "Besides, it isn't Lincoln's bedroom; it is the Lincoln Bedroom, so named to honor a man who was inarguably one of our nation's greatest leaders."

Bowing his head, Tucker stared thoughtfully at the floor. "Let me see if I've got this right. You're saying that no matter how this room is furnished—whether it's with desks and maps and tables, or with a bed, bureaus, and chairs—it's still a room Lincoln once occupied."

"Exactly," she stated forcefully.

"In other words, the name someone chooses to call it is basically immaterial." He lifted his head, centering his gaze on her. "The room is still the same; just the trappings are different."

"That's right," Jocelyn replied, satisfied that she had at last made her point.

"So it's kinda' like you." A corner of his mouth quirked in wry amusement. "The person is the same whether the name happens to be Jones or Wakefield."

"You know who I am," Jocelyn breathed, the shock hitting her like a body blow.

His gently mocking smile chided her. "You didn't really believe that disguise would fool anybody for long, did you?"

"I—I—" She groped for a response, too stunned to notice when he wandered closer. In the end, she settled for anger to cover her confusion. "Who told you?" she demanded. "It was Obediah, wasn't it?"

"It isn't fair to accuse someone who isn't here to defend himself, Jonesy."

The lazy way he said the name and the warm light in his eyes melted some of her anger, and her defenses. Jocelyn fought to rebuild them.

"Don't call me that," she protested.

"Habit," Tucker said with a shrugging nod of his head, his smile widening and warming with intimacy. "And for your information, Obediah didn't reveal your secret to me. I figured it out for myself. When I confronted him with the truth, he did admit it. After all, you've gotta admit it was pretty hard to deny."

Out of desperation, Jocelyn stayed on the attack, conscious of her racing heart and fluttering stomach. "When did you know who I was? Not at the start?"

"No. You had me fooled at first," Tucker confessed and lifted a hand to trace a wave of strawberry blond hair with his fingertips. "It wasn't until *after* you bolted from my apartment that I saw the color photograph of you in the newspaper. From there, it was an easy step to put Jonesy and Jocelyn together."

She searched his hazel eyes, seeing the truth of his words clearly in their bright gold flecks. "Then you knew when . . ." she stopped, doubt rising.

"I met you at the Jefferson Memorial." He finished the sentence for her.

"Why didn't you tell me then?" she accused in frustration, thinking of all she had gone through since then.

"And have you start throwing up invisible walls

between us?'' Tucker raised a dubious eyebrow. "No
a chance.''

"But you backed off,'' Jocelyn remembered with a
sudden stab of pain. "After you realized who I really
was, you backed off.''

"Only enough to let you chase me,'' he replied
with a certain smugness.

"I didn't chase you.'' She was stunned that he could
think she had.

"Really?'' he mocked lightly. "Your memory may
not be so good, but mine is excellent. Let me remind
you that you were the one who kissed *me* outside the
restaurant. And when you did, I definitely didn't back
off from it. In fact, I came back for more.''

He tucked a finger under her chin, tilting it up.
His face dominated her vision, strong and virile, the
light of desire in his eyes. As before, Jocelyn moved
to meet the downward descent of his mouth.

Seconds later, she was wrapped in his arms, experi-
encing again the tingling of all her senses as she
reveled in the dizzying power of his kiss and the strong
security of his arms around her. The sense of belong-
ing strengthened and grew, bringing with it a jubi-
lance of spirit that filled her with a heady glow that
was more intoxicating than the most potent wine.

"Why didn't you tell me that night?'' she murmured, left breathless by his kiss.

"Why didn't you?'' Tucker countered lightly, his
mouth curved in a soft smile.

The answer to that was easy: she hadn't wanted to

Janet Dailey

spoil things. Instead of admitting that, Jocelyn snuggled closer, liking the feel of his arms around her.

"I couldn't," she said simply. "Not then."

"Then why haven't you called me? You knew how to reach me." Again he tipped her chin up so he could see her face, his hand splaying over her cheek in warm possession.

"I wanted to, but—why did you wait until now?" She turned the question back on him.

"Finding a plausible excuse to get in this place isn't easy, you know," Tucker reminded her with a grin. "Not just anybody can get in here."

"That's true," Jocelyn admitted with a touch of chagrin, then wondered, "But what would you have done if I hadn't been here tonight?"

"I thought about that, too." His expression was as serious as it could be, but there was a devilish light dancing in his eyes. "But I've got this clumsy habit of falling over things and banging up my knee."

A laugh slipped from her. "You wouldn't really have tried that again, would you?"

"Why not?" Both eyebrows went up in mocking innocence. "It worked the first time, didn't it? Besides, your father hasn't seen my act. I can be very convincing, you know."

"I remember. But there is a doctor on the premises at all times," she informed him.

Tucker grimaced slightly at that bit of news. "That might have presented a problem, but fortunately I didn't have to resort to such trickery. You were here."

"Yes."

Their eyes locked for a long, long moment. Then, ever so slowly, their lips came together again, the kiss deepening and strengthening into something more than mere desire. Something permanent and powerful, kindled by the kind of fire that doesn't burn itself out.

"Sorry that phone call took so long, but I—"

By the time the hearty sound of her father's voice registered with either of them, he had already walked into the room. As one, they broke apart and turned, caught between embarrassment and surprise, with Tucker's arm still loosely curved to the back of her waist.

"I know how this looks, sir," Tucker began with a touching awkwardness. "But I can explain." He glanced at Jocelyn. Now that her initial attack of self-consciousness had subsided, she suddenly had to fight the urge to laugh. "Maybe I can't explain," he said, then looked hopefully at her father. "By any chance, Mr. President, do you believe in love at first sight?"

A frown puckered her father's forehead, drawing his brows together as he turned his narrowed gaze on Jocelyn. "What is going on?"

This time she didn't try to hold back the laugh, letting it bubble out. "It's a long story, Dad. But the short of it is, I have met Tucker before. In fact, I spent most of Saturday with him."

"Saturday. This past Saturday?" he repeated in disbelief.

"Yes."

"But you spent the weekend at Redford Hall." He stared at her with mounting confusion.

"Not all of it."

Startled by her answer, he said, "But I was given to understand that you never left there."

"That's what I wanted everyone to think," Jocelyn admitted.

"Are you saying that—" He stopped, his eyes narrowing in suspicion. "Was your grandmother in on this?"

"Now, don't go getting mad at Gog, Dad," she inserted quickly. "It was my idea."

"You used that underground tunnel to slip away, didn't you?" he guessed. "Jocelyn, do you realize what—"

"But nothing happened, Dad." She jumped in with the assurance. "Except that I met Tucker, and he's a whole other kind of calamity." She flashed Tucker a quick smile, still glowing with the inner fire from his kiss.

"I think your father might like a drink," Tucker suggested after sizing up the man's mood. "I know I could."

"That's the first thing that's made any sense since I walked into this room," Henry Wakefield declared and expelled a breath that was half exasperation and half lingering confusion. "Let's all go back to the oval room. And after you fix me that drink, Jocelyn, you can start telling me this long story of yours." He turned to retrace his steps, then halted abruptly. "What's that doing here? I don't remember seeing it in this room before." He walked over and picked up the cane that stood propped against the door jamb. "Do you know anything about this, Jocelyn?"

Hesitantly she moved toward him, her disbelieving eyes fixed on the cane's gleaming wood. "It looks just like—" She glanced at Tucker, unable to voice the thought in her mind.

"It couldn't be, though." He stared at it, too, like her, drawn forward for a closer look. "I mean, how could he have left it here?"

"How could who?" Her father looked from one to the other.

"Excuse me, sir." One of the stewards paused in the doorway to the Lincoln Bedroom, drawing the attention of all three from the cane. "The White House operator has a call holding on the line for Mr. Tucker."

"For me?" Tucker drew his head back in surprise. "Are you sure? I didn't tell anybody I was coming here toni—wait a minute," he said, a thought suddenly occurring, one he clearly wasn't too certain about. "Did the caller give his name?"

"A Mr. Melchior."

"Obediah," Tucker breathed the name in amazement.

"But how did he know you were here?" Jocelyn frowned at him.

"How does that wiley old rascal know anything?" Tucker countered, shaking his head.

"Shall I have the call transferred in here, sir?" the steward inquired.

"Please. Where's the phone?" Pivoting, Tucker scanned the room.

"By the bed." Jocelyn pointed to the extension that sat on the round table by the imposing rosewood bed. When his long strides carried him toward it, she followed. "I know it's crazy, Tucker, but—he did tell me his middle name was Nicklaus."

"It's more than crazy; it's impossible." But there was a determined set to his expression when Tucker picked up the phone. "This is Grady Tucker. You have a call for me." There was a pulse beat of silence. "Obediah, is that you?"

"Tucker." The deep bass voice filtering into the room could belong to no other. "I'm pleased to see you succeeded in your mission."

"How did you know I was here?"

Jocelyn edged closer to the receiver that Tucker held, anxious to hear Obediah's answer. "Ha, ha, ha." His chuckle was rich and warm with humor. "A simple deduction, Tucker. I happened to see a bright-red Volkswagen pull up to the White House gates. I doubt there are many such models of your car in Washington. Tell me, have you and Jocelyn worked things out satisfactorily?"

With his mouth slanting in wry acceptance of Obediah's believable explanation, Tucker let his glance slide to Jocelyn. The depth of feeling in his eyes went straight to her heart. For a moment, she let herself become lost in the glow of them.

"If we haven't got it all worked out, we are well on our way to doing it." There was a huskiness to Tucker's voice, and a note of confidence that left no room for doubt.

"I am delighted to hear it," Obediah replied.

"So am I." Tucker curved an arm around her shoulders, drawing her more closely against his side—an action that was wholly natural, and one that evoked a thrilling contentment.

"Tucker, ask him about the cane," she whispered.

Nodding, he repositioned the receiver close to his mouth. "There was something else we were wondering about, Obediah. You see, we found this cane in the Lincoln Bedroom, and—"

A hearty laugh resonated from the phone. "You surely didn't think it was mine," Obediah chided, which really wasn't an answer at all.

Jocelyn reached for the phone. "Let me talk to him." Tucker passed it to her. "Obediah, it's Jocelyn. There was something I wanted to ask you," she began.

"Fire away." His bass voice retained its ring of amusement.

"It's this," Jocelyn said, then paused, suddenly losing her nerve. On second thought, the question suddenly seemed utterly foolish and ridiculous. She darted a self-conscious glance at Tucker, then took a deep breath and plunged ahead, knowing she couldn't stand the thought of always wondering. "Obediah, you aren't by any chance Santa Claus, are you?"

The question drew a stunned and disbelieving laugh from her father. Turning, Jocelyn saw him standing there, still holding the cane and staring at her as if she had taken complete leave of her senses.

"Me?" Obediah chuckled again. "Ah, Jocelyn, I consider myself to be a wise man who worships the Christ Child. Sorry, but I must be going. You two take care of each other, now."

"Yes—" She would have said more, but there was a disconnecting click that told her Obediah had hung up. Lowering the phone, Jocelyn looked at Tucker. "Did you hear what he said?"

"Yeah." He nodded, a little distracted as he mulled the reply over in his mind. "That cagey rascal." He smiled crookedly. "Somehow he always manages to give you an answer that really isn't an answer at all."

"You don't think that he really might be . . ." This time Jocelyn couldn't get the words out.

Tucker sighed heavily. "I don't know, Jocelyn. I honestly don't know."

"What don't you know?" Frowning, her father stared at them both. "And what was all that business about Santa Claus? Who is this Obediah you were talking to just now?"

Jocelyn and Tucker looked at each other, then both started to laugh.

Don't miss SANTA IN A STETSON,
the latest from Janet Dailey,
available now from Zebra!

The rider in the saddle was the personification of male in every way, a dream of a cowboy. He sat tall and erect, matching every fluid movement of the horse—as if the two of them were one. He was lean and muscular, dressed in faded blue jeans and a very broken-in denim jacket lined with sheepskin. On his head was a weathered brown Stetson, pulled low over his face.

As the cowboy caught sight of Rick waving to him, he slowed his horse to a stop and walked it in their direction. Diana watched as he sat immovable in the saddle and listened to Rick. Something in the man's bearing made her think he would refuse to have himself and his horse used as a backdrop for fashion photographs. There was the slightest hesitation before he looked to where Diana was standing beside Connie; then he nodded agreement.

Rick motioned her forward and Diana quickly complied. Precious time had been spent finding a suitable background, and Rick didn't waste any more of it making introductions between his model and his cowboy. Diana didn't even get a chance to study the man up close as Rick hurriedly moved her into position on the right side of the horse and began giving instructions. She was intrigued by the man atop the horse, and in between shots she sneaked quick looks at him.

Rugged guy. He was clean-shaven, with deep grooves around his mouth and a hardworking type of tan. The shadows cast by the brim of his Stetson made it hard to figure out the color of his hair, but she was pretty sure it was brown. His eyes were a different matter. At first glance they'd seemed blue; the next, gray. Yet one thing about him was very clear, and that was his remoteness, as if what he was doing was beneath his dignity. For some reason, Diana wasn't put off by that. If it came right down to it, she'd have to say he fascinated her.

"Put your left foot in the stirrup," Rick ordered, his face mostly concealed behind the bulky professional's camera. "Stand in it, suspended beside the horse."

Diana did as she was told, finding she had to hold onto the rider's shoulder to keep her balance. His sheepskin-lined jacket gave until it pressed against the solid muscle of his shoulder and arm. It was a strange sensation to be so near him. On the ground, she'd thought he was no taller than average, but she realized she hadn't factored in the horse. The man was tall, easily over six feet.

"Now turn and look at him, Diana," Rick instructed.

The man in the saddle had gray eyes. She wondered how she had ever thought they were blue. They were slate gray—no, she reconsidered quickly. They were the color of granite, and as hard and unyielding as granite. Even the contours of his face were angular and uncompromising—too rugged, actually, to be handsome. But too compelling not to be attractive.

There was an obvious virility in the sensual line of his mouth. *Down, girl,* Diana thought to herself.